Crisis Averted

The short fiction of Laura Givens

Crisis Averted
By Laura Givens

Cover illustration: "Wrong Frisbee" copyright 2015 by Laura Givens
Cover design by Laura Givens

First printing February 2016

Nomadic Delirium Press
Aurora, Colorado
http://www.nomadicdeliriumpress.com

This book is dedicated to Jerry Siegel, Joe Schuster, Roy Rogers and Robin Williams and the wonderful ideas they planted in my brain

Contents

Oh, And Another Thing About Laura Givens...

She scares the living bejeepers out of some of you who are holding this book, **Crisis Averted**. It's something about successful multitasking. A fair clue would be her colleague Brom. But we'll get to that anon.

First things first. Ms. Givens pretty much invented herself after attending Ferris State College in Michigan back in the 'seventies. That's a smallish but relatively highly regarded institution located in the North Woods, a land of less daylight and fewer humans. It's near the places where the Affordable Care Act is seasonally circumvented by placing the irredeemably elderly on loose ice floes, setting them adrift in the Lakes to be devoured by snarky walruses and migratory— now largely illegally immigrant—polar bears.

Oh, and another thing about Laura. At Ferris State she all too frequently ate Chinese cuisine in the campus cafeteria. Sometimes four or five times a week. Pay close attention because that seemingly innocuous fact plays a key role later in this narrative.

As will happen in the creative life Laura soon began to figure out where her true interests lay--as a visual artist. And not a digital artist but an artist using the digital media as one key smear of new colors on her palette. Was she to become a Dali, a Picasso, a Wyeth? Perhaps. But likelier, she discovered, to incline toward the classic illustrative talents of a Howard Pyle or John O'Neill or J. Allen St. John, those classic portrayers of the heroic and romantically adventurous bent.

Then—"Eureka, I have found it!" Laura metaphorically exclaimed when she first stumbled upon the extravagant works of art of Frank Frazetta. Bronzed and oiled thews—whatever *those* are. Sharp glittering blades squared off against horrific creatures...

Oh, and another thing about Laura... She learned horrific imagery early on in remote Michigan where she witnessed even the wily kinkajou and the savage opossum struck down and squished to strawberry jam (visually if not tastewise—an effective art lesson in distinguishing the interval between medium and message) by the unstoppable eighteen-wheel lumber trucks.

Even the indigenous wendigo quickly learned to avoid the

8

ravenous timber carriers, but that's a story for another Laura collection.

I was *starting* to tell of Laura's unworldly inclination toward pulp—but *not* the sort of pulp left by roadkill on Michigan's public thoroughfares. No, the pulp of which I speak was the literary sort. She was first made aware of it via Jim Steranko's monumental history of comics.

Oh, and that's another thing… If you don't know your popular cultural history before the dawn of Miley Cyrus—or even Hannah Montana—pulp refers to the cheap, easily-obtainable wood-pulp-based paper used for popular magazines of the genre sort that kept the populace diverted during the depression 'thirties and then through the 'forties and 'fifties. Romance, crime and detective, horror, western, and adventure pulp magazines were all popular, but (oh, heaven!) especially there was science fiction. Discovering the exquisite visual thrill of science fiction adventures was heaven for Laura. And that's why you oftentimes find the peculiar technology of characters wearing Stetsons in space helmets. Now that's some sort of extreme behavior even in Laura's idiosyncratic high-tech illustrative pictures. It shows the future probably not as it will be, but the future as it *ought* to be.

But another thing about Laura's covers, one of my favorites is not a hardware-centered assemblage of glitzy gadgetry—it's instead a viscerally compelling dynamic shot of a ripped hero—stripped to the waist—going up against a presumably ravenous velociraptor armed only with a big knife. The heroic dude, that is. The big lizard looks like it'd just love to tuck into a dish of juicy thews al tartare. That's the cover for Bill Craig's novel, **The Fantastic Adventures of Hardluck Hannigan: The Savage Land**.

Here on **Crisis Averted**, though the Presidential pooch playing whimsically with the altitude-disadvantaged little white aliens' Frisbee-shaped flying machine is no canine Conan, I think Mr. Frazetta would approve. There's a primal dynamic tension depicted, and a true face-off of power.

Oh, and another thing: the power of an unfounded rumor. There is *not* an iotum of truth to the scurrilous allegation that the cover for

Crisis Averted is in any way connected to the cover for the Danish anthology of feline science fiction **Hvad Fluffy Vidste (What Fluffy Saw)**. I know this because I have a story in the Copenhagen book. The kitty-cats on that cover are surveying the midget aliens and their spaceships parked on the parlor floor with true feline disdain. Frazetta dynamics? Forget it.

No, the staging of **Crisis Averted**'s public face is what you might expect from the young woman who, when in college back in Wolverine Country, got her first professional break in art, painting a huge canvas poster of a mermaid for a carnival! What a collectible that would make for a Givens retrospective at the Met.

But now it's time that you read Laura's stories. She's been writing prose fiction for a while now, and it's been like watching a new star forming out of the clouds of creation back there where only the Hubble Telescope can peer unaided.

Laura's been writing short stories and placing them sometimes two at a time in the likes of the anthology **Six Guns Straight from Hell**. While she writes all manner of tales, she's shown a particular flair for the weird western.

For my money, while all the Givens oeuvre is of considerable interest to fans of her art and is an excellent signpost toward her future, I think the mini-gathering of Chin Song Ping tales here constitutes the weirdly beating heart of this whole volume. Ping is a roguish nineteenth-century Oriental gentleman (before we turned to the more politically correct "Asian") who wanders the Wild American West, brushing up against all manner of demons, were-critters, and other supernatural entities as he seeks fortune and love at no little danger to his soul and body. He's a bit reminiscent of Richard Boone in the 'fifties TV western series *Paladin*.

Oh, and another thing—about *Paladin*. The titular hero's first name was actually Wire. That's what was inscribed on his business card:

> "Wire Paladin
> San Francisco"

Enough of this snappy patter and fast badinage. You're here to read this woman's first major collection of stories. So get to it. You'll be amazed and entertained.

Oh, and what I said earlier about Laura Givens scaring the bejeepers out of some people?

Well in truth only the unworthy ones—the folks who sink to the level of ego-threatened mentality that says no one bright and accomplished in *one* pursuit can then turn around and achieve in another. Well, Laura can and is.

So forgive her an abundance of talent. She just draws and writes that way. You'll be happier for it.

Honest.

And another thing. I referenced Brom at the git-go as a clue. The comparison seems apt: (1 Brom is a famed artist. (2 Brom is also the successful novelist of **The Child Thief** and **Krampus**, this last to join your list of holiday classics at the theatre such as *Miracle on 34th Street* and *Elf.* Laura's clearly on the same path.

Oh, and another thing

--Edward Bryant
Fort Wayne
Winter Solstice, 2015

SECTION ONE

COUNTRY FRIED SCI-FI

GRAND OL' SPACE OPRY

At seven years old Ryan James had learned that there were three things he should always do before he went EVA; always go to the bathroom first, the filters could handle your waste but it wasn't very comfortable; make sure somebody, besides yourself, checks your suit; and always give a big old Kentucky-rebel yell as you hit the vacuum.

This last item served several functions; it tested the com system, it helped equalize blood oxygen levels (or so he'd been told) but mostly it gave notice to the universe at large that a Southern boy was coming through, so watch out! At twenty seven he still followed these tenets, especially the third one, especially whenever Silas was on Communications duty.

"Yeeeeeeeeee-Haaaawwww!"

"Damn it, Ryan!" Swore Silas Lapekes! "I told you to cut that crap out!" Ryan exploded out of the hatch flinging himself to the full extension of his tether before he bounced back toward the ship doing a triple summersault and jamming feet first onto the side of the good ship, Molly Brown, where his sticky field soles stuck like well-cooked spaghetti.

"Why, Silas, I'm just following the wishes of my dear, sainted Mamma." Ryan drawled.

Silas shook his head and smiled in spite of himself. Ryan's 'sainted Mamma', Maggie James, was a pop-riveter over on the MacDougal's Folly and she could out-drink and out-curse any twelve marines.

"Well, just show a little consideration, huh? I've had to replace my headphones three times since you came aboard." Silas scratched at the phantom itch between his knee and his prosthesis.

"I can't promise a thing. A lifetime of strict training and discipline is a hard habit to break. As he waited for the next man out, he looked around to see the mountain hovering nearby, squinting his eyes to make out details. "Well, fellas, it's another glorious spring morning in the cosmic Ozarks! I've got me a fresh, new lemon filter in the ol' whiz-womper and PBJ and banana squares in the lunch box, yum! What more could a growin' boy ask for." Joe's head popped out

14

of the airlock and he offered the newcomer a hand. "What's on the old agenda for today anyway?"

Ryan James was third generation spacer and he'd never set foot on any planet, much less Earth - much less Kentucky. His great grandfather, Hiram, had been an eastern Kentucky coal miner and had seen that way of life coming to an end. Coal mining was a dirty, dangerous way to make a living, but it was an honest day's work, and great granddaddy was a proud man. He made sure his son, Earl, got a college degree and learned a trade that would get him out those hollers and into the future.

Hiram's boy became, what was called in those days, an astronaut and granddaddy Earl was one of the first permanent residents of Tranquility Heights, the Moon's premier underground habitat facility. He dug tunnels. He was a miner.

Maggie, Ryan's Mamma, ran away from home at the age of seventeen, heading for the romance of wildcatting in the asteroid belt. She married a red-headed young scoundrel named Billy James and they both just knew that they'd strike it big out where there was plenty of elbow room. Billy promised her the stars but a ruptured plasma tank rudely awakened him from his youthful dreams. He lived for three days with radiation burns covering half his body, but died without ever seeing his unborn son. The void was Ryan's home.

"Joe, you make an interesting point, however I don't think you can really classify Bugs Bunny as a classical transvestite." Ryan said as he planted both his feet into the rock face and heaved at the control lever with all his might. The darned thing had been jammed into neutral by a stray handful of pebbles on an eccentric orbit of asteroid K3N4-55730, AKA Rock 30. He was trying to loosen the stick just enough that his partner, Joe Saxon, could clean out the grit.

Joe replied, "I'm just saying that more than once, that rabbit got himself all gussied up and he's flirting with Elmer one second and then, BAM!, old Elmer's laid out from a hammer up side his head." Joe looked up from his labors and frowned, "Happened to me once on Midas Station."

15

Suddenly Joe's micro jet blasts dislodged the dirt and Drill Site F-1 came dramatically back to life. Huge steel beams swung overhead and the drill shaft resumed its ponderous rotation boring deep into the heart of Rock 30.

Ryan banged his gloves together and smiled at the silent ballet of giants that surrounded him. "The point is, you never saw Bugs get all dressed up when he was by himself, you know, just because he got off on it" He extended his hand to help Joe get out of the drill hole. "I knew a good old boy on my last ship, he liked to wear women's clothing and there wasn't a thing wrong with it. Nice fella, helluva dancer. Now, I will grant you that getting all feminined up and going around hitting people in the head with a hammer, or what have you, though hilarious, is just plain anti-social. Old Bugs did that sort of thing to Elmer whether he was dressed up or not."

Joe took a long sip of apple juice from his helmet dispenser, contemplating the proposition. With a lop-sided grin Ryan added, "Yeah, I guess ol' Elmer should be more careful what sort of rabbit he's got when he's looking for tail."

Joe sputtered and came dangerously close to baptizing his interior faceplate with juice.

Nine months ago Ryan had signed onto the Molly Brown as an able rigger and met Joe, who was on his fourth tour aboard the Molly. They hit it off immediately. Joe was a black man from Detroit, Earth and so qualified as both a gravity hog and a damned Yankee but Ryan tried not to hold any of that against him. Joe was often surly and would just as soon fight you as look at you some days. This was despite the fact that he stood all of five foot nothing and weighed less than Ryan's duffle bag. But, there was no guile in him and he laughed at the same stupid things that tickled Ryan and was mostly pissed off at the right things as well. The two of them could work together all shift long and still find subjects of mutual interest. Rigging wasn't the most intellectually challenging of professions so it was important to have somebody around who could you engage in serious BS.

The day of mere space station building was ending and now the big conglomerates were building entire cities in space. The plan was that these cities would siphon off Earth's teeming masses and be fitted with the new Jablonsky Drives to take them to seed the stars. At least that was the theory. In practice, the three such cities that had been started were nowhere near completion, and belt mining was still a boom industry, supplying all the raw material needed. Mining equipment on this gargantuan scale was supposed to be pretty much automated but it still took a lot of human bodies, and human know how, to deal with the unexpected chaos of mountains in freefall.

The next three hours were relatively uneventfully. Number three coolant line had a leak to be mended and the slag-muncher had bowel trouble again – same old, same old. Then, just as he was ready to call it a day, Janey Doakes came zooming in and grabbed him by the boot which sent them into a pinwheel for a second before Ryan could compensate. "Hey, Ryan, glad I caught you." She said. "We've got an incoming and you and Joe have been nominated to do the honors."

Ryan and Joe both rolled their eyes. "Can't it wait till tomorrow? I got me a date after chow." Joe pleaded.

Trying to be supportive, Ryan piped in, "Yeah, and I've been holding it in all afternoon to preserve my brand new lemon filter."

Janey and Ryan had shared a bunk for a while but that had ended when she had been promoted to pit boss. "Look you two, this order comes down from Humper himself!" She clicked over to a privacy channel, just in case. "Don't think that the Tool Pusher doesn't know it was you that slipped him the helium tab when he gave the corporate big rocks a tour last week. Made him sound like a chipmunk! He can't prove it, but trust me you don't need to give him any excuses to look any harder." Janey clicked back to local traffic channel. "So, gentlemen, do you understand your assignment?" Both men nodded resignedly, "Good, then I want you to sign out a scooter and requisition a couple of mass pushers." Janey pushed off toward the command shack.

"How do I break this to Maude? It's her birthday and I had something real special to give her." Joe sighed.

Ryan nodded his head, "Some folks have got no sense of humor at all."

###

The scout had come into the solar system cold. He feared the reaction of the machines if he were detected. Previous scouts had determined that the third planet of this system was occupied by numerous species, only one of which seemed nominally clever. It had troubled his people that these beings had never ventured off their planet, as that was usually considered one of the signs of actual intelligence by leading scientists. Instead, over the past hundred cycles or so, they had sent machinery out into their system, intricate machineries, many of which looked like mechanical surrogates of the beings themselves. Once you matured and left your cradle world, so the common wisdom said, you put away your toys, such as machines. What was most distressing was that the machines were now dismantling other orbiting bodies to manufacture yet more machines. The implications were staggering! Unchecked, within a mere million cycles they would have converted every bit of usable matter in their solar system into machines that could replicate themselves. After that it was only a matter of time before they would have to search out new solar systems to destroy. The obvious solution was to accelerate this star to supernova and destroy this blight.

The scout, a hero of several expeditions named Brill'thh, was here to execute a daring plan. His assignment was to get close enough to the ravaging onslaught of the machines to analyze their virus-like expansion and determine if they were too wide spread to get past with no loss of life. If only there were some way to safely communicate with the planetary beings what was happening beyond their atmosphere.

Three days ago Brill'thh had instructed his navigator, a symbiotic brain-slug, that he wished to set up base on an asteroid, near the machine colony which lay ahead. The slug was an excellent calculator (and always seemed to be able to find, and scratch, Brill'thh's most out of the way itches). They arrived safely with a minimum of fuss. He had spent his time, since arrival, carefully secreting layer upon layer of lenses with a direct link to both his ocular nerve and his brain-slug's data center. He'd even exuded an atmosphere dome so he could enjoy soothing sounds while he worked. His would be the closest observations ever made of this phenomenon and he was terrified.

###

"Of course I don't think our very language should have been allowed to be changed just to satisfy a fringe group of religious fanatics, but…" Ryan took a sighting on the stray asteroid and Joe jumped right in.

"Hell yeah, that's what I'm saying, 'To go boldly' was correct, not "To boldly go!" he looked satisfied at finally making his point.

"Point taken, but you've got to admit that new Star Trek movie was pretty good. That actress, what's her name, made a great Captain Kirk." He looked again at the reading and thumped the display. "That damned rock just wiggled again!"

"Probably internal gas spitting out," Joe tapped in a new code to compensate – again, "but it is pretty small to have gas reserves."

"That's probably why they sent out a pair of ace troubleshooters like us." Ryan said. They both broke up and laughed themselves silly. Tagging wanderers was a crap detail, five hours out, twenty minutes to set mass drivers to nudge the offender into a more agreeable trajectory, and five hours back. It wasn't like the rock would come within five kilometers of the operation, but the regs (written by a paper pusher at Clavius Three, no doubt) said all objects of this size or greater must be deflected to a twenty five k fly-by. Boring did not do it justice.

"So, if Maude is still speaking to you, are you going to the square dance next week Sunday? I think I've finally worked out the arrangements for those Bob Marley tunes." Ryan asked brightly.

"Hey do I ever miss one when you're calling?" Joe's voice sounded wounded.

###

When mankind first ventured into space, no one could have predicted the phenomenal popular resurgence of square dancing--in Zero G. Ballet, without gravity, was a beautiful thing to watch, but people liked to boogie for themselves as well. Partner dancing usually wound up in collisions and often fights. Then, one night, a drunken theoretical mathematician started working out algorithms for various configurations of human bodies at motion in a freefall environment.

Fellow drunken colleagues felt it necessary to test her equations and everybody had a great time, especially when they added some music. Live music was quickly added to keep things fresh and when it became apparent that the configuration changes were difficult to communicate throughout the group all at once, someone had the idea of a caller. Traditional square dancing tunes worked remarkably well, and were adapted to fit all kinds of tastes, and so was born a whole new popular art form. Whenever a cargo space was scheduled to be free, it would get booked immediately and up to a hundred dancers would show. Things could still get a little wild and everyone had to present their ZG-SQD certification before they were allowed to join in. Ryan James and his Quantum Cowboys were a local favorite.

As casually as he could, Ryan asked Joe, "Janey didn't say anything about coming, did she?"

"Ryan, I don't ever see that dog hunting again." Joe replied in a fatherly tone. "Last Tuesday I saw her down at the Sit and Spin and when I said you'd be right along, she got up and packed her gear. As she left she said she didn't need to share air with such a loser--the loser being you."

Ryan mumbled something under his breath and studied the readouts way more closely than necessary.

"See, that's why I hadn't said anything! Now, Maude knows this girl, over on the Yang-Tze Clipper, who is sweet as an all-day sucker and she's just..." Joe kept talking but Ryan's mind was somewhere else.

Brill'thh settled in on the side of the asteroid facing the machine colony. All his attention was on focusing his lenses toward the large structure which hovered just to the side of the soon-to-be-cannibalized large asteroid. Dozens of drones came and went from it at regular intervals, much like other such mechanisms observed in the past. If he could predict the timings of those comings and goings he might discern the most fortunate time to slip by them. It was a shame he hadn't used one or two of his sense pods to keep up on local affairs, or he would have surely seen the small scooter with two "drones"

20

attached making its final descent around to the far side.

###

"One, Two, Three, throw!" Ryan threw paper and Joe threw rock. "Damn! I guess I get to take a stroll." Joe picked up a mass driver and set a sticky onto the ground. After backing up a respectable distance, he launched himself into space, letting a tether out behind him. "I'll ping you when I've got this set and am ready to head back." It was a silly looking, but efficient way to circumnavigate an asteroid. Place a sticky field anchor then jump to the end of the tether attached to it and let centripetal force carry you back to the asteroid hundreds of feet toward your destination. Turn off the sticky field, reel your line back in, and repeat as often as seems wise.

"Hey! Make it fast and maybe we can catch some sack time before breakfast!" Ryan waved goodbye and started his calculations for where to plant his device, it required some distance between the two for these babies to work their best.

After about four minutes, Joe figured one more jump ought to do it. When he reached full extension on that last jump he glimpsed a structure on the surface off to his left. As he touched down he knew he had nailed the location and proceeded to set up the driver in nothing flat. After a moment of self congratulation he punched up the com to Ryan. "Yo, I think somebody left some gear off to my left so I'm going to check it out." He waited for a reply, "Ryan... Ryan?" Damned curvature! Well, he figured he was way ahead of schedule so what the heck. On his first swing he caught another glimpse but couldn't make it out. The next time it looked like scaffolding with big pods attached. What the hell? His last swing brought him right at it and he still wasn't sure what he was looking at. But, at the last second before he landed he caught a glint off what appeared to be a dome surrounding the weird scaffolding – and he would have sworn that the scaffolding moved. He felt pressure, like an atmosphere, push into his suit as he crashed through the dome and landed helmet first.

###

Brill'thh cursed himself for a fool! He had gotten so involved that the machines had flanked him somehow and were attacking. The drone thrashed towards him in a menacing manner, arms extended

21

straight up and emitting a ferocious roaring buzz. He detached himself from his lens array, shattering several of the more delicate ones, and leaped back. The drone was much smaller than he but there were sure to be more any moment, they were rarely observed alone. He thought that if he could push the thing away, he could get outside the atmosphere field and make a hot escape before they could capture him. He extended a forelimb to its utmost and rammed at the thing using sharp digits to insure a firm purchase. His digits pushed right past the drone's surface layer and into the interior. As red lubricant leaked from the holes, he tasted organic matter on his digit sensors. That couldn't be right. The roar grew shrill and then stopped. Brill'th zoomed in his oculars to see past the spider's web of cracks on the clear plate set into the thing's extruding nub. Was that…? He fed the organic signatures and the visual into the brainslug, fearing the results. The intruder unscrewed its nub and threw it weakly aside. Brill'thh didn't need the analysis after that, it was a being from the third planet that he had impaled and it was now laying at his limbs gasping for atmosphere. After several seconds of frozen horror he did the only thing he could think of, he clamped on a series of glands that would increase the oxygen level and the heat within the field. He rubbed two limbs across each other, emitting a pure tone and then a series of chords. The tones might loosely be translated as, "Dear Maker, what have I done?"

Joe lay thrashing weakly, trying to get air into his lungs but it didn't taste like air. Things were getting black and sparkly and he did the last thing any spacer wanted to be forced to do. On his belt he twisted a small red box which flew off and punched the red button that waited underneath.

The instant he heard the emergency radio screech, designed to penetrate just about anything, Ryan dropped everything and scrambled back onto the scooter and hit the homing lock. He took off, swearing a steady litany of words that would have gotten a stiff fine back at the site. His mind raced ahead of the scooter; a minute for Joe's signal to get back to the ship and go through filtering, maybe twenty minutes to organize a response during night cycle, and at least

22

an hour to get out here at max speed. "Shit!" Whatever was wrong, it was all on him to fix it. Thirty seconds and he could see Joe lying still with no helmet and too much blood floating around him. Standing over Joe was a nightmare brandishing a dozen wicked spikes from three connected pods that pulsated in an obscene fashion. Ryan jammed on the retros, but just enough to slow the scooter down, not enough to make a soft landing. At the last possible second he detached and jumped at an angle to the forward momentum. The scooter crashed into the monstrosity and together they dragged a gash along the asteroid a hundred meters long. Ryan ran to Joe though he had no hope that he was still alive. Kneeling down, his kneepads, like his soles, went sticky to keep him anchored. He started to cry. Through his tears he saw the green LED in his helmet that indicated he was in an atmosphere. He looked closely at Joe's face for signs of decompression--there weren't any. That was impossible! "Screw it!" He got his own helmet off as quickly as possible and started to strip Joe's suit. The bleeding looked bad but the wounds weren't too deep, and it didn't look like any major organs had been damaged, so he grabbed the tube of med-goo from Joe's kit and started filling the holes. When that was empty he dug out his own goo and spread it over Joe's entire stomach and chest. A crust quickly formed and Joe seemed to breathe more easily. Ryan cried openly as he got Joe into a more comfortable position, then through his sobs he heard a scraping noise behind him.

He whirled to see that the creature had returned. It stood wobbling slightly about ten feet away. All its spikes were pointed behind it, away from the Earthmen. On its front surface was stalk with a globe, covered by sliding membranes. It looked, for all the world, like a sad eye to Ryan. Somehow the overall effect was – contriteness. Well, certainly not menace at least.After a moment, two of the smaller limbs unfolded and moved forward, slowly, always pointed toward the ground. Ryan gulped and wished for a fresh waste filter. He could see that the limbs had a roughness to them and when they touched they began to rub which produced a beautiful soaring tone. That tone melted into another and continued till it reached a

23

crescendo then stopped abruptly. The limbs folded back behind him again. It felt like the thing was saying 'sorry'.

A voice crackled behind him and gave him a start. He held up a finger to the alien and said, "Excuse me, I really need to take this. I'll be right back."

Silas' voice came pleading out of the hastily donned helmet, "… an do you copy? We have a rescue launch ready to fly. Do you need anything beyond standard rescue equipment? I say again, do you require any non-standard equipment?"

Ryan toggled over to max power send. "Um, I am not sure, Silas. Let me think. Joe's hurt, but I've patched him up okay for now. A spare suit might be good. Say, could you send up some of that fancy translation software they had a lecture about last month? We've got us a kind of situation up here." He knew there would be a long time-lag before a reply. "Don't reply, just come get us, I think I'm going to be real busy till then. You are not going to believe this, ol' buddy!" He was ready to take off the helmet when an inspiration hit him. "Oh, and send Lucy. That's real important, send Lucy! Y'hear?!"

Once his helmet was off he put his arms behind his back and said to the waiting alien "Hi, my name's Ryan. What's yours? I'm guessing you're new around these parts."

Janey had pulled some strings to be on the rescue flight and now, as the rock came into visual, she felt foolish for doing so. She held a plastic box, hastily grabbed from under Ryan's bunk, on her lap. He'd sounded okay, if a little confused, but why hadn't he kept sending. And why in hell was she here? They'd broken up because he was a drag on her career, a Gypsy rigger moving from job to job with no ambition to be more than that. He was like a fifteen year old, always looking to throw a stink bomb at authority.

"Jumpin' Jesus on a shingle!" The pilot exclaimed as they started their descent toward Joe's emergency signal.

Janey pushed her way to the cockpit where everyone was gawking at a scene they were unlikely to ever forget. An alien (What else could it be) half the size of the launch itself and bristling with limbs that looked made for mayhem. The thing was a dappled bluish-gray with several dark orbs on stalks that were all focused on their ship. A hundred meters or so away was a wrecked skimmer. What really pushed the scene into the surreal was Joe lying on the exposed surface without his helmet, his suit opened wide. And then, of course, there was Ryan, buck naked except for his boots, waving them in like a traffic cop at Mardi Gras.

Janey and the medics piled out and went straight to the sleeping form of Joe. Once they'd determined the extent of his wounds, she turned her attention Ryan, wiggling into his underpants, and their-- guest.

Ryan signaled to take her helmet off. "Janey, I'd like to introduce you to my very good friend, Briddlleydiddleydiddley. At least it's something like that, but I'm pretty sure it's his name." Janey stared-- they all stared--at the first genuine Extraterrestrial ever seen by human eye. Ryan gently relieved Janey of the plastic box she clutched tightly, like a security blanket. Popping the seal he lifted the only family heirloom he had from its protective case. Great Grand Daddy Hiram's fiddle, real wood and lovingly polished till it near sparkled. "Lucy." He sighed. It wasn't a Stradivarius or anything like that but it was priceless to Ryan.

As he tuned the strings he explained, "After a bit of culture shock, that Joe got the worst of, we've been trying to communicate, mostly pointing, waving arms and such. Briddley seemed really distressed by my suit so I figured I'd show him the full Monty, all the original parts so to speak. The notion of being inside--anything--just seems wrong to him for some reason, but he's not freaking at you guys," he glanced at the silent alien, "So that's encouraging." Ryan tucked the instrument under his chin. "I got this idea from something he did earlier."

Ryan had always had a good ear and he tried his best to reproduce the "Sorry" tones as notes on his fiddle. After playing the passage through once he started to repeat it and halfway through Brill'thh brought his limbs together and joined in. The alien played haunting harmonies to Ryan's basic tune and continued when it reached the end. Ryan took a deep breath and started to jam, improvising over the new song.

25

"Crap!" Janey whispered to herself and clicked the device mounted on her shoulder to global record.

For half an hour Ryan followed Brill'thh, even when the alien added other limbs playing weird counterpoint to his main theme. Then they wound down and Ryan looked around him. Joe had been taken into the launch while Janey still stood, smiling and recording. "So, are you getting anything on that translation software?" he asked.

"Not really. I don't think they had this in mind when they wrote this software." She laughed, a bit too loudly perhaps.

Brill'thh made two tones and Ryan turned toward him. Again the two tones were sounded.

Janey cocked her head. "I think he wants *you* to play a tune."

What do you play to an alien? Beethoven, Bach? He couldn't remember how anything started. His fingers took over shortly after his brain failed him, and it was something his Mamma had taught him as a child, old and corny but reliable - Turkey in the Straw.

"They're going to think we're the planet of the rednecks!" he mentally kicked himself, but kept playing and sure enough he had accompaniment almost immediately, and it felt right somehow. He swept right into Blue Moon of Kentucky then just kept going.

The tones produced by the third planet being spoke of joy, freedom and the kind of determination that could, would propel these fragile creatures to the stars. The atmosphere dome suddenly seemed too small to contain this celebration of the meeting of two species. He had no idea what they were actually saying to each other, certainly the buzzing sounds they made seemed to convey everyday information between them, but this was how they must share their higher aspirations and grand ideals. Tiny and squishy though they might be, they truly were people. Brill'thh knew that his people were no longer alone!

Dripping sweat, Ryan finished up with Amazing Grace and drew out the last note and let it trail off into eternity. All was silence as the alien came closer and touched him like he was a soap bubble that might pop at a wayward breeze. Ryan went past the lethal looking limbs and touched the forward pod of his new friend. The pod was hard, but warm and alive, pulsing slightly.

A membrane started buzzing on the second pod, as if trying to find a certain frequency, then a slightly distorted imitation of Ryan's voice said, "Excuse me, I really need to take this. I'll be right back." With that, it scuttled away out of the air bubble. Flexing all its limbs, it took a great leap into the blackness. A few seconds later there was a bright burst and the visitor was gone, headed for the wormhole that had brought him. There was grand news to be spread.

###

Janey helped Ryan back into his suit, neither of them having any words left. Just as they reached the airlock, Joe's voice sounded in their helmets. "It's about time! If you're done auditioning the guy, can we go home and get me patched up before the whole orchestra shows up? Maude would appreciate that." They looked back at the air dome, which seemed to just fade away.

Janey touched Ryan's arm. "You did good, cowboy."

Ryan started laughing hysterically and tilted his head back as far as the suit would allow, "YEEEEEE-HAAAAAAAWWWWW! Now, that's what I call a first contact!"

Ryan spent several more minutes howling at the stars.

THE GREAT DINOSAUR ROUNDUP OF 1903

12, March, 1903

My dearest Bess,

I take pen in hand to inform you of the possible untimely death of your brother, Pete. I know for a fact he loved you dearly and regretted all the things he said that last time in Wichita. He was drunk that night and a man will say stupid things when in such a state. I am still here in Wisconsin; a town called Milwaukee, with the Wild West show and will send his last wages and belongings as soon as old Buffalo Bill settles accounts. I'm certain Pete would want your mother to have them, so please see that she gets them.

I say possible untimely death because Mr. Tesla says, strictly speaking, Pete died a few million years before he was even born. Be that as it may, he was still alive the last time I saw him, though his situation seemed dire enough. Bess, sit yourself down and I'll try and explain, as best I might, just what happened and how Pete wound up trying to break a dinosaur with a Bowie knife.

Well, it all started with the two of us finally getting some time off, so we could take in the local culture of the fair city of Milwaukee.

You'd think that getting massacred at the Little Big Horn twice a day, plus an extra matinee on Sunday, wouldn't be all that hard, but it gets to you after a while. Me and Pete got a little happy before one show and decided that maybe Custer should win that night--just as a change of pace. Now the way it works is the Indians ride around us shooting lots of fake arrows at us. We troopers wear padding under our outfits that those arrows stick into and we stumble around dying heroically. These city folks just eat it up. That particular night we just stayed up, getting shot at until we both looked like a couple of porcupines. Finally, one of the Indians--big old son of a gun called "Cold-Wind-In-Spring"--dismounts and stomps over, picks Pete up by his shirt, and throws him at me. We both go flying right onto General

28

Custer--Bill Cody himself--who gets up and starts whacking us with his hat and using words that I shall not repeat here. So, we had us a week off.

Now, Milwaukee makes some mighty fine beers and, just to be neighborly, me and Pete had us a few more than might normally be considered temperate. Well, we got into a sort of roping match to see who could lasso and hogtie this yahoo in a funny uniform and helmet. I won, and Pete was about to use a cigar as a branding iron when we were accosted by a horde of men in funny helmets. To make a long story short, that yahoo turned out to be a policeman with no sense of humor at all, so we got us a night's lodging in the local calaboose. The next morning, Cody shows up to throw our bail. With him is this real refined gent in a three piece suit, spats and a top hat. That was our introduction to Mr. Nicola Tesla, inventor of the time machine among other things.

After he got us outside Bill blistered our ears for a spell. He finally finished up by saying that if we weren't the best damned straight-up trail hands he had ever seen, he would have let us rot. Luckily for us, it seemed he needed us for a special deal he was working with Tesla. Bill had met the man ten years earlier at the Chicago World's Fair and they hit it right off. Mr. Tesla had him an idea about something he called "time travel" and they had set up a secret base up there in Milwaukee, where land was cheaper. Bill had fronted the money for the whole operation because, it turned out, he'd loved something called "archeology" since he'd met some fella, years ago digging up dinosaur bones out west somewhere.

With this here time machine, me and Pete were going to go back a few million years and round up some critters called Tyrannosaurus Rexes, for the show. Bill is always lookin' for new exotic acts for the show. If we refused to help, we were informed we could spend the next sixty days in the jug and be left stranded in Milwaukee. Cody had us by the short hairs so we were in, whether we liked it or not. Tesla explained it all to us in detail, and I understood not a word of what he said. He is the only man I've ever met more in love with his own voice than Bill.

After a while Pete kind of warmed to the idea and allowed as how it might be fun. You will recall that your brother's idea of fun also included riding your Pa's prize bull through town in hat, spurs and the suit God gave him on his birthday. I remained skeptical but enjoyed the Havana cigars he had offered us.

Traveling through time turns out to be loud and flashy but not as uncomfortable as you might think. Tesla had set up the whole shebang in an abandoned brewery with big old machines with dials and electric lights and wires everywhere. Strangest of all was a whole line of poles with lightning climbing up and down them, made my hair stand right on end. One wall had a huge rolling metal door set to roll up and down like a curtain. Right up against it was a great big cage with three sides tall enough to hold a two story house.

The plan was that we would ride out through that metal door, and on the other side would be those Rexes, and other such critters. Then, we'd herd them back into the cage, the door would drop down behind them and we'd have us some dinosaurs. There was a smaller escape door, on the side of the cage, that me and Pete would be let out through. It sounded simple enough. Bill gave us pictures of what the Rexes looked like and told us that if we couldn't find none of them, we should get a three horned varmint called a Tri-Ceratops. So, we said we'd keep a look out.

I was on a fast little pinto pony, and Pete had him a roan he was particular to, both top notch cow ponies, but the noise and lights had them plum skittish. I've never enjoyed riding a rearing horse but I understood that pinto's point of view. When that big old door started rolling up I thought they would go loco. I certainly felt the urge myself. Up till that moment, I hadn't actually believed what little I could understand of Tesla's explanations. I fully expected that when that big old door raised up I would see the woman selling flowers we had passed coming in. We'd all wind up looking a mite foolish and that would be an end to it. But there, on the other side of that door, looking like something out of a picture book was a jungle all hot and humid, alive with sounds that hadn't been heard on this earth in millions of years. Pete's horse reared up on its hind legs and Pete let out a whoop of pure joy. He set off at a gallop into the forest primeval. Against all good sense, I lit out after him.

Bess, you know how they say the buffalo herds used to be, going on an on as far as the eye could see? Well, that's what this was like, but not just one kind of animal, no, there were critters of every shape and description grazing everywhere or lolling around in watering holes and rivers. It was so pretty, Bess, I wish you could have seen it. We rode around for a while trying to find us a Rex, to no avail, so I suggested we have us a little picnic and see if we couldn't maybe catch one of the little ones running around on two legs. Lure him in with a biscuit and grab him. I pulled out some chicken legs and fresh biscuits, while Pete produced a bottle of whiskey. Whatever else I might have thought of your brother, I always admired his priorities.

We got to toasting one thing and another and Pete fired off a couple of rounds, just to celebrate our not being in jail. I guess he must have winged one of the big old leathery birds that kept flying overhead because it suddenly dived at us like an owl looking for a mouse lunch. I rolled back and grabbed my pistol, just managing to snap off a shot as that vulture snatched Pete's hat--almost took his head along too, just for good measure. I must have stung it though, because it lit out wanting nothing else to do with us. We finished off those chicken legs fast as we could, so we could get back to the job at hand.

Every now and then as we ate one of these cute little critters-- looked like a salamander walkin' around on two legs, bright red, about three foot tall--would get curious about us. None, however, were enticed to come very close by the food we offered. Then, just as we were about ready to ride, one little guy came right up to Pete and offered him his lost hat. That big bird must have dropped it, and this salamander was sharp enough to know to bring it back to Pete. On an impulse I grabbed him up and clutched him to my chest, him squawking and struggling to get free. He was handful but we finally got him quieted down, Pete making soothing noises. I was trying to figure out how best to transport him when we heard a blood-curdling screech and saw something jump from the undergrowth and land a couple of yards away. It was another salamander, but this one stood a good six feet tall and had a spear clutched in one paw. He had a real determined look and his other paw was ready to draw a bone knife from the woven belt slung round his torso. I dropped the little one and put my hand on the butt of my gun, not drawing it for fear of making things worse. There was no telling how many more might be out there. We stood there, eyeball to eyeball, for a good minute, the little one cowering behind his daddy. It was then that Pete put himself between us and made a big show of putting his hat back on and waving back at the youngster. Then, in a stroke of genius, he took a swig from the bottle of whiskey and offered it to that big old salamander fella. Hesitantly, he took the bottle from Pete and sniffed it real good before tipping it back just like Pete had done. It was a mite comical the way he let out a big old belch and started blinking real fast. Well, he took a second swig and then tried to hand it back to Pete. Your brother motioned that he should keep it. That red devil lifted Pete's bottle and let out three blood-curdling whoops, and three more salamanders dropped out of trees. Well, sir, the daddy started makin' all kinds of clicks and barking sounds. We'd both been around Bill Cody long enough to recognize a speech when we heard one-- even if we didn't know what was being said. At the end of his remarks, we all sat down and passed that bottle around till it was bone dry. Then, without so much as a by your leave, they hopped up whipping around fast as lightning and were gone into the trees, leaving the bottle lying on the grass.

Me and Bill stared at each other a moment and then both started laughing like jackasses. After we had laughed ourselves dry, we crawled on our horses and got down to some serious Rex hunting. Fun was fun but we still had us a job to do.

Eventually Pete got bored and started cutting out critters from this group of duck-billed critters with horns on their crests. He was herding them right and left, plying his trade so to speak, when all of a sudden he ran smack dab into a greenish brown wall with four legs and three horns. He had found us a tri-ceratops!

Now, neither Bill nor Mr. Tesla had mentioned how bad tempered one of these things might be. It started swinging its head around right and left, gorging and throwing duck-things all around it. It was about to have a go at Pete, but I rode in through the herd whooping and hollering and blazing away with my colt. The bullets didn't hardly faze that critter none, but I had distracted it enough that Pete could get to a safer distance. Once we had the beast confused with our fancy horsemanship, we just kept at it riding in circles and putting ropes on him till we figured we'd plum tired him out. He was big, but none too bright, and I started to think of him as just another really cantankerous steer. Just as we thought we had him, that three horned devil gave one last huge jerk of his head and sent me and my pinto flying towards the trees. I got up rubbing my back and using foul language. Spying my Winchester on the ground, I determined that maybe I could make a larger caliber impression on that son of a buck with the right tool. All of a sudden, behind me, I heard a roar and a high pitched squeal which ended abruptly. Turning slowly, I saw four horse legs flailing in the air and where its body should have been all I saw were long, pointy teeth and two eyes straight out of a nightmare.

That picture we had been given by Bill was off in several minor details. If this was a rex (and I had a suspicion it was) it wasn't some slow, tail dragging oaf like in the drawing. This thing looked fast and mean as a scorpion on a hot rock. The teeth looked a lot bigger than in the picture, too.

Old three-horn took one look and tore off like a bat out of Hell pulling Pete right off his roan, dragging him through the dirt and ferns. I ran over and grabbed the reins to Pete's horse and was in that saddle faster than a flea on a hound. The one bright spot in all this was that the tri-ceratops was heading right in the direction of that time travel door so I took off after them. Glancing over my shoulder, I saw that the rex was crunching away on his pinto lunch. Nonchalantly, as he chewed, Mr. Rex was studying all the action with his eyes. After a few minutes of hard riding, I spotted the tri-ceratops standing there breathing hard, in the distance ahead of him I saw a dark square on the horizon that I knew had to be the time door. Missing from the scene was any trace of your brother. I made my way carefully around the heaving brute, fearing what grizzly remains I might find on the mouth end, but was puzzled when I found nothing. I had no idea where Pete could have gotten to.

Then I heard a whump in the distance followed by a second and a third and so forth, each one getting louder and closer together. Suddenly, I saw that rex barreling at me, crashing through the undergrowth like a runaway freight train. Three-horn took off like a shot, heading straight for the dark patch. I am ashamed to admit that my pony and I froze right there on the spot. I thought I would soil myself when that big old monster stopped right in front of me and opened wide, letting out a roar that could have stripped paint from a barn. All of a sudden something dropped right out of the branches overhead, landing on the varmint's back. It was Pete, clothes all shredded and covered in mud and leaves, somehow still wearing his hat. He lifted that big old Bowie knife of his, plunging it into the critter's hide. Pete let out howl and held on for dear life as that lizard tried to shake him off. Roused from my stupor, I put spurs to that roan and went off like lightning after the tri-ceratops.

It must have been a strange sight for those boys back in 1903, having a three horned mountain barreling at them--followed by a screaming maniac on a strawberry roan--who was trying to get away from a big old dragon weaving from side to side, ridden by a laughing madman.

The tri-ceratops went right through the big door and proceeded to tear through that cage like pages from a Sears & Roebuck. That critter started smashing machines and lightning poles to beat the band. By the time I rode through there were people running everywhere and explosions like it was the fourth of July. I thought it the better part of valor to get out of there fast as I could. As I made for the cage door, I turned one last time and, through the fireworks, I could see Pete still on the other side of the big door, riding that wheeling, bucking tyrannosaurus rex, with one hand waving in the air, singing the "Yellow Rose of Texas" at the top of his lungs. Just before the smoke got too dense to see, I would swear I saw a spear hit the beast right under one of its tiny arms. I heard three loud whoops as I was unceremoniously shoved through a side door, and out onto an overcast Milwaukee street corner.

Once we were out, that building started shaking and tearing itself apart. It finally just up and imploded into itself with a big old whump of air. By the time the volunteer firemen showed up there wasn't much left to see. Men in white coats gave statements to bewildered policemen as I sipped a beer offered me by an understanding soul. Nicola Tesla was off to one side, covered in dust and debris scribbling madly in a notebook that was now charred slightly at the edges. Buffalo Bill sat hunched up on a curb, hat in hand, crying softly for his lost dreams of dinosaurs at a dime a head.

So, my dearest, Pete is gone. The professor says he will rebuild his machines one day-- Bill says not with his money he ain't. So rescue seems out of the question. The common sense thing to assume is that your baby brother is long gone, a meal for monsters. But Pete was never one much for common sense. I lay awake some nights wondering if, somewhere back in pre-history, Pete didn't manage to bust that Rex after all. If so, then maybe my old partner has managed to start himself the world's first and only dinosaur ranch. Never count a cowboy out till he's six foot under, that's what I always say.

Hug the children for me. I will be home from my travels in the spring.

Your loving husband,
Sam

GO WEST, YOUNG MARTIAN, GO WEST

I swear, you'd think Martians had never seen a horse before.

"Mr. B'Sham," I shouted, "sometimes you have to work the reins and holler at the critters some. And that whip there beside you on the seat -- that is not there for you to kill flies with. I promise you, sitting around singing to your team and trying to establish one of your 'telepathic rapports' will not get these nags moving."

This was becoming a regular, and annoying, event. Every time the wagon train came across a creek, a river, a rugged patch of land, anything that might naturally give a horse pause, you could count on B'Sham to try his mumbo-jumbo instead just showing his nags who was boss. It slowed the whole train down, and folks were starting to get irritated.

"Good wagon master Wilde, you must forgive me once again, but I was sure I had touched the mind of our lead horse, Nellie. If I can once accomplish this, and convince Nellie of the importance of our journey, I might never again have to resort to intimidation and pain in dealing with her. Is this not a worthy goal?" The Martian cocked his oversized head and smiled a very human smile.

Five years ago, the Martian pod-ships had fallen out of the skies all over the world. Lots of countries figured it was some sort of invasion and, in many places where they'd come down, they were slaughtered by the hundreds. The Martians in the pod that landed in the Mediterranean were condemned as demons by the Pope and infidels by the Arabs. That pod had weapons, though, and was able to defend itself. They somehow made it to Gibraltar eventually and proclaimed a new state – or so I'd read.

The ones that had come down in New York Harbor were just filled with your garden variety Martians, who were about as meek as lambs. Someone up high in immigration showed uncommon good sense that day, and decided to treat these Martians as just one more group of folks coming to America to find a new life. Just like my Pa and Ma had done forty years earlier.Like a lot of families had.

I had reluctantly taken B'Sham and his six brood-mates into the wagon train at St. Louis. This was the sixth bunch of settlers I'd seen through to Oregon, and I thought I'd gotten used to the peculiarities of foreigners. So I decided, why not.

Martians were a whole new kettle of fish though.

"Now, I suppose old Nellie is a right fine conversationalist, once you get to know her," I said, "but maybe you could put off all the mental jaw-boning till after we get past the Rockies? We are on a bit of a schedule here, sir."

Part of me wanted to tell him to just hold back and wait on the next wagon train, but I wasn't so sure he'd be welcomed with open arms.

Surviving Martians from all over the world had flocked to the U.S. and there were Marsey-towns springing up in cities back east. I'd been to the one in Chicago and the smell about made me puke. They had been forced to take squalor to a new low in order to survive. Martians were despised by the local citizenry, regularly beaten and hung, scapegoats for every misery that befell the Windy City.

B'Sham nodded agreeably. "Ah, my fore-mind sees the wisdom of such advice but my hind-mind gets lost in the miracles of the under-realities, as usual. I will do my best to…" He was interrupted by two sets of tentacles exploding from the interior.

"Skil'Tha is putting his nasal appendage in my water again!" A voice shrieked out of the wagon.

All three of B'Sham's eye stalks swiveled back to see what was going on. "Skil'Tha, stop that this moment! Bla'Me, keep your cup under your hood so he can't do that. You shall both walk this day if you do not behave."

Soon things had quieted down in the wagon and the Martian's team was moving once again. As I rode away to see to some other small crisis, I couldn't get over how different these folks from the stars were, and yet, how much like us they were, in so very many other ways.

A wagon train is about eight parts boredom and two parts planning. There are always likely to be personality clashes and differences of opinion, which is why everybody agrees to some pretty basic rules before they can become a part of the train. The rules

37

change from train to train, depending on the parties involved, but sticking to them is what makes things work.

Not stealing, and keeping your pecker to yourself, are almost always high on the list rules, so I was taken totally aback the night one of the young Martian brood-mates was accused of stealing Jake McCoy's dog and fornicating with the thing.

It had been a long day and I'd settled in early when young Tad Jenkins shook me awake. "Mr. Wilde, you gotta come quick. Mr. McCoy and the Jones boys are stirring everybody up, sayin' they aim to string up them heathen Martians."

I hissed out an oath or two and was up at a run, over to where a crowd had gathered outside B'Sham's wagon.

There was a tug-of-war going on between the Mars born Patriarch and the Jones Boys. The rope in this contest was a Martian young'un named B'Li who had wrapped himself around an old hound dog I'd seen running alongside Jake's wagon. I hated wasting a perfectly good shotgun shell, but I needed this to stop immediately, so I shot up into the air.

"What in tar-nation is going on out here? Has everyone lost their damned minds?"

McCoy strode forward as the Jones boys reluctantly gave up their side of the struggle. "That damned little Leather-lips there stole my dog, Duke, who I'd just tied up for the night, and we found him," he pointed at B'Li, " hidin' behind some barrels, stickin' his wheedle right up ol' Duke's ass -- brazen as you please. That's just plain ol' against the laws of God and nature."

You could cut the moral outrage with a butter knife.

"I... don't know what it could be, but I'm betting we should all hear B'Sham's side of this mess before we go stringing anybody up." Even I had to admit that it all sounded damned nasty.

The Martian hugged his tiny brood-mate closely. "Wagon-master Wilde, Mr. McCoy, I don't understand what is going on. I assume this involves the Earth custom of sex but that would involve sex organs and we have none... at least not in the way you mean."

Several women clapped hands over the ears of young children and hurried them away. The men became even more agitated.

38

"Okay, hold it down." I said loudly. "Let's see what the kid has to say for himself. Maybe we can get this all cleared up without the need for ropes and I can get back to sleep." B'Li had released Duke into the wagon and now he wriggled free of his elder's grasp. "Well youngster, speak up." I prompted.

Shyly, he answered. "I was passing the wagon of Mr. McCoy when my hind-mind felt the anxiety of the dog, Duke. She is soon to deliver off-spring and did not wish to do so, tied up out in the open. That is not the way of her kind, so I was helping her to find a more suitable place."

"Duke's a bitch?" asked Fred Jones. No one bothered to answer.

"All right," I encouraged the young Martian. "So, what about the other thing?"

"I have seen that it was the custom, among dogs, to sniff out the anal openings of one another. She had sniffed mine and I reciprocated with my own nasal appendage." He pointed down between his leg stalks.

There was silence for a long, ponderous moment before Jake broke the silence with a laugh that would have done a donkey proud. "If that don't beat all?!" The laughter got contagious and soon we were all about fit to bust a gut. Just about then, B'Sham informed everyone present that smaller dogs were emerging from the larger one in his wagon. Well, that got people laughing even louder, and that brought more folks, and every time the story was told, the merriment grew. Next we knew the necktie party had become a camp wide wing-ding, celebrating the birth of Duke's new puppies. It was probably midnight when things broke up. Last I remembered, Jake was insisting that B'Li have one of the pups just as soon as it was weaned.

But, mostly, boredom was the order of the day. We fanned out the wagons whenever the land permitted it, so no one would have to eat too much dust or start feeling like they were constantly bringing up the rear. B'Sham had gotten better at communing with Nellie and she was getting good at leading the others in the team. Folks had even started to seek out his help in dealing with unruly animals -- with mixed results. It wasn't like Martians could actually talk to critters, he admitted to me one day, but they could *touch* them it seemed. Folks were plum tickled when he did manage to figure out a bug bite in a horse's nose causing it to act skittish, or why a chicken wasn't laying.

Then one day, we spotted the Rocky Mountains and that got everyone a little excited, especially the Martians.

"There is a great uprising of land on my world, much larger than anything on Earth, but Mars has nothing to rival the drama of your mountains." B'Sham told me as I rode alongside his prairie schooner. "It was atop this rise that the great machine, which flung us to this world, was erected. It makes me sad that those we left behind are surely dead by now."

Not a lot was known about why the people of Mars had abandoned their world all in one great wave as they had. It was a disaster of some sort, but that was usually about as much as they'd say.

"It's got to be hard losing your home, all at once like that." I offered.

He smiled sadly at me. "Would you like to know about why we made such a perilous trek? It's not a secret, just something painful to discuss with outsiders." I wasn't sure what to say, so I waited to see where this might go. "You have been kind to me and my brood; perhaps the sharing of this tale will make you even less of an outsider to us."

"I'd be honored, sir."

"Mars was once much like Earth, but all that ended a very long time ago. We were the last generation of that age and we knew that our world could no longer sustain us. Our leaders decided that we should enter vast hibernation facilities to wait till scientists had figured out how to renew our dying planet. There were less than half a million of us at that point, and there seemed no other choice." He shook his head and adjusted his enormous hat to shield his eyes. "We were to be awakened when the world was new again, but that day never came. The scientists failed and we slept for, I am told, more than a million Earth years. Finally, the machines that kept us in slumber failed as well, we awoke to a world we barely knew, desolate and dead. The scientists had left us one last desperate gift, the great impellers which threw us toward your planet, and a half completed

40

fleet of survival pods. It was a mad scheme, in retrospect, and many of the pods did not survive the journey, but this was our last resort."

"So now, you and your family are flinging yourself off into the great unknown again?" I smiled at him and he returned the gesture.

"Yes, but this time we have one who is brave and fearless to guide us in our pilgrimage, so how can we fail?"

I could tell he had been practicing his sarcasm.

"Mr. B'Sham, just call me Moses, and tell Nellie that she needs to pick up her pace a bit." I put spurs to my roan and lit off to see what was around the next bend.

We were nearing the foothills and people were getting antsy to get started up the mountain. They knew it was a hard road but the sooner we were at it, the sooner it would be done. As the wagons were circled for the night, there was a tension in the air.

Back east, the dime novels have convinced a lot of folks that you circle the wagons to fight off wild Indians and that just is not the case, for the most part. Mainly, the circled Conestoga wagons provide a corral so that the animals can't wander off, and to discourage the odd Indian brave, wishing to enlarge his number of ponies. This was usually about as close as things came to an Indian attack.

That night the Martians were all out, long after everyone was asleep, soothing and reassuring the horses and livestock against the ordeals of the next day. I was fast asleep, so I didn't see this next part with my own eyes.

A young brave from one of the local tribes had crawled under a wagon and had his sights set on two of our best ponies, probably to impress some girl. But, when he climbed up on the first one's back, he found him a small demon from another world, dressed in denim and flannel, perched on the animal's neck. He let out a scream and so did little B'Li. They slapped at each other in terror as the boy's feet urged the horse into a galloping leap over the tongue of the nearest wagon.

This might have been the end of the affair, with B'Li dropping off, and the brave getting away with a handsome trophy for his bravery.

Luck is a fickle dance partner though.

41

That horse managed to land smack into the middle of a bear snuffling around the camp for food. The thing reared up, throwing horse and riders to the ground. This commotion had men, including myself, out of bed on the run, snatching rifles as we pulled on pants. The Martians had beat us to the punch, though, and had formed their own circle around the bear, the Indian, the horse and their tiny brood-mate. I couldn't get a clear shot in the darkness but I could see the Martians moving in a slow clockwise dance singing a soothing song. At first it seemed to work, the bear was wary, but calmer, then Joey Jones let off a shot, by mistake, and the bear went insane.

That behemoth backhanded the Indian youth and I knew he was dead instantly. Then he made for the circle of singers and before they could react, the beast had mauled two of them and taken B'Sham's head clean off his shoulders. I froze in horror, I'm ashamed to say, but the animal turned its rage toward us humans and would surely have several of us before we could get off a shot -- except that the remaining Martians had leapt onto its back and seemed to be stinging it with barbs that had emerged from the tips of their tentacles. Once we came to our senses, we all shot at once, aiming so as not to hit our fellow travelers.

When it was done, only the three smallest brood-mates were still alive; B'Li, Skil'Tha and Bla'Me.

The trail is supposed to harden a man up, but I cried like a baby that night and so did a lot of other folks.

We spent another day camped by those foothills as we buried our friends, and the young ones did a ceremony over their graves. At the end of the service, little B'Li sang a song in English of how glad B'Sham and the others would be, knowing that they had sacrificed themselves for the brood, not only those born on the home-world, but those who had become brood along the trail West.

Jake and Sarah McCoy sort of adopted those alien kids after that. They spread the new family over both wagons and somehow managed to make it work. Most all of us made it to the Oregon Territory that year and I was sad to take my leave when the time came.

When I returned to St. Louis I found more than twenty five broods all outfitted and waiting for someone who would lead them.

42

That trip I took five human families, along with the broods. I had a pretty good feeling about how things would go.

TASTEFUL

"What in God's name possessed you to hire the man? He looks like a vulture." Edward Sullivan wiped ink from his hands as he nodded toward the hunched-over scarecrow of a man who shuffled his feet down the hallway, peering furtively into each doorway he passed. "Man gives me the willies just looking at him."

Fred Bonfils shrugged into his fur coat as he gave Ed his patented *trust me* grin. "That's the beauty of it. You've been pestering me for a night guard for the past three months. It's nineteen-oh-one, a whole new century, and folks in *this* century love a paper to read over breakfast. We dropped the 'Evening' from the *Denver Evening Post* and started doing the lion's share of printing at night. That makes you a mite concerned. Quite understandable... consider the problem fixed."

Ed rolled his eyes. "Yes, a guard. Someone big and dangerous-looking who can handle all the deranged nut-jobs you manage to piss off with this here paper. I'm the one stuck here all night with a target painted on my back and you declaring it's hunting season. When twenty guys with sledge-hammers and guns break in here to destroy the presses and shoot me dead, what good is *he* going to do?" He jerked his thumb nervously in the direction of the human vulture.

Bonfils patted his chief-printer's shoulder reassuringly. "Don't you see, Eddie, we publish a couple of articles about the West's most famous cannibal patrolling these premises every night, armed only with a knife and fork, and it'll scare the bodily fluids out of any would-be hooligan. Makes for a damned fine story too, if I do say so myself. It'll be the sort of thing that sells papers... *Alfred Packer, Colorado Cannibal, Hungry For A Challenge!*"

Suddenly the hunched form was there, between them, smiling shyly. "Actually it's Alferd... 'ER' not 'RE'."

Both men jumped back with a start.

"Just so, just so." Bonfils adjusted his coat, and harrumphed loudly. "Well, both you fellows keep up the good work. Morning news waits for no man and all that. Good evening." His walking stick tapped out hurried measure as he sprinted for the front door.

Suddenly it seemed to Sullivan that his boss was in a mighty big rush to face the Colorado snowstorm that awaited him on Denver's narrow streets.

Edward Sullivan stood there for a moment examining the ceiling and walls in great detail – anywhere that was not in the direction of Packer's damp, red eyes. "Yes, *Alferd*, the presses must roll if we're to tell the good folks of Denver what to be appalled about tomorrow. Murder and scandal, scandal and murder. Yup! Folks just eat that u…" Now it was Ed's turn to harrumph. "No offense."

Packer just tilted his head too one side like a dog trying to understand the Declaration of Independence.

The printer turned to his right, to where the massive presses were housed. "You can expect the folders and bundlers to wander in about 3 a.m., but things should be pretty quiet till then." He turned back to see Alferd's crooked smile. "Not quiet, quiet, of course… the presses can get pretty damned loud, actually." Sullivan chewed at his lip."Have a good… guarding."

Something about the man made Ed want to run for the safety of his printing presses, but he didn't. His pace was defiantly casual. Edward Sullivan would not be cowed in his own kingdom. He had almost pulled off his dignified escape when he heard a thin voice from back down the hallway.

"Don't you worry none, sir. I became a vegetarian whilst I was in Prison."

Ed glanced over his shoulder, but the vulture had flown.

"Sir, is the city treasurer really a Satan worshiping Sodomite?" Tim Smith poked his nose up over the tear-sheet he was examining. His voice echoed in the cavernous room that housed the now-stilled presses.

Sullivan sighed. The presses had churned to a stop five whole minutes ago and if he couldn't get them back up and running—and damned soon—there'd be Hell to pay. It was always something.

"Timmy, lad, how many times must I tell you to just see how things are printing up. You'll ruin your mind if you actually read the damned paper."

Timmy was a good kid, 14 years old and already a fine mechanic and printer's devil. He was eager to learn the trade but a mite too earnest for his own good sometimes.

"Next week we'll probably print a retraction on page 7 saying that we only meant to imply that the treasurer is a Republican." Ed rubbed his eyes. This was going to be a long night.

Tim folded the tear-sheet, laid it aside and grabbed another. "How can we get away with printing something like that if it ain't true?"

Sullivan looked down from atop the press where he had been adjusting a tension bar. "Well, I've been with this paper since I was your age, so I can remember the days when we ran factual, well-reported pieces that truly informed the public. Trouble was that nobody bought the damned thing back then except to wrap fish in. Then along comes Fred Bonfils and Harry Tammen, and the *Post* starts filling its pages with gruesome killings and hair-raising scandals. Bingo, and we are now the number one rag in this ragged old town." He scratched his chin and winked at the boy. "Every now and then, though, a fact slips past and gets into a story. Thus do I sleep soundly, secure in the knowledge that we are still providing a service. And that, Timmy lad, is how I am able to face my morning shave without cutting my own throat. It's a grand life."

Young Mr. Smith nodded his head sagely. "Okay, but what's a Sodomite?"

Ed rubbed his eyes again, harder this time. "A Sodomite is what old Bonfils will do to us if we don't get these presses back on line and printing his paper. Crawl under the cutter like a good lad and see if there's another dead cat caught in there again."

Two dead cats and raccoon later, the metal giant was once again chugging away noisily, spitting out wood pulp paper covered with ink and imagination.

With all the racket Sullivan's ears had been subjected too over his 40 years of running printing presses, he often thought he should be stone deaf. He wasn't... especially where his presses were concerned. To him the cacophony was a symphony and he knew every note by heart. The High reeds of a bearing that needed a drop of grease; the

46

steady beat of bass drum rollers as they pressed paper tightly between them; pistons clacking away like Spanish castanets; the slice of sharpened steel blades cutting through flimsy pulpy, white flesh providing a constant cymbal clash of finality at the end of the line. But, something was out of tune tonight. Something was clicking that shouldn't be.

Sullivan knew that snowstorms would drive animals to seek shelter in the warmth of the moving machinery but three dead cats in one night would be a new record. He bent down low to check under the great machine. The view through to the other side was fairly clear here by the driver belts. No obvious small critters. Then he saw cloven hooves walk past on the far side of the array of moving gears and chains.

His head shot up and hit a metal gear box. He staggered to regain his balance. It wasn't such a bad storm as to drive in a horse. How would it get in anyway? No, horses didn't have cloven hooves. A goat? Ed shook his head to clear it. Couldn't be a goat, way too big for a goat and he'd only seen two hooves.

Then Tim Smith backed right into him and they both managed to stay upright only through a set of very elaborate dance steps. Without looking at Ed, Tim croaked, "Mr. Sullivan, sir? Last week you said that my job as your assistant made me the printer's devil around here, right?"

Sullivan nodded and blinked to clear his eyes of the last remaining stars. "Yup, that's how you're referred to in the trade. Started out that way myself, I did."

"Then what does that make him?" The boy pointed a shaking finger at the figure just now rounding the back end of the metal printing behemoth.

He was tall, well over six feet, and a flowing satin cape mantled his shoulders. His complexion was a darker shade of red than Ed had ever seen on any Indian. He had a goatee, a forked tail, furry legs and a set of cloven hooves that would have done any billy-goat proud. A sulfurous vapor swirled around him as he strode toward the shocked duo. Tim feinted dead away.

"Y-y-you can't be in here." Ed yelled. "You'll have to come back during regular business hours." He could feel his knees turning to churned butter.

"Yes, yes, yes. Sorry, but I am booked solid these days. I apologize for the theatrics but my client, the honorable Harry Snowden, insisted that I look the part." The red man hadn't spoken loudly yet his voice cut through the din like a bloody bowie knife.

"Treasurer Snowden? Holy crap!" At least the paper wouldn't have to retract that part. "Well, if you are Satan, where are your horns?" Sullivan bellowed. Now that he'd gotten over his initial shock, he was starting to doubt the entire scenario. This was the twentieth century after all, and Ed was a man of reason.

Satan snapped his fingers and two sharp, long, gleaming white horns appeared on his forehead. "It's true, isn't it? The devil's in the details."

Ed fell back hard onto the gear-box. His fingers fumbled frantically into the open front of his shirt. He shakily pulled out the little crucifix his grandmother had given him when he'd left Ireland and mumbled a quick prayer. "I c-c-comand thee, Satan, to get... something... oh yeah, hence!

The lord of Hell stepped gingerly over Tim's prostrate form and nudged Ed aside. "Sorry, can't hear a word you're saying." Satan's fingers rubbed the gear box, as though trying to polish it. "You know, I've been thinking about getting one of these contraptions myself. Ever since that Guttenberg fellow started putting out my rival's memoirs, he's been doing better than ever. Why, with some good writers I could do a monthly magazine instead some book that nobody ever reads all the way through." The Lord of Hell yawned and cracked his knuckles noisily. "Almost a shame that I'm contractually obligated to kill you gents and destroy this mechanical marvel."

Ed whimpered softly. All those Sundays spent genuflecting on wooden pews and where was God when you needed him?

Just then, a small vulture-like form fell from the top of the press onto the demon's shoulders. Before Satan could react Alferd Packer had grabbed the sharp white horns. He leaned forward with all his body weight and the horns snapped off like dead wood. As the king of the damned screamed in rage, Packer jammed the points of the horns into Satan's infernal eye-sockets.

The demon staggered back, and tripped on Tim.

Packer rolled off, a gleam in his eyes.

The Dark One lashed out blindly but his hooves got hopelessly entangled in the long cape. Satan roared. "Mortal, I shall have your soul flayed before the combined legions of hell."

In reply, Packer hacked out Satan's tongue with one of the razor-sharp horns and threw it aside.

"I ain't been troubled with a soul in decades. Heh, if you find that damned, shriveled, worthless piece of ectoplasm, you're welcome to it. Never did do me no good."

Fire danced across Lucifer's fingertips but Packer grabbed his arms. He swiveled Satan around until he could jam the demon's hands between two enormous rollers. Then, with one deft stroke Alferd sliced off the red, pointed tail and tied the hooves and hands together like a rodeo steer. He then lost no time in using the broken horns to carve away large steak-sized hunks from hell-spawned arms and chest.

Packer licked one horn with a shy smile. "Some days I do regret becoming vegetarian."

Sullivan fell to his knees as he watched the rest of the grizzly slaughter. He'd never considered himself particularly religious, but had always had a healthy respect for the prince of lies and evil in general. His head spun with the moral implications of what he now witnessed. Overcoming evil was a good thing, right? Did that make this demented cannibal an agent of God? If the Devil was evil, did that make Alferd Packer good? Certainly he was a good butcher.

Just as Packer sliced off the last remaining decent cut of devil meat, the demonic cadaver disappeared along with the pile of juicy red steaks and their puddles of blood.

Only the crimson-stained horns remained, still firmly grasped in Packer's gore-covered fists.

Over the mechanical din of the still churning presses a booming, disembodied voice roared out in fiery exasperation. "Snowden can keep his damned soul for all I care! *The Denver Post* can print whatever it sees fit -- most of what you print are my kind of stories anyway – just keep that crazy man away from me!" Flame spat along the ceiling though there were no scorch marks in its wake.

Ed felt a pressure inside his head and thought it would burst. With a rush of wind and a rumble of thunder, the building shook to its very foundations. Then all was quiet. Not quiet, quiet since the presses still clattering along usual, but normal.

Packer carefully slid the horns into his coat pockets before cleaning his hands with an ink stained rag. "If that's all then, Mr. Sullivan, sir, it's time for my lunch break. I made myself a nice green salad with vinegar dressing and home-made bread. I'd hate to see it sit too long and go stale."

Ed looked up from his prayerful stance and just nodded his head. Packer was right -- no one liked a wilted salad.

Eventually, Tim came to, embarrassed at having dozed off. He wanted to tell Sullivan about the strange dream he'd had, but the folders and bundlers showed up just about that time, stomping their feet and complaining of the horrible weather.

Ed never spoke of the incident again, not with Alferd or anyone else. *The Denver Post* never did run any articles touting their cannibal night watchman, but somehow word got around and there were no more incidents as long as Alferd was on the job.

Mr. Edward Sullivan, too, became a confirmed vegetarian.

THE LAST BATTLE HYMN

Hardly five feet out of the barn door and the mule just stopped. Plopped down without a by your leave. No amount of cajoling or cursing by the young black farmer had moved it one inch further.

The old woman sat rocking and knitting on the front porch, doing her best to pay no heed to Joe and his labor dispute.

Ninie Ann Jacobs was somewhere in her nineties now and could sympathize with that mule's point of view. Texas had proven to be a dry, harsh land but, after a life spent picking cotton under the Louisiana sun, at least it was *their* harsh land.A smile lit her eyes despite herself. Freedom was a wonderful thing but it came with its own challenges

"Ninie!" Joe shouted from the barn, "Old Hepzabah done made up his mind that his work day is over before it's even begun, but I still got a third of that field left to plow!" He cocked his head in defeat. "Help"

Ninie laid her knitting aside and strode out into the harsh morning sun. It was all she could do to keep from laughing at the look on Joe's face.

"I recon me and this mule need to negotiate some." She gazed deep into Hepzabah's eyes and, after a moment, the animal averted its gaze with a visible shudder. She'd learned a thing or two over the years about dealing with critters. Something like this didn't need no full-on hexing though, so she stood on her tiptoes and whispered into Hepzabah's ear. Then she turned around and marched back to her knitting. After a moment's consideration, the mule stood up and resumed his weary gait.

Joe slapped his knee and took off after Hepzabah. "You are queen of the negotiators, Ninie!"

Waiting on the porch, eyes wide with wonder, stood Little Joe, her eight year old great grandson. Ninie settled herself in the rocker where he tugged at her sleeve till she tilted her head his way.

"Ninie, Ninie! What did you say to Hepzabah?! You put the whammie on that ol'mule, sure as sugar. Didn't you?"

"Now, that's somethin' you don't need to know nothin' about."

But eight year olds are tenacious. Finally, Ninie set down her needles. "Well, I'll tell you, I only said two words to that critter. " The boy leaned in close. "Mule stew!'" she whispered.

Little Joe stared for a second then laughed and twirled himself dizzy. After a moment he jumped from the porch in pursuit of two scrawny chickens.

A sudden wind made Ninie's hands shiver. Her eyes scanned the low hills that marked the horizon. The wind came from out there— nothing good ever came from out there.

Jed Creed hated Texas. It was just like the Hell his Mamma had always preached about. If it wasn't for all that cattle money that filled its banks to overflowing, he'd never have been tempted by the damned place.

"Godalmighty, Jed!" Roy moaned, "We shook 'em. We ain't seen that posse for hours and this wound in my leg ain't feelin' no better."

His other associate, Clyde, looked ready to fall off his horse— pitiful. Jed missed the war.

He slowed his horse, "All right, all right!" he hissed. He unslung his spyglass and surveyed the horizon. "There looks to be a house off towards the horizon, I suppose we can hold up there for a bit."

Jed turned his horse in a three sixty degree circle, squinting his eyes for signs of pursuit then spurred the animal towards the distant house. He was a proud man--Proud to have ridden with Bloody Bill Anderson and proud to have been part of the war against slavery. John Brown himself had once shaken his hand. It galled him that he had been forced into common bank robbery by a country that now called him a murderer, no better than Southern border ruffians like Quantrill and his pack of dogs.

"Afternoon, sir. Anything we can be of service with?"

Joe had seen the riders approaching from a mile away and quickly shrugged out of his plow rig. Most folks were neighborly enough but he made sure Ninie and Little Joe were inside behind closed doors.

Jed smiled—never a pretty sight--and jerked a thumb at his

companions. "We ran into some trouble a ways back, one of my men took a bullet in the leg, nothing serious, but we could use some water, maybe some linens and such, to patch him up. We've been riding pretty hard."

"Trouble?" Joe asked. "We heard something about an Apache raiding party last month but I figured they were gone. Not much around here worth raiding."

Clyde piped up, "Yep, it was Injuns, Apaches by the look of 'em. Meaner than a coyote in a corner."

The door slammed open and Little Joe bounded down the stairs in a jump. He raced to see the wounded man, an awed light gleaming in his eye. "Gee, mister, real live Apaches? Did they try to scalp you too?"

Roy smiled a wicked grin and pushed his hat back to reveal a billiard ball of a head. "Just let 'em try, boy, God done beat' em to it"

Clyde let out a belly laugh, and Little Joe joined in. Joe smiled nervously.

Ninie slipped out of the house and caught Captain Jed Creed's eye. They stared at each other for a long moment, neither wished to be the first to look away.

An hour later, wounds had been bound and the three riders sat in the sparse shade of the farm's one scraggly tree. They sipped from canteens and gnawed on Ninie's biscuits.

"Lonely kinda place, isn't it?" Clyde said through a mouth full of breadcrumbs.

Roy worried at his bandage and offered, "Still, it beats the hell out Kansas. These niggers got it pretty soft now that we done liberated them from the chains of slavery."

"Negroes." Creed growled.

"Yeah, that's what I meant."

From out of nowhere, Little Joe plopped down in front of them.

"My daddy says you fellas fought for the union in the war. Says he could tell by them pants ya'll wear. Boy, I wish I could have been there fightin' by your side and killin' Rebs." A puzzled look crossed his face. "Say, were any of those Apaches Rebs?"

Jed set aside his canteen. "Well, first off there weren't no coloreds in our regiment. You can't just go mixing the races up that—the men wouldn't have stood for it." A far away look came into his eyes. "I wasn't much bigger than you when my Pa moved us to Kansas so it couldn't become a damned slave state, but I never even spoke with a negro until the war was over." Jed thought briefly of the jailer whose throat he had slit the night he escaped the stockade.

The boy shifted uneasily at the look in Jed's eyes.

Ninie strolled over to the tree and grabbed Little Joe by the ear, "Boy, you got chores need tendin'." She slapped his rear and sent him on his way. "My, my but you men sure did tear through those biscuits. I'm sorry we don't have much else besides beans." She looked at the ground, not wanting another staring contest with the man the others called Captain Jed.

Jed scanned the old woman from head to toe and thought, *Good men bled and died for the likes of her.* A bitterness rose up in his throat and settled into his eyes. *God ordains that men go to war, I just wish he would explain it sometimes.*

Ninie gazed up into those eyes and took a step back in spite of herself. Her hands shivered again though no wind stirred the stillness.

There was some commotion out behind the house and the men looked furtively at each other.

"I know you gentlemen wants to be leaving," her voice quivered, "I've sent the boy out back to see that your horses are ready and that your saddles are nice and tight, we got snakes in these parts will spook a horse something fierce."

Clyde smiled, teeth full of crumbs. "Mighty good biscuits, Ma'am. I recon I'll see what the boy's up to."

Eyes locked again but this time Ninie's were filled with fear.

Clyde's panicked voice came from the back yard. Captain, I think you need to get back here!"

Creed exploded, "Damn it, old woman!" He shoved her aside like a small child and ran to the sound. Roy followed at a fast limp.

She staggered around the side and a terrible tableau awaited her. Everything seemed to happen in slow motion. She saw little Joe fly through the air propelled by the anger of Jed's clenched fist. Gold coins spilling out of the saddlebags and bounced everywhere in a sparkling chaotic pattern. Then she heard the sound of an eight year old body slamming into a wooden wall--a terrible crunching, wet sound. And then he lay still in the dust, his limbs at angles they were not meant to be.

Ninie screamed like banshee wailing out all the horror in the world.

Joe came storming around the opposite corner of the house, a hastily grabbed axe swung high above his head. Three guns simultaneously barked out their song of death and Joe fell to his knees, anger and surprise lit his eyes briefly before he flopped to the ground. For a moment all was silence.

Roy raised his head and surveyed the area. "What in tarnation happened to the old lady?"

Creed shook with rage. "She's run off--damn her black soul anyway. Let's make sure she's got nothing here to come back to."

Jedediah Creed watched the flames dance and remembered all the other houses, barns, cabins and storefronts he had watched burn in his career. He put spurs to his steed and never looked back.

Their path led them into a parched creek and when they emerged on the other side a figure stood waiting.

Jed's horse reared up and almost threw him back into the gully onto Roy and Clyde. After a moment's confusion they rode over the edge again. There stood Ninie wrapped in a ragged old black shawl, surrounded by a circle etched in the sand and bordered by weird objects, many of which were disturbing to the eye.

"Old woman, get out of our way or I'll kill you where you stand!" Jed thundered in a voice that would have done John Brown proud. All three horses whirled and bucked wildly for a moment until they could be brought into line.

Ninie stood quietly and watched. Creed took aim and shot. The bullet missed its mark so he fired two more, to no effect.

Ninie glared. "I have what you call a talent." She croaked out. "Unlike most, I came into my talent late in life. I've known others who had these gifts, but they tended to piddle them away on frivolous things, love charms and such."

55

Clyde dismounted and stormed towards her. "You're a witch, that's what you are you old black scarecrow." He stopped short ay the circle.

Roy stayed on his horse and screamed, "What the hell do you want?!"

Ninie ignored both of them and kept her eyes locked with Jedediah's.

"Bein' older I had learned how to let my pain and anger simmer at a low boil. You know why you never hear of no big magical things that rip the world asunder for everyone to see? I'll tell you why--a spell like that takes a long time to prepare and not many have the patience and focus to do such an awful thing." The wind picked up around them and dust started to sting their eyes. "I said I'd already learned patience and the focus was easy. Master John Jacobs focused me real good. That man savaged my daughters and then sold them off like livestock. That man, who we had to call "Massa", chopped off my husband's hand. What he done to me ain't even worth mentioning."

Creed sneered.

"So it took me over four decades," she continued. "But I slowly, and with great care, gathered my mojo and crafted a spell that would gain me a vengeance such as has never been witnessed by mortal man..." She flexed her gnarled hand and the cracking of her knuckles was thunder. "But then the war came and afterwards, freedom. Massa Jacobs was a pitiful, droolin' old fool by that time, and I couldn't hardly see the point no more." She raised her head and looked at the setting sun. "So, as it happens, I still have that spell sittin' around like a loaded shotgun. I figured I'd never have a use for it." Then she hissed in a voice that could barely be heard, "That changed today!"

Creed bellowed. "You and your kind should be kissing my feet! I fought for your freedom, I bled for you, I rode with John Brown!"

Ninie let out a dry raucous laugh, "Ain't you heard? Old John Brown's body is moulderin' in its grave." She waved her skinny arms and all hell broke loose.

The wind swirled around her and buffeted the three outlaws.The sand and dust swarmed like angry hornets rising toward a suddenly dark and threatening sky. The noise was like an oncoming locomotive.

As the last bits of dust swirled into the sky, a sudden calm replaced the fury. The old woman was gone and the men coughed to clear their lungs. Clyde stepped into the circle where all that was left was the black shawl. He blinked the sand out of his eyes and nudged at the shawl with his toe. "God damn…"

Clyde's words were cut off by a shriek that split the sky. A solid column of blistered air and dirt spun out of the clouds, the furious fist of some dark twister god.

It struck square in the circle and tore Clyde's head and arms raggedly from his torso. The arms, fingers still twitching, flew into the sky, but the half stripped skull landed dully at Jed's feet. Clyde's eyes were frozen wide in terror, his bloated tongue choked on a half delivered curse.

The column continued to rotate wildly. It crushed the remainder of Clyde's carcass into a reddish brown paste.Stones and sharp grains of sand smashed into the petrified outlaws—tears and blood stung at their eyes and torn flesh.

Somehow, over the roar of the wind the men heard the whisper of the old woman. "Run…"

Creed and Roy lit off in opposite directions.

Jed glanced back and saw the dust devil head off after Roy's limping form. He could hear Roy's screams above the mighty roar of the wind as he mounted his frightened horse.Spurs dug into the animal as Creed screamed in rage and frustration.Roy's body flew past as the wind knocked the Captain off his horse.The form swung wide in an awful arc till it stopped and rotated, upside down, above Jed's head. Most of the man's clothing and swaths of skin had been rudely ripped away, but his face moved in such a way that proclaimed him still among the living.

"Kill me." The plea came as more of a squeal than a true voice.

The sand and wind had formed a whirling wall around the two men. The captain bared his teeth. There was a cracking sound above his head and he could see Roy's legs forced apart as if by some invisible hand, a wishbone that would grant no boon. Bits of un-named gore hit Jed's cheek as the two sides of Roy flew into the swirling mass of sand.

"What?!!!" Jed screeched, "I've lived my life in righteousness and all I've ever been is spit on! I deserve better than this. Face me, witch!"

Ninie stepped slowly out of the maelstrom. Her shoulders slumped in a great sadness.

"We weren't hurtin' nobody. It weren't like we was gonna take your gold. Why… my boys…" She dropped to her knees.

Creed roared and lurched toward her but a rock, the size of a fist, hurled out of the sand and struck his forehead. He dropped to his knees and the two stared at each other.

"You just like hurtin' people. You say you was a soldier but I don't think it really mattered much to you which side you fought on—long as you got to hurt people." She pushed herself up. "I thought when I finally got me some revenge it'd feel good, righteous… All I done was waste forty years. Ain't no justice here, just puttin' down rabid varmint."

The wall of grit closed in on Creed. It engulfed the old woman till he could see nothing more of her. Who was she to judge someone like him? As the terrible wind ripped at his skin and tore the flesh and muscle from his face he lifted his voice in song, "Mine eyes have seen the glory of the coming of the Lord, He hath trampled out the vintage where the grapes of wrath are stored, He hath loosed…"

Ninie made little piles of stones over the charred bodies of her grandson and great grandson, too tired to dig proper graves. She sat vigil through the long night rocking back and forth in her rocking chair, which had somehow survived the flames.Joe and the boy were truly free now—maybe she was finally free too. She wondered if men like Creed ever found freedom. When the first rays of morning came, she was gone.

58

MANDOLIN WIND

In Mandolin, Kentucky there was a saying, "The only men that go down into the ground are either coal miners or dead, or both. It started with a disaster. Fifteen good men were caught in a methane explosion a mile under the ground. When they were finally dug out they found seven men who had died instantly and eight who were not as lucky.

Rumors of sub-standard practices flew like rotten tomatoes but the Big Lock Mining Company maintained a firm stance that no one could have predicted or prevented the tragedy. Coal mining was a dangerous and dirty endeavor.

The folks of Mandolin just hung their heads and made ready to bury their dead. There hadn't been such a large-scale disaster in those parts since the thirties, but men died down there every year and that was a fact of life. That Sunday every church in town would have more than one casket lined up waiting to have words spoken over it and the pews would be filled like it was Easter Sunday.

I felt a gentle nudge on my shoulder and came awake like a startled owl. "Son, this is your stop. I told you we'd get you here on time." The Greyhound driver had been a good listener the night before, pretending not to notice when my eyes had gotten teary when I told him why I was making this trip, said the dust did that to everybody.

I blinked my eyes a few time to get my bearings. "Thanks Mr. Hollings. I'd have slept straight through to New York." He helped me get my bags and I bit my lip as he drove off into the rising sun carrying twenty more souls somewhere east, away from Mandolin. I'd spent the last three days and nights riding one bus or another to get back here. I was twenty years old, and had come back from studying at the School of Mines in Golden, Colorado. I was here to help my Mamaw bury my daddy. I was going to be an engineer, the first member of my family to go to college. Daddy had said if I was so God-damned determined to work in a mine, I sure as hell was going to do so in a tie and carrying a clipboard.

The town was just waking up and I figured I'd better put myself together some if I was going to make it through this thing. I went into the little general store that acted as the town bus station, to use the facilities.

"Well, look what the cat drug in!" I knew that voice before I saw the face. Old Lou Hascombe, a big friendly bear of a man who used to sneak aside Superman comics for me. He came around the counter and shook my hand like it was a pump handle. "Johnny, your Mamaw has been in here every couple of hours for the past two days, wanting to know when you was coming in."

I nodded and stifled a yawn. "How is Mamaw holding up?"

Lou poured me a cup of coffee. "Well as can be expected I suppose, like the rest of the town." He said and gave me the key to the washroom.

Now, Mamaw wasn't my grandmother but rather my great-grandmother. She had lived to see her husband, my Papaw, and all three of her children die and now she was laying her only grandson, my Daddy, to rest. They'd all taken, one way or another, by the mines. Papaw and their eldest had died in a cave in-back in 1935 and my great aunt Esther passed the next year of a broken heart, so they say. Grandpa got the black lung in the early Sixties and five years later we lost Grandma to influenza. Momma died the year I graduated high school.

As I walked up the front porch steps of the house I'd grown up in, I tried to avoid the squeaky spots so I wouldn't wake anyone. I should have known better. Mamaw was sitting in the porch swing holding her old mandolin tight to her chest--so quiet I would have missed her if she hadn't spoke up. "Praise be, I thought you was your daddy there for a second, in the morning light." I went over and sat down by her, intending to hold her and give her comfort, but she pulled me close and let me cry into her white hair.

No one knew how old Mamaw was, but all the stories told about her alluded to her growing up wild out in the hollers, the youngest daughter of the infamous Black Jack Dougal.Folks swore that most nights, if you were real quiet, you could here her play her mandolin up somewhere in the hills, from the front porch of her run down shack, accompanied by a fiddle and a banjo—though it was said

60

Mamaw never had visitors after Papaw died. All my life I had heard the tales of evil eyes, love potions and hexes of all manner and shape. Parents would frighten children with tales of the wicked Dougal clan.

To me, though, she was just Mamaw, the sweet, wrinkled old lady who showed up on Sundays and holidays and always had a piece of candy, a warm hug and a twinkle in her eye for me and my brother. She smelled of biscuits and peach preserves and I knew I was home.

As I sat there on her left, my kid-brother, Billy, came through the screen door and sat down silently on her right and nestled his head into mamaw's other shoulder. We'd talk pleasantries later--how was the trip, how's school treating you—but right then we just needed to hold each other. Billy was a sandy-haired, gangly young heartbreaker, the star pitcher of the Mandolin High School team, and the apple of Mamaw's eye. He and I were all Mamaw had left, and she was all we needed right then.

As expected, the Third Baptist Church of God was filled to overflowing, but folks carved out a place for us. Mamaw wasn't a regular church-goer--in fact she and her heathen ways were a favorite topic in the local gossip-go-round—but Mandolin stood together, united in their grief, on this awful day.

It was cold and gray outside, wet and miserable as only an east Kentucky October day could be. We all stood when the preacher finally stepped up to lead us in a hymn. Brother Ellis Cob was a hellfire type, but that day he mostly spoke about heavenly rewards and the wickedness of men. He didn't come right out and name the Big Lock Mining firm specifically, but he got a lot of rousing "Amens" anyway. He was just getting really wound up when he stopped abruptly. The bells over at the Episcopal Church had started pealing and, considering the time, that was peculiar. Then we all got to whispering among ourselves as more bells joined in the chorus: Lutheran bells, Assembly of Christ, Methodist and when the big bell over at the Catholic Church let out its deep bass bong, folks jumped from their seats and mothers held their children tight as men edged their way toward the aisles. Suddenly, a man covered in coal dust burst though the double doors and announced in anguished tones, "There's been another cave-in!"

Now, the mine was temporarily closed while mine inspectors were checking out the repairs. Time was money and Big Lock needed their report so that they could officially get the mine opened up, quick as possible. It was nine of those inspectors and two Big Lock officials who'd been trapped this time, in another methane explosion down near elevator shaft #2.

Jake Stuart was a foreman, as well as a deacon, and he got the men organized as best he could. He came over to me and hung his head. "Bobby, I know you ain't no certified engineer yet but I'd take it as a blessing if you would get in on this. All the regular company engineers are down in Bowling Green this weekend learning about new safety protocols."

I looked at Mamaw. She was holding tight to Billy's arm but when she looked in my eyes she let go of him. "I know I can't argue either of you out of this, so go on." She moved aside and Billy and I joined the stream of men and women heading toward the mine.

I somehow wound up giving orders to men who'd worked this mine their whole lives. It wasn't a role I coveted, but everyone looked to me as someone with knowledge of the big picture. Too many of the men who would normally be sought out in a crises such as this were laying in pine boxes, in churches all over Mandolin. Men like my Daddy.

Working in teams, we made good headway getting machinery and men into elevator #1 for trip after agonizing trip down to where the inspectors and company men were trapped behind a wall of boulders and splintered wood. Despite all our best efforts, it was pandemonium. Dust was everywhere and all communication between the surface and the efforts below were sketchy at best. I grabbed old Jake Stuart, who had just returned to the surface, and asked him how it was actually going down there. "Bobby," he wheezed, "I just can't say. There's lot's of rock, lots of dust. If you ask me, I'd say there's eleven dead men behind that wall of stones." He shrugged away and headed outside for some well-deserved fresh air. I looked around, feeling helpless. Normally the mine ran like a well oiled machine but necessary equipment was down for repairs and no contingency plans had ever been made for a situation so unthinkable.

62

What happened next started out as a low rumble that we all felt more than heard. Everyone's eyes went wide with terror. Suddenly the sound became deafening. Smoke and dust billowed out of the #1 shaft like a steel mill chimney. Everyone in the elevator scrambled out just before the cable snapped and the cage plummeted like it was a freight train bound straight for Hell. That was the last thing I saw clearly.

After what seemed like an eternity of coughing and staggering around in the dark, I stumbled out of the entrance into the dismal gray afternoon--into another nightmare. Smoke and dust billowed all around as women ran frantically, screaming the names of husbands and sons. Grown men sat like broken puppets beating on the ground with impotent fury or simply standing with downcast eyes. Children grabbed tight to the legs of their parents, squalling in terror at what was happening. I called for Billy and ran around snatching at every blackened figure that was about his height and build. He wasn't there.

Jake Stuart laid a hand on my shoulder and shook his head until I thought it might fall from his shoulders. "Son, there were a whole lot of men still down there." He sighed. "I'm afraid your brother was headed down, last I saw of him."

From behind him I heard a brittle, dry choke of a scream and saw Mamaw collapse like a rag doll carelessly dropped to the floor by a petulant child.

I knelt down beside this frail, ancient woman who seemed to have imploded into herself. Putting my ear near her mouth I expected to hear sobbing or a prayer for mercy. Instead, what I heard was a hiss of sheer fury and one word repeated over and over, "NO! NO! NO!" Jumping to her feet my Mamaw knocked me backwards and lifted her hands to the leaden sky. "No more!" she shouted. "I'm done playing by your rules you son of a bitch! Do you hear me? Done!" Her eyes blazed with a knowing madness and she wailed in a voice I barely recognized as hers. The words she screamed were in a language I hadn't heard since she sang ancient lullabies to Billie and me, when visited her cabin. Momma didn't like her singing them to us, so Mamaw sang them to us when Momma wasn't around.

A wind came up from nowhere, causing black dust devils to

dance all around us. It knocked folks off their feet and took their breath away. Only Mamaw kept her stance, head reared back and howling something that was neither curse nor prayer. Lightning played across the sky, repeatedly striking at the iron rods set near the crosses on the roofs of every church in town. Bells rang in a mad symphony that could barely be heard above the deafening howl of a wind that sounded like the very hounds of Hell were hunting for wayward souls.

Then I saw them coming through the blinding dust and debris, fifteen men with waxy faces and Sunday best coats snapping crisply in that awful wind. They came stiffly, but determinedly, down the main road from town and converged from the various churches scattered around the community.

Nothing seemed to impede their charge through the miniature cyclones, black as any strike breaker's heart.They strode through the townsfolk who were hanging on for dear life to anything they could. Their gate was staggering and inhuman but glimpses of their features were horrifyingly familiar. I struggled to my feet to follow them. Others clawed their way to standing so that they could follow as well. The looks on the faces of the citizens of Mandolin ran the gamut from bliss to utter horror. I made it into the mine just in time to see the last two of the fifteen climb down into what was left of elevator shaft #1. They crawled down into the darkness clinging to the walls like lizards or spiders, finding hand and foot holds no mortal could grasp.

"My God!" Jake whispered next to me. I hefted a fallen beam and made for the shaft, with the whole town close on my heels. What we had just seen was insane and what we were about to do, even more so. As if by some silent command, men started rigging block and tackles and scrounging around for cable and rope to assemble slings that might hold an injured man without causing them too much more damage. As we worked we could hear sounds from deep in the shaft, rocks flying and shifting as though a pack of dogs were digging up bones in a rabid frenzy. Maybe the Hellhounds *had* been loosed upon the world.

Twenty minutes later the rig was as ready to go as it ever would be, still we were silent. Each man looked at the shaft like a schoolboy afraid of being called upon by a hatchet-faced teacher. I remembered Daddy telling me once that if you looked the devil square in the eye, you had him half beat every time. I took a miner's helmet off the man next to me, and stepped up to the rope sling suspended from the hastily constructed pulley system. "Just don't let go of me, boys." I knew I should have said something more profound, but that was all that I could think of. Two men eased me over the side and I started my descent.

Almost immediately I was in a world that came in headlamp glimpses. The fear of smashing into a wall without warning had my heart beating like a trip-hammer. The only tangible thing in that place was the rope that I clung to for dear life. Next stop, Hell.

After about 86 bottles of beer on the proverbial wall, I could see what had to be the bottom of the shaft and heard a series of ragged coughs. I saw three men prone on the ground, laid out as neatly as any hospital ward. As soon as my toes touched down I unlimbered the rigging I had brought from above so I could secure this end of the pulley system. As I pounded the last spike into place, my headlamp spotlighted something out of a horror movie. Three of the fifteen waxy faced men staggered toward me, their hands and fingers scraped to the bone, crusted with dirt and coal dust, their faces pitted and gashed by cruel pebbles. What had once been Sunday go-to-meeting suits were in tatters and covered in filth. Staggering and awkward, they moved with a purpose, all the more disquieting because their eyes were shut tight. Cradled in their arms were three more miners, battered but alive. I froze not knowing what to expect but they ignored me and with blind precision managed to secure their charges into the makeshift rigging. One turned to me, his head at an unnatural angle, and pointed up. I edged around him, fearing what he might do if I came too close, and gave the rope three tugs.

Those unconscious men ascended into the waiting darkness like prayers to the ears of God. I knew it would be a while before I could send up two more so I checked the men lying on the ground to be sure they were okay. Once I was satisfied, I turned to follow the sightless, ragged figures as they made their way toward the sound of digging. After about thirty steps my light played over the other twelve. They were hefting rocks and debris that should have crushed them, digging with hands that were heedless of the terrible abuse they were taking. All of them moved with a speed I would have thought impossible and a stamina that was not human.

Suddenly, as I watched in awful fascination, they broke through to another pocket of air and several of them acted as inhuman braces to shore up the opening while others crawled in and out, gently pulling man after man to safety.

I turned and ran back to the lifeline just as it lowered into grabbing distance. Two of the fifteen had followed me back and between the three of us we strapped two more men in and sent them on their way. More men were brought out and I saw to their comfort while they waited patiently for their turn at salvation. After the ninth and tenth men had been sent on their way, something deep in the earth roared out its anger, causing chunks of rock and dust to fall all around us. Several of the sightless men came lurching back, using their bodies as struts to hold up the walls.

It was obvious that time was of the essence and still there was no sign of my brother. We found a way to rig three men into the next load and went on like that until only the walking dead and I remained. I started to cry as I realized all our efforts had not been enough to save Billy. How could I ever face Mamaw? When the rig descended one last time I started to latch myself in as another shower of dust stung my eyes. The undead miners closed in all around me, holding me fast. I panicked and hit one of them on the jaw. They held me tight. Then, through a wave of dust, the last of the fifteen staggered into view carrying a boy so gangly and frail, I thought my heart would jump right through my ribs. The battered, sightless man who carried him was covered in soot from head to toe and seemed to remain standing only as an act of pure will. The ragged forms released their hold on me as he gently transferred Billy's weight into my arms. Then he did something unexpected-- he stretched his neck to plant a soft kiss on my forehead. I knew the feel of those two lips from a thousand nights of being tucked into bed. As they always had, they banished all my fears and doubts, making the world a place worth living in again. I secured Billy beside me, then turned to the last of the fifteen and pleaded, "Come on, Daddy, there's room!" But another deep rumble sounded and he grabbed the rope, giving it three tugs. The last I saw was a flickering of forms trying futilely to hold back the movement of the Earth. I tried, as best I could, to shield Billy from the avalanche that had been unleashed all around us. When I looked back down again, there was only a rumbling blackness where I had stood the moment before.

As we reached the surface hands quickly released us from the ropes and we were hurried out into the light. The whole mine seemed determined to destroy itself and all we could do was flee its death throes.

Once out, I saw stars and the full moon in all their glory. The terrible wind that had summoned those buried below had become a warm, soothing breeze. Everywhere there were people holding each other as if to make sure they were real. Those poor mine inspectors and company men were truly lost, but no son of Mandolin died that day. I reluctantly left Billy in the hands of people setting up impromptu medical tents. I had to find Mamaw and tell her Billy was all right.

I found her right where I'd left her. She lay silent and still upon the ground, her eyes closed forever but there was a smile on her lips. I knelt to stroke the wispy white hair which fluttered over her translucent skin. I stared at her, and realized that though this woman had been there all my life, I'd never really known her at all. A phrase came unbidden into my mind: "Those who sow the wind shall surely reap the whirlwind." Mamaw's wind had harvested life from the deep furrows of death.

The mine never reopened and Mandolin soon became just another deserted collection of ramshackle buildings. For some reason, a lot of townsfolk wound up in Michigan, making cars and furniture. Billy played several seasons for the Detroit Tigers before opening his own car lot. He married a girl from Mandolin and they raised two gangly boys.

I still make a living going down into the earth, trying my best to make sure men can survive their shift. It's a dirty and dangerous business. But, sometimes, when I'm down there alone, I swear I hear music, like the gentle strum of a night's breeze across the strings of Mamaw's mandolin.

SECTION TWO

CHIN SONG PING AND THE FIFTY-THREE THIEVES

Chapter one:
Land of Opportunities

As near as he could figure, Ping had fallen into one of the levels of hell. The sun stripped all color from the barren landscape. The mind-squelching heat seemed to assault him from below and above equally. The horizon stretched farther than he would have thought imaginable only a year before, and there was no relief in sight. This level of hell had a name, and the name was Arizona.

He wasn't terribly surprised at being in hell. His mother had always said it was where he would wind up, after all. What he did resent, though, was *walking* through this place of damnation while leading a magnificent white stallion that refused to be ridden.

For the eighth time that day, he stopped and bowed to the stallion. "Great and honorable steed," he said, "I realize you are far too noble to be ridden by a scoundrel such as my humble self, but we may move out of this place much faster on your four feet than on our six collective feet." He bowed lower and added, "Please?"

Ping clambered into the saddle resting on the broad, white back of the animal. He did all the "giddyup" things he had seen white riders do, to no avail. For the eighth time he slid to the ground, thinking that the problem was speaking Chinese to an American horse. He was naturally good with languages and understood English well enough, if it was spoken clearly, but the best he could manage to remember right then was, "Horse, go now, please!" and that had just seemed to irritate the animal.

So he walked, heading southeast for no particular reason other than that it was away from the railroad.

###

It had begun a year ago, when his all-too-brief career as an acrobat ended badly following private instruction in contortion from the wife of the head acrobat. He decided that women and his

70

handsome face were a formula for failure. So he became a gambler – a very male-oriented profession, indeed. After an early run of good luck, he had the bad luck of continuing his winning streak in a game of chance with several brothers in the local Tong. An upturned table, an escape through a window and a daring chase across the city's rooftops had led to him blending in with a group of men gathered at the docks. He subsequently found himself herded onto a ship headed for America. He was to become a railroad worker. He wasn't sure what, exactly, that meant, but it was a career he had not tried before.

Being a Chinese worker for the Central Pacific Railroad was back-breaking, demeaning and boring work, so he again took to gambling most nights, just to keep his skills fresh. At first, he gambled only with other Chinese, but they had very little money. So as soon as he learned enough English, he sat in on poker games with the Americans. It was another bad career move. Drawing four aces to Chauncey O'Donnell's three kings had put him on the work-gang foreman's permanent bad side – so much so that Ping had found himself in the basket three days later, when blasting into a hillside was required.

A unique method of planting explosives had been developed by the Central Pacific. You lower a Chinese worker over the cliff side in a basket to set the explosive and light the fuse, and then you haul him up as quickly as possible. Often, the man even survived. Ping kept his eyes closed during the descent and quickly planted the charge and lit the fuse. He screamed to be pulled up and was raised a couple of yards before his ascent stopped. He hollered and looked up to see the smiling face of Mr. Chauncey O'Donnell.

"Looks like you ain't so lucky today, China boy!"

Stunned, Ping reached down to snatch the fuse, but he was too far away. Laughter wafted from above. He started his basket swinging while keeping a close eye on the sizzling fuse. As it reached its last sputter, he leaped from the basket at its highest arc, tucking into a ball and rolling with the blast as it sent him high into the air. At the moment he felt himself begin his downward plummet, he went spread eagle in an attempt to impede his fall. He landed square on the head engineer's large, snowy-white tent.

71

Extricating himself from yards and yards of canvas and cursing white men, Ping sensed that this might be the time for another career shift. Perhaps horse thief. He grabbed the large water skin hanging off a post and leaped onto the engineer's beautiful white stallion. He'd never ridden such a beast before, but the situation provided the necessary learning incentive. He took off like a shot. Random gunfire and angry yells receded as he urged his stolen steed in the direction that he had seen whites point toward and call Arizona.

Chapter 2:
Dances with Dogs

Deep in a cavern, in the mountains south of Tucson, a man with sly features and ancient eyes danced. He danced not in any particular step known to the feet of man but a mad dervish of joy and self-congratulation. He giggled at his own cleverness as he danced.

Behind him were four cages of a size and strength to hold a human being. The two cages in the middle held two young women who sat in despair, one black and the other Oriental. Though clothed in elegant attire, all hope had fled their expressions, and tracks of tears, long spilled, streaked their lovely cheeks. To the side of the cells was a natural hot spring, large enough to bathe in. It bubbled and hissed sulfurous odors, and an unnatural glow shown from deep within. Louise, the young black woman, spat vehemently at the pool.

"Why don't you just get this over with, Moses? At least then I wouldn't have to watch you try to dance, you crazy ol' dog," she hollered.

The sharp-featured man stopped in mid-gyration and ran to Louise's prison. "Don't pout so, my Nubian beauty," he purred. "Your time will come, and there's always the chance the baron will come through with your ransom." He sighed. "Now, that would be a pity. This is working out so well."

He snaked his nervous hand through the bars to touch the hem of her dress. Louise kicked at him. He withdrew and licked his fingertips like he was finishing a Sunday chicken dinner.

"I swear I can just taste the power inside you." His eyes rolled up in their sockets in pure ecstasy. "Today, however, our celestial princess shall be the star attraction." He nodded toward the other cage, where the young Oriental woman sat dejectedly. "A pity she refused the opium though." The girl whimpered slightly.

"I hope you aren't so foolish when your time comes, dear Louise. I do so hate to see a dumb animal suffer." With that, he jumped across the bubbling stone cauldron and shouted, "So much to do, our guests will arrive any moment now!"

Red light filled the cavern, casting weird shadows wherever

Moses Castle danced. Sometimes the shadows were of a man, sometimes of a dog. Some of the shadows bore no resemblance to anything found outside a nightmare.

Louise reached through the bars of her cage to May Song, the girl in the next cage. "We still here, and we still got a chance," she said soothingly. "My mamma used to tell me stories about princesses who was in lots worse jams than this." May Song gripped her hand tightly. "They's always a hero in them stories somewhere. He's coming, we just got to hang on till he does." She smiled tightly. This wasn't a fairy tale, and she knew there weren't any heroes in real life.

Chapter 3:
Dust and devils

At least it wasn't flat. After a night's march farther, Ping had finally come to the boulders scattered around the foothills of a mountain range that stretched to the north. He saw a cloud of dust approaching from the east and was unsure of what course of action he should take. In desperation, he thought to consult his traveling companion.

"Great and honorable steed," he said, bowing, "there are many men coming our way. They may be our salvation, or they may be our doom." The horse nodded. "They come from the wrong direction to be those who might chase us, but there is the mystery of the telegraph, which could have foretold our coming. They might also be those known as Apaches. I am told they have no sense humor in these matters." He wrinkled his brow. "Of course, any random band of white men might also find distraction in disposing of me and acquiring you."

The horse lowered his head and shook it distractedly. "Yes, you are wise, oh noble one. Let's hide!"

Soon he and the horse were concealed behind a boulder. Ping peered through the heavy brush.

The dust cloud soon became a large group of hard-looking white men led by three men with dangerous expressions and red sashes around their waists. When they came to a rock face near where Ping lay hidden, they sat to let the dust settle. Then the three leaders wailed loudly, like amorous wolves or coyotes on a moonlit night. The ground beneath Ping rumbled as the rock face pivoted upward with a frightening majesty that froze most of the riders and frightened their horses.

When the way was completely open, the men with sashes swore and gestured wildly to move them all into the cave. Once the rest of the group had vanished into the hillside, the three whooped, shot off their pistols and galloped after the others.

As the stone slid slowly back into place, Ping sat wide-eyed and slack-jawed for a few heartbeats. America was such a strange place, and Arizona doubly so. However, as odd as what he had just seen was, what he smelled was opportunity.

He bowed briefly to his steed and said, "Stay!"

Ping ran around the boulder, legs pumping in a way that might have prolonged his short career as a messenger many years ago. He dove for the diminishing opening, tucked into a roll and propelled himself into the dark interior which, he belatedly admitted to himself, had all the makings of a fine tomb.

He stayed in a crouch as his eyesight adjusted to the gloom. He was alone.

But somewhere farther down in the Earth's bowels came a grumbling of loud, masculine conversation. A faint reddish glow made his surroundings even more surreal. The smell of opportunity had been replaced with the unpleasant whiff of sulfur. He glanced back at the now-closed stone wall. He took a deep breath and moved forward in a cautious, but determined, trot.

It wasn't a straight course. Several times, he thought he was surely lost, but then a snatch of echoed conversation or scratches of hooves on the floor steered him back onto the correct path. Finally, he came to the entrance of the main hall where the voices were loudest. He was about to peek around the entryway when a man's hat brim came into view, followed by a long arc of tobacco spit.

Ping thought retreat was a wise tactic, so he backed away quickly and silently until he tumbled down a short flight of roughly carved stairs into a smaller chamber. He dusted himself off and made sure his bones were sufficiently intact. In this chamber, the red glow had taken on a more golden hue. Slowly, he perceived the room was filled with stacks of paper and piles of things that sparkled or glowed with a warm luster.

Gold, jewels, American money. He lost no time in stripping off his shirt. With the practiced movements of a one-time escape artist, he tied off the sleeves and neck openings with strong knots and filled it until he thought sure the seams would split. Finding quality garments was difficult on a railroad worker's salary.

Ping smiled broadly and was about to make a hasty escape when, through a ventilation hole in the wall, he heard a woman cry out in fear and anguish. He stood and glared at the ceiling, reciting under his breath all the reasons he should keep going. He was a career thief now, and he had to learn to harden himself to his more tender impulses.

Then there was another scream and a woman's voice pleading for help, in Chinese. This was followed by loud, coarse laughter and jeering whistles.

Okay, one look wouldn't hurt. He dropped his loot and scrambled up a massive pile of gold and into the ventilation hole. A series of twists and turns brought him to a wooden-grated opening that overlooked an enormous cavern and four cages.

Chapter 4:
The Cowboy Way

Moses Castle stood on a platform, resplendent in a crimson robe, and faced a room full of trail-hardened men. He dangled the young Asian woman over a steaming, water-filled pit as his audience of desperadoes whistled and cheered. The girl's wrists were bound, held high by only the robed man's strong right hand. Every few seconds, he dipped her low enough for the bubbling water to scald her feet, causing her to scream. The men hooted their approval every time.

"I am Moses Castle and, like that Moses long ago, I will deliver you into the Promised Land!" he shouted.

The crowd went wild.

"You have been chosen to carry out my law in this land, and my law is chaos and violence! You will do this, not for my pleasure but because it is your pleasure!"

More cheers and hooted laughter rang off the cavern walls.

"You 50 men will wear the red sashes that will make you my special brand of cowboys, and you will be invincible from this day forward. That invincibility does not come cheaply though, it requires sacrifice."

Moses frowned, then threw his head back in a loud laugh. "Not a sacrifice by you, my friends, but *for* you!"

He turned to the young woman whose life he held so literally in his hand. "A shame to waste one so lovely on such a pack of mangy curs, but it's for a worthy cause," he crooned in flawless Chinese, a glint in his eye. May screamed as loud as she could.

A long gleaming knife appeared from nowhere in Moses' left hand. With a movement as quick and devious as his features, he cut the woman's delicate throat, sending a streamer of blood across his audience. Then, with a flourish, he let go of her bound hands. She dropped into the pit. Water splashed over the sides in a hissing tide of deep red as she disappeared into her churning, watery grave.

Eerily, a searing red light erupted from the water's depths and cast Moses' shadow in stark relief on the far wall. It was no human shadow but that of some great beast howling at an unseen moon.

As the commotion in the audience slowly died down, Moses produced an armload of virgin-white strips of silky cloth. He dipped each one into the bloody pool until it came out soaked, dripping red, like a bandage used once too often. These he handed to the three men who already wore such sashes.

Like deacons, the three moved through the throng offering an unholy baptism to their congregation. At each new initiate, a soaking red sash was wrung over the man's head, then tied around his waist with the snarled word, "Brother." After all the men had been so anointed, Moses ascended his platform and let out a mournful wail to recapture their attention.

"Boys," he drawled, in a decidedly less formal tone, "You're cowboys now, and that means you step aside for no man. If you want it, you take it! No one can hurt you. You can laugh at bullets and eat knives for breakfast, as long as you wear those sashes."

Several men looked at their waists with dubious expressions. "Oh ye of little faith!" Moses shouted with glee. He pulled a .45 Colt from his robe and shot the man nearest to him. The owl-hoot looked frantically at his chest for a wound, but there was nothing but a small hole in his shirt. Wide-eyed with delight, he joined Moses and the throng in a good laugh.

Soon, men were shooting one another and generally having themselves a good old time. The walls echoed with thunder and mad laughter.

After a while, Moses set his feral features into a mirthless grimace and howled once more for silence.

"With you men, we are now 150 strong, and we will keep growing. We are going to be a god-damned army!" No longer able to contain his joy, Moses jumped up and down, whirling as he did. "Now get the hell out of here," he screamed, "and don't let me be hearing anything good about you. You got that?!"

The cowboys ran to their horses, tied along posts at the rear of the cavern. They laughed and punched one another's shoulders until the last men were saddled up. As one, they rode into the stone maze that would lead them to the outside world – and glory. The clattering echo of hooves mingled with yelling and the rumble of stone grinding on stone until the cacophony receded into silence.

Moses could barely contain his sense of self-satisfaction. He wished that there were two of him so he could shake his own hand and pat his own back. Instead, he settled for dancing around the cave. When his revels brought him close to Louise's cage, he stopped dead in his tracks and sat on the stone floor.

Moses turned to Louise sitting stolidly in her lonely cell. "Cry havoc, my dear, for I have just unleashed the dogs of war."

Louise sneered through fresh tears.

"What must you think of me?" He sighed. "You've watched me kill three women so that I could give power to men not worthy to stroke your cheek."

Louise looked him straight in the eye. "I ain't afraid of you. You just some crazy man likes to watch folks suffer. I seen your kind when I was a girl – night riders with torches and masks. I see through your mask!"

Moses clutched his hands to his heart. "Girl, you wound me deeply! Can you not see the enormity of my plan? Each of you lovely creatures was chosen with great care, stolen away from your destiny with infinite guile and cunning. A recipe this big requires only the best ingredients." He leapt into the air, clicked his heels together and held up a single finger.

"Let's see, there was Susan Bright Water, snatched right from her wedding bed – the unconsummated bride of the Sasquatch chief himself. Can't go wrong stealing from Sasquatch." He giggled. Gloating was half the fun.

A second finger joined the first. "Lady Carmady, plucked at the height of ripeness, fresh from a holiday in the haunted woods outside Salem. I wonder if her coven is still looking for her."

Louise shook her head. "That girl today, May Lee, she weren't nothing special. She was just a mail-order bride for some big shot owns a telegraph company. Why'd you have to go and kill her?"

Moses pushed his face to the bars of the cage, screaming gleefully at the top of his lungs. "Because I hate telegraphs!"

Several deep breaths cleared the madness from his eyes so he could continue. "What place is there for mystery and magic when just anyone can speak to anyone else over such distances? Those wires strangle every bit of the romance this land once knew." He wiped drool from his lips. "Besides, she is a seventh daughter of a seventh daughter, and those are always magical. You, though, my dear, are my crown jewel. When I sacrifice you, it's going to be quite the soirée. Your grandmother was hot stuff in her day but she's gone. Marie Laveau is dead, and everyone is going crazy looking for little Louise Laveau, but I've got you! You are mine, mine, mine!"

Louise rolled her eyes in disgust. "I keep tellin' you I ain't got no special powers. I don't know no voodoo hoodoo."

Castle looked ready to split a gut, he was so happy. "Baron Samedi says he'll pay handsomely for your return — but I never liked that skull-faced bastard, so I think I'll just stick to plan A!"

Just then, they heard the faint echo of a howl and felt the grinding tremble of the great stone door opening and closing.

"What the hell did those idiots forget this time?" Moses listened for the sound of hoofbeats, but none came. "That's peculiar."

He scratched his neck as he went to the middle of the room, cocking his head to listen. Nothing!

As he turned back to the cages, he heard a pop. A flash of light exploded in the middle of the chamber's doorway, leaving a thin veil of smoke. Then a second and a third until the entire doorway was a thick, hazy curtain of vapors. Through this curtain strode a short, young man with strong, handsome features and an oriental slant to his eyes. He was wrapped from head to toe in a loose toga of fine heavy silk. His wavy black hair flowed around his shoulders. The newcomer's face was split from ear to ear by a warm infectious smile as he bowed low before his robed host.

Moses snarled in perfect Chinese, "Who the hell are you, and what the hell do you want?"

81

Chapter 5:
The Not-So-Great Escape

Ping watched in horror, through the wicker ventilation grid, as the man in robes slit the young woman's throat. He could not hold back the anguished cry of anger and frustration that exploded from his lips.

That might have been Ping's undoing, except that he was entirely drowned out by the general pandemonium that now reigned on the cavern floor.

The only person who heard him was the young black woman trapped in the cage below him. Her head snapped up toward Ping, and their eyes locked. Hers were the most wonderful eyes Ping had ever beheld, dark and gleaming with sudden hope. She was darker than any woman he had ever known. The red luminosity from the pit gave her an aura of sensuality he had never imagined. He fell in love immediately. This was terrible timing for one looking to start a career as a hardened criminal.

He put his finger to his lips then motioned that she shouldn't look at him, but they couldn't keep their eyes off each other.

He mouthed, "My name is Ping."

She returned, "I'm Louise."

Louise. That was such a wonderful and exotic name.

Out in the cavern, a strange and unholy ceremony was being performed, but all of Ping's thoughts were focused on those large, luminous brown eyes.

His mind raced. He had been the student of one of China's great escape artists, so he ought to be able to pull off a simple rescue/escape. True, his master had let him go when he proved to be inept at picking pockets while the great man was performing, but he had learned much in that month and a half.

He ran through his options.

He could smash through the grill, leap onto the cages, climb over to the prison of his new beloved and … be cut down by a room of madmen. Terrible escape plan.

On the other hand he could … what?

When the shooting started, Ping was snapped from his reverie. Plans were overrated anyway, he thought. He would figure out something. With a final blown kiss to Louise, he crawled backward through the ventilation shaft. With no room to turn around, he fell back into the treasure chamber, where he tumbled down the mound of gold to land lightly on his feet.

He grabbed his improvised sack and was almost out the door when he spied a roll of intricately printed silk propped against a wall. In a flash of inspiration, he grabbed the richly woven cloth and bounded up the stairs three at a time. It wasn't a plan exactly, but it was a start.

As he sprinted back the way he had entered, he tried desperately to remember the correct turns. He soon came to the dead end that marked the cave's entrance. Spinning around like a top, he spied a dark alcove he had failed to notice earlier and lunged into its scant protection.

His back pressed against the cold stone. He stashed his stolen booty at his feet. The cleft in the rock provided some semblance of shadows, so Ping closed his eyes, breathed deeply and willed himself to be as insignificant as possible. He listened to the echoes of gunshots, trying to recall his brief training as an actor.

"Be the rock, be the shadow, be invisible," he whispered.

After what seemed an eternity, he heard the rumble of riders and horses. Eyes squeezed tighter, he said a silent prayer. The sound was almost upon him. Over the din of hooves, hammering on solid stone, 53 voices were raised in a howl of sheer, murderous delight. Ping's knees felt wobbly. The wall trembled against his bare back as the great stone rose.

He thought he might soil his only pair of pants.

The din eventually died down until there was only the grind of stone on stone. He risked opening one eye.

The door was more than half-closed, with no sign of the horsemen. Pretending to be invisible had actually worked. Perhaps he should have continued with his acting career.

He scooped up his ill-gotten gains and ran for the narrowing gap between earth and door, where he flung his burdens ahead of his own tumbling body, escaping much as he had entered.

Ping leapt to his feet and saw the retreating men turn into a wave of dust and heat. They were riding hard for some luckless destination to test their new invincible status.

Breath came hard as he dragged his spoils toward the large boulder to his right. To his great surprise and relief, the white stallion was still there.

Ping dropped to his knees and started to kiss the horse's feet, before thinking better of it. He looked into the animal's soulful eyes, then at its swishing tail. A smile crossed his lips as another facet of his plan popped into his head.

He bowed until his forehead touched the ground. "Oh noble one, please forgive me for what I am about to do, but I do it in the name of true love."

The stallion merely shook his lowered head.

Chapter 6:
Gentleman's Wager

Ping bowed low, trying his best to look nonchalant.

The stone door had been ridiculously easy to open once he figured out the trick. Though he had never tried his hand at being a tailor, he had dated a royal dressmaker who had showed him many interesting ways to drape silk fabric. He hoped he looked suitably impressive.

He had found chemicals in the engineer's saddlebags and, with knowledge gained in his short but exciting career in fireworks manufacturing, he had managed his flash-powder entrance.

It felt good to unbraid his hair, and it seemed to fit the role.

"I am Chin Song Ping, a humble sorcerer from the celestial lands across the great water," he intoned.

Well, he had been a sorcerer's apprentice for a time, but he had hated the hours, and the potions gave him a rash.

"In my dreams, I saw a vision of the wonderful plan which you have wrought here in the Americas," he continued. "I thought how delightful and gratifying it would be to meet one with such a bold and devious mind." He laughed. "So, I determined I would drop by for a visit. I trust I haven't come at an inconvenient time."

Ping raised his head to see Moses, chest puffed out and a grin on his face, looking like a kid ready to show off new toys.

"Welcome, welcome!" Moses cried. "It isn't often I have a guest of your obvious intelligence and insight. Come, sit." He waved at the platform, and it became a table and two chairs. "I haven't much hospitality to offer. I suffer from a sensitivity to strong spirits and try to stay away …"

From a fold of cloth, Ping pulled a bottle of fine sipping whiskey – another saddlebag find.

"… But perhaps I could make an exception for such a festive occasion." Moses' face lit up, and two glasses appeared on the table.

After a couple of toasts and some friendly chitchat, Ping sighed. "This is most pleasant, but I wonder if you have ever heard of this American game called poker? I've always wanted to learn it, and I do so enjoy a friendly game of chance."

No sooner had the words left the young man's lips than an unopened deck of cards appeared in Moses' hand. "I've heard of the game." A gleam of cold steel appeared in his eyes. "I'm told it's customary in poker to make wagers as you play. What shall we play for?"

From various folds of cloth, Ping withdrew diamonds, rubies and golden trinkets. Soon, a substantial pile had formed on the table. "I have these few baubles, will they do?" he asked innocently.

Moses' mouth watered. Ping was pleased the man hadn't recognized his own stolen treasure.

As Ping poured Moses a third drink, he noticed that the other man was starting to rock gently back and forth. For some reason, those who trafficked in magical doings often turned out to be cheap dates. Ping had once seen his magician master pass out while summoning a demon, under the influence, leaving him to entertain the monster for 45 minutes, waiting for the spell to wear off.

After several losing hands, Ping's pile had diminished some and the bottle was half-empty. Moses raked in another pot and giggled sloppily.

"You know, Ping ol' buddy ol' pal, I like you! I'm going to let you in on a little secret. My name isn't really Moses Castle." Sly eyes darted around the room, making sure no one lurked nearby. Beside himself with glee, he continued. "It's actually Coyote! I'm something of a god around these parts."

Sweat broke out on Ping's upper lip, but his face remained calm. "A god?"

Coyote/Moses tilted back in his chair. "Yeah, well I was very big with a lot of the tribes who lived in these parts for thousands of years, but these days … white men, black men, even celestials such as yourself." He sighed. "It's all changed." He looked wistfully at the bubbling pit. "But I've got my plan, and it's going pretty well so far. I'm thinking of renaming this whole part of the country Coyoteland. Has a nice ring, don't you think?"

Ping shuffled the cards and looked over his adversary's shoulder at Louise, who nodded in sad affirmation. "Hmm, a god, that must be very nice for you."

For a god, Ping thought, Coyote/Moses was a very poor cheat, but he continued to pretend not to notice. He lost a couple more hands before he said, as casually as he could, "I fear, oh great Coyote, that your plan is so wonderful in its subtlety that I don't fully grasp its logic." He laid aside two cards and got replacements. "Why didn't you just bestow your wondrous red sashes upon your native followers so they might rid this land of foreigners themselves?"

Coyote looked thoughtful, closing one eye and then the other in an effort to make the cards come into focus.

"I could have done that, but it would have been a rather mundane solution, don't you think? This way, my plan is intricate, subtle, like you said. I build my army of cowboys and send them out to pillage, kill and rape, lots of people dead or scared out of their gourds, high-tailing it back east. Eventually, the land will be free of foreign devils, a good thing all around I'd say."

The self-proclaimed god fanned himself with his cards. "Then, just when the cowboys think they have triumphed, I command all the sashes to choke their wearers like cloth pythons. They're all pieces cut from a single strip of cloth woven, 50 at a time, from the webs of Iktomi, the spider-spirit, a pal of mine. He had them lying around, so I sort of borrowed them last time I had dinner with him. Of course, last time I borrowed something without telling him, he set my tail on fire, but ..." He blinked to clear the sweat that ran into his eyes. "What was I talking about?"

Ping took a sip of whiskey. "Something about slaughtering your minions?"

"Oh, yeah, yeah, yeah! I figure between the raping and gruesome deaths of the cowboys, no white man will ever dare set foot here again for at least a hundred years.

"After that, we get to the best part. I step forward, claim due credit, and the tribes regain their lands and worship me again, as I so richly deserve." His eyes misted over in nostalgia. "Now, I wouldn't be greedy, mind you. I'd just rule this southwest part of Arizona and maybe some of Mexico. Coyoteland! There's still plenty of territory for Iktomi and all the others who want to bring back the good old days. There are more out-of-work gods, spirits and unholy entities on this continent than most folks think. Of course they aren't as clever as me, but I say 'Be generous in victory.' Everyone wins!" He waggled his tongue between his lips. "Say, talking all this Chinese is getting to me. Would you mind if I make it so you can speak something easier – English, maybe Lakota?"

"English would be pleasant." A firecracker seemed to go off in his brain and then he was simply able to converse in English. "Thank you, I had meant to do just that before I came."

"A plan should be fun, don't you think! Here's to the plan." Coyote grabbed his glass and emptied it at a gulp.

Ping smiled a fragile grin of agreement and lost another poker hand.

Soon, both the whiskey and Ping's pile of treasure were nearly gone. He stretched and yawned as Coyote counted his winnings.

"I fear I haven't given you much of a challenge, and for that I apologize." Ping sighed and smiled warmly. "Perhaps it is because we play for mere baubles rather than things of true value and power."

Coyote's ears pricked up. "What do you have in mind?"

From a fold in his sleeve, Ping drew a long, stiff white hair that fairly glowed in the weird light. Summoning up all the knowledge he had gained during his time as a seller of rare antiquities, he began his pitch.

"This is a hair plucked from the chin of the great and holy Jade Emperor, may Buddha bless his name. Just before he ascended to heaven for his thousand-year reign, he called in his royal barber to groom him properly one last time. It is well-known that there are no decent barbers to be found in heaven. The barber, knowing the vanity of his lord, merely plucked one hair from the august personage's beard – this hair." Ping rolled the white hair between finger and thumb. "With that, he declared the emperor perfect and fit for heaven. From that day forth, whoever possesses this whisker is blessed with great handsomeness."

Coyote cocked an eyebrow at Ping and the hair.

"Ah, you think that I am good-looking but not devastatingly so." Ping continued, "But, before I acquired this hair, I was so ugly that women would throw rocks and children spat in my face. My warts had warts, and I looked as though someone had beaten me about the face with a chain. This face is the best the holy whisker could do for me. The mind reels at the glory it would bestow on one already as handsome as your own godly self."

With a drunken gleam in his eye, Coyote shoved his loot onto the table and said, "Let's play!"

Ping shock his head. "You insult me, sir! I offer a priceless wonder, and you would match it with mere baubles?"

"Name your stakes then!" Coyote cried, eyes locked on the hair.

Ping leisurely let his gaze wander around the room until it fell on Louise, sitting quietly in her cage. "The girl. She is pleasant to the eye, and I sense that she has some value to you." Pin nodded once, firmly.

Coyote plucked the key to her cage from around his neck and added it to the pile. Ping laid the white hair on top of the rest and shuffled the cards. Coyote cut the deck twice, one eye locked on his guest.

Ping dealt five cards to each of them and sat a moment, studying his hand. "The wager still seems somehow lacking. How would it suit you to wager something more personal, in addition to our existing bet?"

Coyote hunched into his cards and snarled, "Like what?"

"If you win, I will perform for you one service, no matter how unpleasant or demeaning. If I win, you pledge to do the same."

Coyote looked at his cards, then at the hair, then back at his hand. He smiled slightly. "Agreed."

"Ah, then I shall draw two cards. How many would you like?"

Moses Castle, the great Coyote, shook his head.

Ping drew two cards and frowned.

Slowly, dramatically, the Southwestern god lowered his cards to the table. He was holding two fives and three kings.

As he gazed into Coyote's eyes, Ping laid his cards down one at a time: a king, followed by an ace, and then another ace, and a third, and finally, with delicate precision, a fourth ace.

Coyote's face went white, even in the red light. "I've been tricked," he whispered. He shoved the table toward Ping and stood, taller and broader than he had been a moment before. He bellowed his rage. "I am Coyote! I'm the prince of tricksters, I don't *get* tricked!"

Ping jumped to his feet and hurried to the other side of the table, where he bowed in seeming supplication.

Nostrils flared, the trickster raised his hand to deliver a mighty blow to Ping's exposed back. Suddenly, the young man exploded forward and slammed into Coyote with a savage head butt to the god's groin.

The blow sent the god reeling backward until he stood pin-wheeling at the edge of the pool. For a moment, before plunging backward, screaming, into the natural cauldron, the look on his face seemed to say, "Not again." As he sunk, the pool burst forth in a great plume of hissing steam and water sloshed over the floor.

Ping snatched the key from the table and raced to Louise. The door was flung wide, and they embraced with a passion fueled by fear and relief. When they kissed, even the red lighting became more intense. The eventual need for air seemed the only thing that might part them.

"Ahem!" came a voice from over Ping's shoulder.

Ping shoved Louise behind him as he braced to continue the battle, though head butts were about the extent of his martial-arts repertoire.

"You didn't have to do that you know," Coyote said.

There on the table sat a sopping wet, slightly mangy, small coyote. Its fur was singed away in several places, and painful-looking blisters covered its reddened skin.

"I was just a little angry there and got carried away," Coyote said. "I wouldn't really have hurt you much. I always pay my debts. No need to get rough about it."

Ping bowed slightly but kept his narrowed eyes on Coyote. "My apologies."

"So, you have the girl. I guess I can always find another." A long-suffering look came over his canine features. "What service can I perform for you?"

Ping knit his brows in thought. There were so many things that a being like Coyote might do for him. "I humbly ask that you remove your spell of invincibility from the ruffians you call cowboys and never seek to use this evil plan again."

Coyote ran in tight, tiny circles on the tabletop, cursing in languages not yet invented. When he stopped, he looked as though he might cry.

"Oh, come on! Anything but that! I really like this plan, and you can't actually care all that much about what happens to these American white devils!"

Ping sighed. "Perhaps, perhaps not. But I intend to stay in this land for a while, and an army of homicidal, rapacious, invincible thugs might prove truly inconvenient at some point."

Coyote, sullen, licked at a blister on his left paw. "It was probably a dumb plan anyway."

The defeated-looking god turned to go with shoulders slumped, his tail tucked between his legs, but turned and gave a wide grin.

"I can turn off the sashes just by destroying the pool, so consider that taken care of." He vanished before Ping could lodge a complaint.

With a deep grumble, the cave started to shake itself apart. Echoing off the walls was a yipping noise that sounded suspiciously like laughter. Ping mentally kicked himself. He should have included a clause in their agreement about surviving all this.

Chapter 7:
By a Landslide

Ping shouted to Louise in his now-fluent English, "Run! Go swiftly to the cave's entrance. I left a trail of yellow thread to follow. This humble pilgrim shall join you there anon."

Louise, eyes wide in terror and bewilderment, rushed from the room. Ping spared just a moment to stare at the gold, jewels and single white hair on the table. No! He had to keep his mind on the bigger picture.

With practiced muscles, he leaped to the top of the cages and made a running dive into the vent hole on the wall. He smashed through the wicker grating like so much kindling and was gone. Yips of laughter spurred him on.

Louise made it to the entryway in good time, considering the fallen boulders she was forced to circumnavigate, but the stone wall was closed, of course. She had no idea how it worked, and Ping had neglected to share how the thing opened. It was a dead end. Her eyes stung from falling dust as she spent long minutes banging her fists on the stone edifice and feeling uselessly for some nonexistent locking mechanism.

She screamed as a huge section of the cave's ceiling crashed mere feet from where she stood. Finally, as dust filled her eyes and throat, a wracking cough shook her body and despair overtook her. She sat down hard and cried, with rocks and dirt falling around her.

With all that had happened to her in the past few months, being snatched from her home, the hideous deaths, the abuse ... Why had she foolishly pinned her hopes on the smile of a handsome stranger? A glimmer of hope, snatched away like a shiny penny that turns out to be a brass slug – it was too much.

Then out of the dust and debris came a sound, "Awooooo!"

The stone door began to shiver and move.

"Awoooooooooo!" louder this time.

Ping broke through the falling debris, wearing only tattered pants and a layer of dust. He blinked to clear his vision and coughed dryly between howls. Behind him, he dragged an enormous silk bundle that would have given Father Christmas a hernia.

Their kiss was no less passionate this time, though necessarily shorter. He motioned that she should help drag the bundle. She grunted at the weight but was overjoyed by the shaft of sun that filtered under the great stone and the first whiff of fresh air that streamed in under the slowly rising door.

"Stay close. I fear that calamity may come just as easily in the last hand as in the first." Ping choked through the grit that still filled the air.

She grinned fiercely and replied, "You like a hero from some ol' story book, you know that?"

The door lifted only about a foot and a half from the ground, and there it stopped.

"Crawl!" he croaked and pushed Louise through the opening.

With tears in his eyes, he poured out the contents of his bundle until it looked like it might squeeze through. He would have to content himself with being very rich instead of filthy rich.

He emerged into the sunlight where Louise waited. She pulled on the shrunken sack of treasure, understanding the need to keep moving for fear that the mountain itself would shake apart onto their heads. Coyote was petty and spiteful, but he was also thorough.

They reached the brush-covered boulder that hid the white stallion as the door fell ponderously under its own weight. It seemed to take half the cliff side with it.

Louise laughed and wrapped her arms around Ping, smothering him in kisses and tears of joy. Ping looked relieved and dazed. He stared, goggle-eyed at the fallen wall of stone. The yips of Coyote's laughter no longer echoed in his ears.

"We made it." His eyes rolled up into his head as he fainted dead away into Louise's strong arms.

Out somewhere in the merciless Arizona desert, a scraggly grey form chewed on a hapless rodent he had caught for dinner. As he masticated, he puzzled over a long white hair clutched between his paws. He couldn't make more of his invincible cowboys, but a new plan already was forming in his tiny brain. He had once heard an old medicine woman's prophecy about a place, in the land called Holy-Wood, where one day the beautiful and handsome would rule as kings and queens. When that day came, he would be the handsomest of all and therefore a king among kings. That sounded pretty good. He studied the hair more closely and wondered how to get the darned thing to work.

CHIN SONG PING AND THE DRAGON MERCHANTS

Ping ducked as the hatchet whirled out of the fog embedding itself into a ragged playbill for a theater that had burned down the year before. Fog didn't really do justice to the heavy, gray atmosphere that covered the land, making walking a dangerous activity and running a sure recipe for disaster. Despite this fact, Ping ran headlong into the ubiquitous gray swirl--and ran smack into a wall. He staggered for a moment but his head was cleared wonderfully by the knife-wielding maniac that appeared in his path. Dropping to the ground, he slid neatly through the maniac's widespread legs on a loose layer of wet garbage and slime, bowling the ruffian over in the process. Behind him voices screamed curses, muffled somewhat by the atmosphere. Tonight the fog was so thick one might be tempted to call it a heavy drizzle though the constituent droplets seemed to defy the dictates of gravity, hovering as black pepper would in a soup. And it was cold! He should have listened to Louise and packed his woolen coat. A thermometer was useless to describe the numbing cold that penetrated into the bone as a result of the swirling miasma freezing the soul more than ice possibly could. As another hatchet sliced past his left ear, severing the queue Ping had worn his whole life, two thoughts came into his mind. One was, "I was getting tired of wearing that ponytail anyway." The other was, "God, how I hate San Francisco!"

Ping jumped up onto a box that had materialized before him, launching himself into the air where he hoped he might find a friendly fire escape, but this was Chinatown, where one rarely found such luxuries. What his hands found instead was a clothesline. Suddenly his face met with wet undergarments stained in places that he found entirely unsettling. Ping disliked Chinatown even more than San Francisco proper. He used his momentum to propel him in an arc around the line, hurtling him far down the alley where he landed, rolling with the impact. How many years since his career as an aspiring acrobat had been cut tragically short by a slight indiscretion with the master acrobat's wife? But this was neither the time nor place to indulge in pleasant nostalgia.

Over long years, Chinatown had been built haphazardly. It was a wooden labyrinth of false fronts and secret passageways leading to hidden dens of iniquity that lured the depraved, no matter their skin color. It was a maze that had Ping thoroughly lost. If only he had a moment to sit, collect his thoughts, and get his bearings. 'Most unlikely,' he thought. Behind him, he heard the sound of one of his pursuers tripping over the box he had used as a springboard. As a knife whistled through the air, ventilating his jacket, he felt a rumbling beneath his feet and heard the insistent clang of bells in the distance. In San Francisco that meant only one thing, a cable car!

Perhaps he could survive this night after all.

He burst onto a busy avenue populated by a colorful array of humanity dressed in gaudy silk, ragged canvas and dapper, if unimaginative, western suits and dresses. This many whites had to mean that he wasn't far from the Stockton Cable Car line. So, he ran through the brightly lit fog, jumping over displays of fruit and vegetables, pushing through tourists and residents alike in a mad dash for the safety the moving fortress on rails that he heard ahead.

Just as he thought his lungs might burst into flames, he saw the wooden and iron vehicle pulling away from its stop, heading for a steep descent. In one last desperate burst, he flung himself at the cable car and just managed to grasp an iron pole as the vehicle picked up speed. Swinging one foot onto the running board, he hollered "Duck!!"

A hail of hatchets and knives dug into seats and running board. Fortunately, the passengers were few and nimble, so there were no casualties. The gripman deftly dodged a small hatchet while urging the car on its way. The conductor emerged from the cabin, plucking various sharp implements from wooden panels. He tossed them into the street with a certain jaded disdain as he made his way to Ping.

"That'll be two bits, pal," he said very matter of factly.

Ping reached into his pocket and retrieved a twenty dollar gold piece, his good luck charm. "I regret sir that this gaudy coin is all I have at the moment. Perhaps I might persuade you to accept it as an inducement to ignore the next several stops normally scheduled for your most noble vehicle."

The gripman and the conductor exchanged a look. They took judicious note of the sharp instruments still embedded in the seats and walls. They also made assessed the group of angry men who had taken pursuit of the vehicle. After due consideration the conductor took the coin and winked at the gripman. "Enjoy your ride, sir," he said as he motioned Ping to take his seat.

The hike from the end of the Stockton line to a rather seedy looking bar on the so-called Barbary Coast had left Ping feeling stiff and morose. Pulling off his left shoe as he sat down, he extracted a five-dollar bill squirreled away for just such an emergency. The smell of the bill was somewhat unpleasant, but in such surroundings the bartender barely noticed. Chinese were not served at many Barbary Coast establishments, however the Limping Dutchman had never observed such niceties. Four drinks later, Ping was sobbing softly as a burly man with a bristly mustache sat down loudly beside him.

"Barkeep!" The man roared, "Whiskey--your finest--and another round for my sorrowful friend here!"

Ping turned to look at the man, one eye drooping slightly. "Sir, you are a gentleman of great gentle...osity." He shook his head to sort the wool that had gathered within. "You have a look of intelligence about you. May this humble one ask an opinion about a dilemma in which he finds himself?"

The man laughed heartily and slapped him on the back. "Lad, I doubt many would agree about my intelligence these days but all my mental resources are at your disposal for the next..." He looked at his pocket watch, "Five minutes and thirty five seconds."

"My name is Chin Song Ping and I am a man who has always placed a high esteem on my freedom, yet now I am to be married and thus shackled to a life of connubial servitude. I care greatly for my beloved, Louise, but I know not whether I'm ready for such a commitment. I am a coward!"

"Nonsense! You are a man in your prime and this marriage would be quite a blow to your routines and rhythms. Have you thought of merely living with this woman? I know that the oriental mind can be liberal toward such things." His mustache bristled even more and he adjusted the glasses, which perched birdlike on his nose.

"That was my very point!" Ping perked up at having found such an understanding soul. "For almost twenty-five years we have lived together happily, and I would not want to see us split asunder by something like marriage." The man sat open mouthed and staring. "If the strain of marriage were to prove too much for us to bear, whatever would become of our five children?" The man's elbow, which had supported his chin, slipped off the bar and might have caused a lesser being to fall off his stool.

"Five nights ago," Ping continued, "Louise's grandmother, a powerful voodoo priestess long dead, came to my love in her dreams and said we must marry, and very soon soon. Granny Loa dictated that Louise be wed in a beautiful white and lavender gown in a grove of blossoming cherry trees... or the world is doomed." Ping sighed and sipped at his drink. "Both Louise and myself are quite fond of this world... so here am I in this wretched city trying to find a suitable dress for the great occasion."

The man's eyes narrowed. "Sir, a woman entering her middle years will come up with many strange notions. Though I sympathize with your desire to accommodate the lady's wishes, I have grave doubts that the world will halt its tread should you not wed. Has the lady in question been experiencing hot flashes?"

"Ah, just so!" Ping nodded his head vigorously, "You and I, as sane men of the world, might find such a claim outlandish, but who would tremble at the faint threat of world's end when faced with the real and present fury of a woman contradicted?"

Ping and the man both upended their drinks. "Bowing to fate's dictates I have searched the city for two days to find a white and lavender dress fine enough to be worthy of saving the world. An hour ago I spied such a dress in a shop window but before I could find my way in, the dress was sold and gone. I chased the buyers to Chinatown, following them through back alleys and hidden tunnels to implore them to have pity upon my plight. I thought I had lost them when I heard music through a thin wall. I noticed light coming through a crack and endeavored to peek in. There, much to my surprise, I saw Pan Sai Kow--who I recognized as a chief of the Boo Hoo Dow Doy hatchet sons—dancing around, admiring himself in a mirror while wearing the dress I sought for Louise. In my shock I crashed through the flimsy wall, startling the hatchet chief. He quickly hopped out of the dress and called for his men to kill me for defiling his privacy. I managed to escape but am now plagued by the feeling that this might be an inauspicious sign. What do you think?"

Before the man could speak, six aged Chinese gentlemen dressed in stark black western suits flooded through the saloon door. "Mr. President, you will come with us!"

Ping squinted one eye at the mustached man who had jumped to his feet and assumed a boxer's pose. He leapt to his feet beside the embattled President and assumed a similar pose, though he had never boxed anyone in his life. "Mr. President Teddy Roosevelt, forgive this lowly one for not recognizing your grand self earlier. You seem much shorter when perched atop a bar stool."

Roosevelt grinned fiercely, "Bully for you! Heathen you might be, but I thank you for standing with me." Ping gulped as several more Chinese pushed their way into the room--young men, tall and burly, with wicked smiles and sharpened blades at the ready.

"Perhaps this would be a propitious time to summon your Secret Service legions? I have read that such men were always around you."

"I had to ditch them. They would have insisted I not come here to personally meet an informant. Damned nuisance sometimes, being the President!" T.R. ducked a heavy-handed blow and jabbed his opponent in the solar plexus as Ping hopped onto the bar behind him to escape a slash from a curved knife. Leaping out to a rather shabby looking chandelier he swung through the goon squad and landed in the midst of the aged gentlemen. His thought was to use one of these six as a hostage and secure safe exit for himself and the President.

He grabbed a particularly frail looking old man by the throat, "I have no wish to harm you but if you do not stop this I will snap your neck like a twig in winter." The old man twisted and broke his hold so quickly and easily that Ping almost cried out in alarm. Suddenly, he felt himself flying through the air, thinking, not for the first time,

"Am I the only wretch from China who does not know martial arts?" He crashed into the mirror over the bar and felt himself blacking out as soon as he hit the floor. The last thing he heard before oblivion was Teddy Roosevelt bellowing, "Take that, you Celestial son of a bitch!" He could not recall if he had voted for the fellow or not.

Ping awoke spluttering through the water splashing into his mouth and nose. A hand yanked him upright by his newly shortened hair and snarled. "Where is the President, you slant-eyed runt?"

Over the years, Ping had learned to ignore racial epithets as products of ignorance and unwarranted arrogance. He would not tolerate such remarks to his children or wife--his modest wealth and status did afford some measure of dignity--but when directed at himself he was willing to be more philosophical. "Pardon my ignorance in this matter, but I seem to have been on another plane of consciousness when that most worthy gentleman left these premises." His inquisitor backhanded him, leaving Ping to spit out the blood pooling in his mouth.

This man was tall and muscular, dressed blandly and had obviously eaten large amounts of garlic with his evening meal. "We have reports that the President was seen being dragged from this bar by a bunch of Chinese, and you're Chinese. So where is the President?" He let Ping loose and pulled out a badge which said, 'Secret Service.' "I can make matters very unpleasant for you if you don't start cooperating!"

Ping straightened his clothing and pulled back his disheveled hair, "Ah, when last I saw Mr. President Teddy Roosevelt, I was attempting to do the job you are paid for!" A dangerous twinkle formed in the agent's eye. "Please do not take my word, you need but ask the worthy keeper of this bar. Surely he saw it all." The man let out a snort and jerked his thumb down the bar where another man in an apron lay in a pool of blood with a hatchet imbedded in his skull.

"He's not talking so good right this minute. So that leaves you as our only lead." Two more nondescript men came behind the bar and Ping could only assume that their scientific questioning techniques might include the brass knuckles one was fitting on his hand.

100

Had he paused a moment to consider the alternatives, he might have taken the beating and hoped for the best. Instead he did a near perfect back flip over the wooden bar, landing feet first on a table filled with half empty beer mugs. These he kicked into the faces of the gawking Secret Service men and was out the door before they could even react.

###

Ping had already surmised that the six old men in black suits had to be the heads of the six families which comprised the Consolidated Chinese Benevolent Association, though why they should kidnap the president was beyond him. This meant a return to Chinatown and probably more hatchets, but the honorable President Teddy was the only one who might clear his name--and there was still the matter of the dress.

As the agents rushed past his hiding place, which consisted of shadows and trash in a nearby alley, he made himself as small and insignificant as possible and considered the problem of disguise.

In China he had briefly been understudy to one of the greatest actors in the land, Ooh Long, celebrated as the man of one thousand and eighty-seven faces for his skill with makeup. One night, half way through the comedic farce 'The Emperor's Chicken' Ping finally made his stage debut when Ooh Long complained of stomach pains. He was a hit with the audience until interrupted by angry merchants demanding payment for a long list of services rendered to one Ooh Long. Ping swore that he was merely the understudy and quickly removed his makeup to prove the fact. Sadly, it seemed that the unscrupulous actor had disguised himself as Ping when running up his enormous bills. Young Ping barely escaped ten years labor in a mine by ducking under the stage and escaping in the leading lady's favorite yellow frock. Though that ended his promising career as a thespian, he had learned much about the craft.

Simplicity was always best. He had worn his best western-style suit for the shopping expedition. So first, he removed his cravat to tie his hair back into a pale ghost of his former queue. Next he ripped the silk lining out of his jacket and made a colorful--though ragged looking--shirt of it. His white western shirt became an apron, which

101

helped secure the lining in place. He kicked off his shoes in favor of a barefoot motif and used smudges of mud to create a credible mustache, beard and uni-brow. It was, at best, a ludicrous, eccentric outfit. In other words, he should blend in rather well in San Francisco.

At least he had a destination. The Benevolent Association boasted a veritable palace at the heart of Chinatown, a fortress some might say. Ping looked at the fog-shrouded hills rising in his path, the path to Chinatown. Among his many other grievances toward this city, the three dimensional nature of its geography surely ranked high right then. "I should have stayed at home and let the world end," he grumbled.

If the alleyways of Chinatown were an inscrutable maze, then the rooftops were an ever-shifting minefield of loose wood, broken shingles and hidden holes. Ping, thankful for his months of training as a blindfolded tightrope walker, threaded his way onto ever-higher summits of treacherous footholds. The Benevolent Association headquarters was naturally the highest structure on the tallest hill in Chinatown, thus easily found even from this perspective. He thought to himself that he should always traverse Chinatown in this manner, the visibility was much clearer and the stench was almost bearable. To the southwest he saw a flash, as if it were lightning, but it seemed to come from the sea itself rather than overhead and there was no thunder which followed. Probably some new marvel being tested, electrical he shouldn't wonder. This New American century was only in its sixth year but seemed to show no sign of slowing down. Carriages without horses, men flying about like birds--Ping considered himself a liberal thinker but he sometimes wished all this science would slow down just enough for his brain to keep pace.

He came at last to a small skylight, situated over a tiny dark room. This would be the third story flush toilet, so highly touted in the Chinese newspapers a year ago, which was the pride of the Six Families. It was proclaimed as the ultimate symbol of how progressive Chinatown had become. Nimbly lowering himself, he felt one foot descend into wetness and prayed to a merciful deity that the thing had been recently flushed.

After drying his toes and smelling the towel, he eased open the door to find a hallway, silent and dark. Without a sound he made his way to the stairwell where he heard angry voices arguing below. Stairs were tricky. No matter how careful, one would always seem to find a squeaky board, so he opted for sliding down the banister. The voices seemed to emanate from behind a closed door with light leaking out from below. It felt terribly exposed, but he could see no alternative. Quietly, he cupped his hand to his ear and leaned in close to the wooden-paneled door.

"Kill him, I say!" a nasal voice whined, "This Roosevelt has made many enemies. Someone shot his predecessor. Maybe no one would notice if this one disappeared as well."

A dry voice hissed in reply. "You speak like an ass braying!" There was a sharp thumping sound. "If this President knew of our plans, how many more might also know? We were lucky we managed to intercept the traitor, Chang, before he could fully disclose what will happen this night. Otherwise, the Emperor's dreams of a new, progressive China would be destroyed forever and the Empress Dowager..." Ping heard the sounds of multiple expectorations hitting the floor, "...would keep our ancestral homeland trapped in a feudal cesspool to be abused like a cheap whore by the west. We must tread carefully."

A low rumbling voice added, "Roosevelt is a crusader. We are simply one more thing against which he can rail to proclaim himself a champion and defender of the people. His cities are overflowing and must be fed. The unfeeling industry that has grown up to meet this demand abuses its power, callous to the deaths and misery it also manufactures. He fights against tainted meat because that is the cause of the day. He merely sees another potential target in our endeavour."

Ping's blackened eyebrows knitted together as he whispered to himself, "Tainted meat?"

The rumbling man continued, "If we can convince him that what we offer is not tainted in any way, we may gain an ally where once we had an enemy."

There was a murmur of agreement. "Then we are decided. We

shall tempt Roosevelt with a deal he can hardly refuse--and kill him if he does refuse."

Ping dropped to the floor at the sound of footsteps and started scrubbing as hard as he could with his apron/shirt. When the old men emerged, sure enough, they did not defile their dignity to take notice of a lowly servant. All six filed by him, followed by a burly bodyguard who gave Ping a perfunctory kick just on principle.

Confused but undaunted, Ping followed the others at a discrete distance to a sub-basement where he saw the President pacing like a cornered lion in a small cell. T.R. stopped cold in his tracks when he saw his captors. "I hope you fully realize the ramifications of your acts. This heinous behavior constitutes nothing less than an act of war!"

"Most honorable Mr. President Teddy Roosevelt," the whiney man stepped forward. "No doubt we were overly enthusiastic in our misguided efforts to secure a private audience, but rest assured we never meant for any harm to come to your august personage."

The rumbling man continued, "We would merely offer this great country, which we also love, a new dawn, a way to feed your masses, to repopulate your plains with something more wonderful and enduring than the buffalo at its prime."

The President stuck out his chin defiantly. "I have been informed already of the abominations you offer, sickly things that your country can hardly sustain. Now you would foist your rejects off on America--shameful, sir, shameful."

The old man rumbled in reply. "I humbly offer that you were misinformed. We have at this very moment, tethered off Mussel rock, just south of the city, one magnificent male and four enthusiastic females. They were sedated with opiates during their journey here, but I have telephoned my people to revive the leviathans most expediently, so that you might see them for yourself. Imagine, these great beasts roaming free on the vast American prairies, breeding to become great herds. Cattle and swine would pale by comparison as a rich food source for a ravenous nation." Roosevelt relaxed somewhat but remained wary. "They are wild and savage beasts," the old man continued, "but easily subdued into docility by simple burnt opium. In the wild they are the preferred hunting game of emperors for over a thousand years."

Roosevelt's mustache twitched as his eyes twinkled with a far-away light. "Gadfry! I've always dreamed of bagging a dragon."

Ping almost choked on his tongue.

Dragons had always held a special place of dread in Ping's mind. As a child, his mother's favorite threat at misbehavior was that she would summon a dragon to swoop down and bite his head right off his shoulders if he continued to act out in some unruly manner. Indeed, as he was usually unruly in one form or another, he spent his early years constantly looking over his shoulder for an imminent dragon attack. He was deeply relieved to discover, upon leaving home at the age of fourteen, that dragons were merely a fairy story to frighten children. They were a myth, although a powerful one. What village or city did not have a colorful cloth dragon wind sensuously down its streets at least once a year?

During his brief time as a seller of rare antiquities, he had managed to part a wealthy merchant from a sizeable bag of gold by simply convincing him that two polished marble balls were thousand-year-old dragon testicles.

Then here in America, there were tales of monstrous dragons fought by European knights. Why, Mexico even had a great, feathered serpent as a national symbol. And here were powerful men who calmly discussed the beasts as a given. The concept that real dragons might somehow be introduced to his adopted country was enough to send a chill through his bladder.

Theodore Roosevelt was accustomed to riding in an automobile, and considered himself a brave man, but even he was unprepared for the driving abilities of the deep-voiced old man called Chu Chu Chang. Chang drove at breakneck speeds of up to forty miles an hour over fog slick roads paved with cobblestones, or not at all. The vehicle barreled through streets that had grown up with little sense of planning or safety. Visibility was almost nonexistent, even where the lamplights gave off their faint ghostly orange glow. Roosevelt was also gaining a new respect for the depth and passions of Chinese curses as Chang kept up a running commentary on the stupidity of pedestrians, wagons and other autos, which narrowly dodged his progress.

All six aged Chinese patriarchs and their burly bodyguard were also crammed into the auto, discouraging any hope of escape as effectively as the iron chains binding Roosevelt's hands and feet. His emotions were as torn as his shirt cuffs by the naked iron.

To set himself against such a magnificent beast with only his wits and a very large caliber rifle was the dream of any red-blooded sportsman… On the other hand, did he want to be responsible for introducing such monsters into the open plains of America? He could see where ravaging behemoths might be a hindrance to potential settlement or mining interests. Also, he could not help but wonder if dragon meat were as nutritious and untainted as these gentlemen insisted, why China wasn't the best-fed nation on earth. It was a puzzle that he felt inadequate to solving under present circumstances. Perhaps when they reached this Mussel Rock, and he could more clearly see the situation, he would evolve a bold and decisive plan of action--something Presidential, by God!

Clinging tenaciously to the rear spare tire, Ping kept his eyes tightly shut, murmuring a long string of halfhearted prayers to every deity he had ever heard of. The thought kept running through his mind that Chicago was not so far away by rail and doubtlessly carried a much larger selection of fine wedding dresses.

As the auto screeched to a brief halt to allow a cable car the right of way, Ping opened his eyes and thought to slip away, allowing events to unfold as they would without his further interference. As he eased one foot to the street he glanced at the three men stalking along the sidewalk in the soft gaslight illumination, thinking that one looked very familiar. As he met the man's eyes, he realized that his disguise was not as good as he had hoped, for he saw instant recognition in the eyes of Pan Sai Kow, chief of the Boo Hoo Dow Doy hatchet sons.Ping lifted his foot just as the auto roared away; sparing him from the hatchet that had been aimed squarely at his fake uni-brow. This whole affair was becoming decidedly unpleasant.

City streets eventually gave way to barely paved coastal trails boasting wild stretches of hairpin turns and sheer drops to jagged boulders. Once he saw a great spume of vomit from the passenger's side which he thought had a presidential cast to it. The roar of surf on stones was so loud, it blotted out the auto's engine and even the sharp voices of the old men as they argued and lectured. He had learned a few facts, though, during the earlier parts of the journey and was trying to make sense of them now.

Dragons were big. The male of the group that had been brought to these shores was said to be a quarter-mile long and twice as large around as a grain silo. Long centuries of inactivity had grown them to proportions never imagined in the old tales.

Dragons were strong.A tale was told of a dragon who had a nightmare as it slept its opium-induced slumber and had taken to twitching its tail. This had removed the top of a small hill, as well as killing three hundred attendants whose organs were turned to mush by the great vibrations produced as the tail hit the ground. In nearby Tibet, temple gongs rang out though no hand had struck them. This story was not repeated in English for Roosevelt.

Dragons could fly. They were filled with thousands of gas bladders, which allowed them to hover just off the ground, making the monsters as easily maneuvered as soap bubbles--or so it was said. Hundreds of thousands of feathered flaps served as wings that could propel the leviathans at great speeds, but only for short distances. The wings were kept clipped and were only in use at feedings. Like great hovering cows, dragons ate grass.

Dragons breathed fire. The gas produced to allow them to fly was belched forth occasionally and would be ignited should a dragon gnash its great stony teeth, eliciting a spark. This was a common occurrence, it seemed, as they dreamt their dragon dreams. It was the main cause of death among dragon attendants.

There were not many dragons left in the world. A thousand years before, the dragons had been subdued and domesticated, retained against the threat of invasion, but they had died for lack of activity. All except a few. Ten of the great beasts survived and grew to

107

enormous size, kept secluded in a remote corner of the kingdom. They were a secret and ultimate symbol of the Emperor's power. When the west had made its great incursion from across the ocean, two dragons were awakened and sent to destroy the invaders while still at sea. Exploding shells from a gunboat made short work of China's defenders, turning the gas bladders into huge fireballs. China stood defenseless and jaded in their long, smug assumption of power. Ping had not seen his native land in over a quarter century but this saddened him and explained much about China's present standing in the world.

Between the chill in his fingers and the icy hand which clutched at his stomach, Ping was again ready to abandon his quest when, all of a sudden, the automobile skidded to a sudden, gravel-plumed stop throwing the passengers forward and dislodging Ping from his perch. He was thrown to the side and was afraid of discovery until he saw what had made the driver stop so precipitously. From a small island, off to the right, there came a fireball, arcing through the night toward the auto. The doors opened, spilling out passengers scrambling madly for safety. Ping froze for only a second before he used the rear fender as a springboard to propel himself at the manacled form of the President. As the fireball hit the hood of the auto, Ping bore the President to the ground, covering him as best he could. Shaking his head to clear it, Ping removed a pin from Teddy's lapel and made short work of the locks at his hands and feet.

It was amazing how much he remembered from his long ago affair with the great lock-pick, Zhing Zhoh. He hadn't had much occasion to use those skills since he had helped her steal a nobleman's great jade turtle yo-yo from a locked tower.

Ping helped the president to his feet and they saw the flaming, misshapen form of a man, which had fallen from the sky to destroy the auto's engine so thoroughly. That small island he had noted before was suddenly alive with flame and screaming which was heard even over the roar of the ocean. Roosevelt leaned heavily on his shoulder as they hobbled to the cliff edge along with Chu Chu Chan and his brethren. "Perhaps waking the brutes wasn't such a bully idea after all." Roosevelt offered as he looked out to sea.

They beheld a large steamship moored to the island, battered and burning, with four dragons circling overhead and spitting flames. Chan wailed out that the ship was the one that had brought the tethered giants from China. A fifth dragon, the largest, undoubtedly the male, lay huddled on the great rock island watching his harem wreak devastation. As they watched in disbelief, an American gunboat appeared over the horizon speeding to the rescue of the ocean liner.

Chan and the other old men waved their gnarled hands wildly, yelling at the top of their lungs for the gunboat to go away.

The President turned his head, squinting hard at Ping for the first time. His lips spread into a fierce grin. "Why, you're the fellow needing a dress to save the world!"

Back down the dirt road came the sound of screaming engines and savage war cries as two carloads of men brandishing hatchets flew over a hill, barreling toward the dazed group of Benevolent Family heads, their captive President and the bedraggled Ping. "Let me guess, this would be the cross-dressing hatchet fellow and a few of his friends." The president intoned.

Ping shrugged, "So it would seem. How did you know?"

Teddy flexed his fists and threw off his jacket to make ready for battle. "Seemed as reasonable a guess as anything else this night."

Over the hills to the east, the sun's first rays broke through the fog and brought the sound of a giant mosquito. A small flying machine buzzed in topping the hills, coming in low over the cars filled with hatchetmen forcing them off the road. One went flying off the cliff and the other into a boulder. Teddy laughed and pointed as the flying machine flew on toward the flaming island. "Ain't she a beauty?" The president waved at the pilot, who Ping recognized him as the Secret service man who was so fond of garlic. Ping deduced the man had probably managed to track down Mr. Teddy by simply flying around the city until he spotted them. Very scientific, if a bit late.

The commander and chief beamed with pride. "Had it made from some plans the Wright boys drew up for me. That's what brought me out here in the first place, to give her a test run and, by Gadfry, she's all I could have hoped for. I think I'll call her my Air Horse One!"

Ping thought that those elected to such a high office should be thoroughly and regularly examined to determine their continued sanity.

He pushed the President aside and ducked as the foot of an elderly man in black threatened to take his head off. As the foot sailed by, Ping launched his own foot squarely into the old man's groin. This was clearly not an honorable move, but it worked.

The flying machine had banked out over the ocean and was headed back toward them when the Earth lurched. The huge form of the male dragon separated itself from the rocks of the island, to give chase to the machine. Everyone was thrown off their feet when, an instant later, the winged device sailed over them and an immense form crashed into the cliff side below.

Somehow, Pan Sai Kow, chief of the Boo Hoo Dow Doy hatchet sons, had managed to stagger forward through the car crash and the great Earth movement. Such was his fury to destroy the outsider who had seen him indulge his enthusiasm for beautiful things--such as western women's dresses--he had barely noticed the pandemonium arrayed around him. Running and screaming, he saw Ping at last. There would be no escape this time. Kow pulled his largest hatchet from his belt and threw it straight at Ping's back.

Ping stood at the cliff's edge shaking in terror. Up the side came a feathered face with a wide mouth and huge luminous eyes, not quite focused but clearly agitated. All strength fled Ping and he fell to his knees just as the eyes crested the cliff. From behind him, a large hatchet whirled past, sticking deep into one of the enormous orbs. Surely the shock more than the pain sent the dragon into a thrashing frenzy that flung men and battered autos flying into the air as the very Earth moved once again.

From the island below, the coast guard gunboat let out with several rounds of large caliber gunfire. Four great fireballs lit up the still shadowed shoreline, signaling the dazzling demise of the four female dragons.

The male halted his thrashing for just a moment and Ping could

110

see the torment in the great eyes as the dragon launched himself into the air. Ping glanced behind him to see the hatchet chief raise another weapon.

Again, had he thought for a moment longer he might have taken his chances with a hatchet to the head, but instead he turned back and leaped as hard as he could over the cliff, grabbing a handful of feathers as the mighty creature propelled itself toward the falling ruins of San Francisco.

The air was crisp and biting as Ping clung for dear life. He had always supposed dragons to be scaly, perhaps slimy, but the creature was soft as a downy featherbed, providing innumerable hand and foot holds. So he climbed. After some progress he dared look ahead, just long enough to ascertain that he was indeed near the head of the thing for he saw what must be an ear. He looked to the Earth below and saw devastation stretching to the horizon where minutes before a great city had sprawled. The dragon let fly a stream of flaming bile onto the city, causing Ping to cry out. He had never cared for San Francisco or Chinatown, but he had also never wished to see such devastation dealt to the city and its citizens.

If ever a living being had cause for terrible vengeance, surely it was this dragon. The old tales spoke of sages who could reason with dragons, moving them to pity for the plight of poor deluded mortals. Ping was no sage but he had to do something, so he crawled toward the great ear, hoping he could find words to stay the wrath of a force of nature.

Drawing himself close to the opening, he screamed at the top of his lungs. "Noble lord of the land and sky, this humble gnat seeks your benevolent notice!" Another rain of flames flew down from immense mouth, engulfing yet another part of the city. Ping closed his eyes and screamed louder. "You seek to redress wrongs done to you and your kind for a millennium but this is not worthy of your magnificence! Your kind are all but gone yet you waste your wrath upon those who have done you no harm. You have shown your might and none will ever forget the awesome fury you have unleashed, but if you continue you will be destroyed by forces you cannot comprehend." Another gout of flame lanced at the wreckage. Ping wept but kept up his screamed plea. "Think, oh ruler of the heavens! This is folly! In the land of our births there are still two dragons, if I understand the math, and only you can free them to become a mighty nation once again!" The dragon slowed its momentum and seemed to hang there in the air contemplating the words of the frightened gadfly, Chin Song Ping. Slowly the immense form pivoted in a sky filled with billowing black smoke and gouts of crimson, both from the conflagration below and the angry sky overhead. Majestically, the thing oriented itself toward the ocean stretching endlessly to the west. Ping almost lost his hold as he slumped back in relief.

First he thought how much he enjoyed being a hero but decided that he shouldn't overdo such behavior as others might come to expect it of him. Then his thoughts became more practical. He was flying on a dragon out toward open water and below lay only ruin, leading to that savage sea. His planning, he decided, might have been a bit more foresighted.

Suddenly a small hail of large metal pellets scorched the air above his head sending several feathers flying. He looked up and heard a loud buzz as a fragile canvas and wood craft slowly descended from the cloud above. "Damn it man, how can I get off a decent shot if you keep waggling these wings back and forth like an epileptic goose?" a voice boomed as a huge iron rifle barrel slipped over the side of the craft.

Ping was never one much for social niceties but he understood well enough that one should never ignore a Presidential invitation. He sprang with all his might at the wheel axel that was right over his head, shouting in what was left of his ragged voice. "Mr. President Teddy Roosevelt, sir, DO NOT SHOOT!"

In the following days, volumes were written about the great 1906 San Francisco earthquake, but no mention was ever made of dragons or Presidents. The Secret Service was good for something after all. The power of the Tongs and the influence of the Chinese Benevolent Society was broken with the destruction of Chinatown, which was eventually rebuilt in a manner more understandable to the western mind.

Roosevelt's reforms against tainted meat were enacted as the law of the land. Thousand-year-old Chinese dragon meat was not the only cause worth his ardor, it seemed, and Roosevelt was off to champion something else before the ink was dry on the bill. Without the monies from the sale of dragons as foodstuffs, the Emperor Guangxu failed in his coup to wrest power back from the Empress Dowager Cixi. The Quing Dynasty died five years later leaving China to almost half a century of civil wars and ultimately the rise of Communism.

###

"I do." Ping said breathlessly and kissed his beautiful bride. They were a picture of splendor, he in a white silk suit and she in a frothy creation of whites and lavenders hastily erected by an army of the finest seamstresses in Washington DC. Her smile was dazzling against her rich coffee-brown skin and her beauty hadn't diminished in the slightest since he had first laid eyes on her across a garishly lit cave twenty-five years earlier.

"Well," She laughed as she threw her hands around his neck, "Everything's still here, so it looks like we saved the world again! And this time was so much easier."

Perhaps Ping would finally find time to share the details of his dress-finding excursion tonight, in their honeymoon bed.

Abruptly, five laughing children, aged fifteen and down, engulfed them in a weave of arms and legs. Fireworks went off overhead lighting up the cherry blossoms that fell all about. Ping still couldn't recall for sure if he had voted for Roosevelt in the previous two elections but vowed to vote twice for him the next time he ran.

CHIN SONG PING AND THE FISTS OF STEEL

The monster stood at least 6 1/2 feet tall, easily the tallest, most terrifying individual Ping had ever seen. In his mouth was a large smoldering stick, and from his nostrils smoke emerged. He was a being with deathly pale skin, glowing green eyes and flame-red hair, as wide as he was tall. Surely he must be a demon.

Ping, a mere 14 years old, had never dreamed of such a creature as now towered over him where he lay sprawled on the busy, cobbled thoroughfare. The monster offered him a hand up.

"Dreadfully sorry, my lad, I should have been watching where I was walking." The demon spoke Chinese in a refined but odd accent.

"Oh no, great demon," Ping managed to sputter out. "It is I who must apologize for my lowly clumsiness. I did not mean to cause consternation to one such as yourself!"

The demon laughed heartily and pulled Ping to his feet. "I've been called many things in my time, lad, but never a demon. Allow me to introduce myself. Daniel O'Flay, gentleman promoter of pugilistic pageantry on three continents, at your service!" He swept off his top hat and bowed to the boy in a most courtly manner.

Ah! Ping thought, *an American demon.* He had heard tales of such creatures. He had also heard that such creatures were usually eccentric and rich.

"Forgive my ignorance, sir. I am called Chin Song Ping, a humble wanderer in search of gainful employment. Perhaps I may act as your guide if you are a stranger in this city. My rates are quite reasonable."

Ping was an industrious fellow and felt strongly that every man should know a trade. He had spent the past three weeks since he had left home endeavoring to learn the trade of picking pockets. In fact, he had been trying to lift the demon's wallet when he had tripped over the American's large, booted foot. He seemed to possess little talent as a criminal mastermind, and saw instantly that becoming a guide to foreigners promised to be a more lucrative career path than pick-pocket.

The American scratched his whiskers. "Well, perhaps such an enterprising young man could come in handy. I'm seeking the workshop of one Ho Lai, master craftsman of clockwork wonders."

Ping straightened his tunic and smiled broadly. "Good sir, you were most fortunate to happen upon me. The den of Ho Lai is several streets north, but you were heading south and would soon have encountered all manner of rogues."

O'Flay peered at his handmade map with puzzlement until Ping rotated the thing 180 degrees.

"Bless my soul, I do believe you're spot on there, my boy."

A bargain was struck, and Ping took charge of the man's enormous steamer trunk, previously hidden by his girth. Ping was small of stature, but the thing had wheels, and Ping was determined to be the best guide ever. He led the way through crowded, twisting streets, struggling and huffing over the cobblestones.

"Please pardon my unworthy curiosity, sir, but why has one such as yourself traveled so far from his native shores merely to have a clock made?" Ping puffed. "Are there no such craftsmen in America?"

O'Flay let out another loud laugh. "Clock? I should say not! Word is that this Ho Lai fellow has contrived a mechanical, clockwork warrior that fights better than any living man. It would make your emperor's army obsolete if such automatons were to be produced in large numbers." The man put a finger to the side of his nose and winked. "Old Ho Lai won't sell to the emperor though. He says his creation is destined for a greater purpose. I am offering him the greatest purpose imaginable … fame and wealth."

"How wonderful," Ping replied flatly as he wiped his brow and gave the trunk an extra heave.

"Ain't it though!" the American exclaimed. "By god, I mean to see this wonder of the East square off in the ring against the mighty Goliath, a steam-powered titan of my own devising! Sweet St. Patrick, but I can smell the money flowing in already."

###

"Just how much money are we talking about?" Ho Lai had been skeptical of the scheme until the American pulled stacks of cash, local currency and greenback dollars, from his inner pockets. "My Iron Tiger is not some toy to be displayed at a yen a head."

"My good man, the beads on your abacus can't count high

enough to describe the riches we stand to reap."

Ping could see a gleam in O'Flay's eyes that reminded him of his uncle Pao when he was winning at mah-jongg. The American was on a roll.

"We'll start with a tour of your homeland, billing the match as the ultimate showdown of East and West. I'll promote the whole affair, no expense spared. I'll have every manjack on this continent, yellow and white, convinced that his very life depends on being there to see the outcome."

Ho Lai stroked his beard so hard that Ping thought he might dislodge it. "And you say that we can do this all over the world as well?"

"Sir, in America we will tout it as the fight of 1876, the centennial slaughter! We'll wrap my Goliath in the flag and bill your boy as the Iron Menace. After that, we'll tour Europe and have tea with every blessed crowned head they've got. We, sir, will become the stuff of legends." O'Flay leaned back, smiling, and put his feet up on his steamer trunk. "That is, of course, if this mechanical man of yours is as good as you say. I look around me at these marvels you've created, and I've got to say, they all look a mite … fragile."

"Toys!" The inventor swept his hands dismissively at the mechanical birds, cats, clocks and fanciful contraptions that littered the room. "These are mere toys meant for the jaded palates of those too wealthy for their own good."

He leapt to his feet, beckoning Ping and the American to follow. They wound through rooms of obscure purpose, stocked with tools unheard of by the common man and half-built wonders that defied the imagination. Finally, they came to an enormous courtyard filled with trees that might once have been lovely but were now smashed and splintered.

In a corner stood a statue – 12 feet tall, glittering and terrible in martial aspect. It was half-buried under shattered tree limbs. The old man rummaged in his voluminous pockets for something he seemed to have misplaced. The more he searched, the more frustrated he became, until he looked like he might rend the robes to pieces. He stopped, extricated his hands from their fruitless search, and screeched at the top of his lungs.

"Min!"

In less time than it took for Ping to look around, a young woman emerged from a door in the wall behind the statue. She hopped nimbly over the pile of ruined wood, holding high a large brass key. Her raven hair, unfastened and wild, bounced behind her like a battle flag. She came close and bowed, offering the key to her master.

The girl took the old man's hand to guide him over the debris. He made a dismissive introduction as he took charge of the key. "This is Lee Min. She assists me in my great work. She is a woman, but that cannot be helped, I suppose. She does possess the cleverest and tiniest of hands, a useful asset in my trade."

Min smiled a roguish smile, and Ping's heart skipped several beats. She was not as pretty as the street girls he saw every night, but she had fire in her eyes and a stance that set his young libido ablaze.-

He bowed deeply but never took his eyes off hers. "I am Chin Song Ping, pugilistic promoter in training, at your service."

O'Flay gave the boy a gentle wrap with his cane to remind him of his station.

Ho Lai inserted the key into the great statue and turned it with all his might. "Iron Tiger possesses not only the ability to move and fight but also the ability to think."

O'Flay laughed. "Think? Damnation man, but that is a bold claim!"

"Yes, bold but quite true. I have given him the capacity of thought by virtue of the millions of infinitesimal gears that fill his head. He also possesses hundreds of variably chaotic spring drives, allowing him to cope with any situation. Iron Tiger can plan and reason and even learn new skills." The inventor paused in turning the key to stroke the polished metal. "When wound up, he is a veritable philosopher/warrior, able to speak his thoughts as well as any man. But I assure you, he is no fragile plaything. His internal works are wrapped in several layers of raw silk and further protected by a layer of shaped bamboo and an outer shell of brass and steel. I just call him *Iron* Tiger because I like the way it sounds."

The key would turn no farther, so Ho Lai removed it and tossed it to Min. The clockmaker pressed a lever and jumped nimbly to the floor.

"I present for your most worthy consideration, Iron Tiger, the first great wonder of the modern world!"

The statue came to life in flowing motions that cleared away the surrounding fallen branches and trunks as though they were made of rice paper. Iron Tiger went through a series of movements that emulated a flesh-and-blood tiger's speed and aggressiveness. With the last of his foot movements, the metal man flicked a section of tree trunk into the air, where it was met by an enormous, gleaming black-and-red fist. The courtyard was filled with a thunderous sound as the wooden obstacle exploded into splinters and sawdust. The mechanical man bowed to his audience and spoke in a voice like a music box. "I am composing a poem on the nature of rust. Would you like to hear it?"

O'Flay whooped and tossed his hat in the air. He shook the old man's hand so hard that Ping felt sure the inventor might rattle to pieces. "Sir, let's talk turkey!"

Why they should speak of birds at this time Ping had no idea – but he didn't really care, either – as Min took him by the hands and danced around joyfully. Ping was in love.

"I think I found an arm," Ping called out as he dug through straw and paper.

The warehouse was enormous and echoed with the sounds of his voice. A half-hour before, 20 heavy wooden crates had been delivered to this place that O'Flay had rented for the upcoming event. Goliath had been shipped in pieces from America, and Ping had been enlisted to assist in assembling the behemoth.

"Good lad!" the American barked. "Use that winch, and let's see how Goliath looks with both his arms."

This new career involved more physical labor than Ping cared for, but the task was an interesting one and held the promise of more dancing with the lovely Min.

"Mr. Daniel, sir, might this humble one inquire how exactly the great and wonderful Goliath will move once he is whole? Though I have seen gears and pulleys as we have assembled him, I've seen nothing of the sheer complexity we were told went into Ho Lai's Iron Tiger."

O'Flay maneuvered the arm deftly into place. "Well, I'll tell you. Goliath is a lot like me, simple but powerful. What powers him is steam."

Ping grunted as he held the arm steady to be bolted into place. "Full of steam – yes, I can see the similarity."

O'Flay eyed his assistant, then laughed. "Just so, lad, just so!"

At midday, there was a knock on the warehouse door. Ping volunteered to answer it.

"Even great promoters of pugilism must eat," he said.

It was Min. She removed the wrap from a tray of turnip cakes, rice balls and a steaming assortment of vegetables. Ping had not seen its like since he left home. Indeed, it was a close thing whether he was gladder to see the food or the girl. Fortunately, they came as one package together.

"Well, bless my soul, doesn't that smell good." O'Flay came up behind him. "I suppose it is lunchtime at that, but my stomach is of a delicate disposition when it comes to local cuisine." He made a courtly bow to invite the young lady in, and Ping belatedly followed suit.

"Then this food shall go to waste, and my master will be cross." She sighed and moved toward an overturned crate.

"I should be most grateful to sample your morsels." Ping sighed.

Min tickled his chin. "I can offer only the morsels on this tray. Anything else, you should discuss with my master."

Ping turned red, and Min giggled.

O'Flay winked at the girl. "I have boiled beef and cabbage waiting for me in the back room. Why don't you two eat this, and old Ho Lai need be none the wiser." The American waddled off.

Ping filled his mouth with a rice ball as he scrounged up two smaller boxes to sit on. They ate in silence – Ping ravenously, Min less so.

Min looked at her turnip cake. "Forgive me for saying so, but you seem young to be involved with such a grand scheme."

"I'm 16!" Ping lied through a mouthful of vegetables. "I am the fourth son of a good family." At least that was true. "I intend to make my mark on this world. I will not be like my older brothers who had their destinies handed to them on a platter of gold. I left home so that I might experience the greater world for myself."

Min nodded thoughtfully. "Ah, so your parents threw you out."

Ping almost choked on the vegetables.

"It makes no difference to me. My stepfather sought to sell me into prostitution, but Ho Lai bought me first. I was meant to be his concubine, but a man so old is rarely interested. In the end, he found me more useful as an assistant than a plaything."

Ping sat open-mouthed, then smiled. "I think we are, both of us, lucky that we have the opportunity to write what we will in our life's books." It was something his old teacher had once said to him, and it sounded wise.

They ate again in silence until the food was gone. As Min gathered dishes, Ping pulled out a stack of handbills advertising the upcoming fight.

"Yesterday, I put these up all over the city. Everywhere I went a crowd gathered and asked me questions as though I were someone worth speaking to. A week ago, I was little more than a street beggar. A month before that, I was a worthless, lay-about fourth son with no prospects whatsoever." He twirled in delight, arms flung wide. "You and I are a part of all this now. People will know our names."

Min looked at the ground. "They will know my master's name. I am merely his property."

Ping grabbed her hands. "Then I shall become rich and buy you from Ho Lai! We shall marry, and I will learn how to make mechanical men. You and your wonderfully clever hands will help me, and the world shall be at our feet."

They danced around the crates and metal body parts, and Ping wished for a time when they might do more than dance.

It took the afternoon, but the steam-driven man was almost finished. Ping was ordered to bring a bucket of water. He dumped it into the boiler in the behemoth's metal back.

The American produced a large, ornate key and unlocked his steam trunk.

"And here we have Goliath's very heart." He held up what looked to be a small log. "These are what fuel the fire. They are my own invention and are comprised of wood chips, coal, beeswax, bourbon, oil and a few secret ingredients." He tossed one to Ping for his inspection. "This will make Goliath's furnace burn like the sun itself and pressurize his steam to an unheard-of capacity. I tell you, lad, springs and fancy gadgets will be no match for the pure power of steam."

As the fire heated the water, Ping was given an oversized metal pot with slits cut into it to attach at the top of Goliath's frame. He scuttled up the hand and footholds in the side of the body.

"Sir, again I am confused," Ping said. "If this is our champion's head, where is his brain?"

The kettle attached upside-down to a hinge on the shoulders near two rows of buttons that would be under the pot when it was locked closed.

After Ping descended, O'Flay climbed up and punched the buttons seemingly at random. As he did so, a marvelous thing happened. The right arm and then the left shot out at lightning speed, powered by pistons releasing a faint hissing screech of steam. O'Flay slipped from his perch but grabbed at the hinged head to steady himself.

Goliath stepped forward, and the punches continued at uneven intervals. At the press of more buttons, the giant turned toward one of the taller packing crates and punched it full of holes. When the box was almost demolished, Goliath stepped back and raised a mechanical leg behind him. With a high-pitched sound of metal scraping metal, the foot came down and delivered a mighty kick to the crate. It flew the length of the warehouse and exploded into splinters.

Twisting a recessed valve, O'Flay released the trapped steam in a great plume and clambered down.

"Ain't he a dandy?" he asked.

Ping stood stunned. He had never witnessed such a display of sheer, raw power.

"So, you act as the brain for Goliath," Ping said. "Forgive me for saying so, but are you insane? You could never fit in that kettle and would be exposed to Iron Tiger. ... Wait one moment. You don't mean to have me be in that kettle, do you?"

Ping widened his eyes, and he felt the blood drain from his face. This career path was looking less appealing every minute.

"Hmm, you would just about fit ..."

Ping turned to flee.

The American grabbed his shirt. "I'm joking!" He roared with laughter.

Ping sighed in relief as the man went to the steamer trunk and produced a large cage. In the cage was a black rooster with a fiery comb and wicked spurs. Now Ping was truly confused.

"Meet Goliath's brain, the most vicious fighting gamecock in all Vinegaroon country, Texas." He poked a finger at the bird and almost got it snapped off for his effort. "I got the idea at an Indiana carnival where a fellow had taught a chicken to add up totals by pecking on the keys of a cash register. This is the same principal. This noble fowl has incredible fighting skills bred right into him, so all I had to do was teach him to express his talent for mayhem by pecking at the buttons that control our ferrous gladiator. I can't put him in right now without an opponent to strike at. Lord only knows what he'd do. But I assure you he will be hell and hotspurs when the time is right."

Gingerly, O'Flay returned the rooster to the trunk. "Don't just stand there, my boy. We have leaks to be sealed and lots of oiling ahead of us if we're to be ready to take on that giant celestial windup toy next weekend."

As Ping hauled away empty packing crates, he thought of something else his old teacher had once said. The old man had yelled it at him – many years ago – when he had been caught in the act of drawing pictures on a priceless scroll. Something about Ping living in interesting times, but he had shouted it as though it were a curse. This was a time much more interesting than anything that had ever happened back home, and it was most enjoyable! Crazy old man. He shouldn't have left the scroll lying around like that.

Ten days had transformed the warehouse into something fabulous. Rows and rows of long steps had been erected for people to sit on, and everything was draped in brightly colored paper. Torches and lanterns transformed the cavernous edifice to noontime brilliance. It was a very large space, but the excited crowds threatened to fill it to bursting.

For two weeks, urchins on every street corner had been given rice in return for shouting about the fight of the millennium. Colorful handbills covered every square inch of every public wall. Prostitutes were paid to whisper in their client's ears as they slept about how they must see this once-in-a-lifetime battle. No betting parlor was without long odds one way or the other on the fight's outcome. People wagered their life's savings on which contender would emerge triumphant. This was the crowning jewel in Daniel O'Flay's promotional career.

"What the hell do you mean, the rooster doesn't feel like fighting?" O'Flay yelled at Ping as he coaxed the gamecock into the steel head.

"I think, perhaps, the crowd has dampened his enthusiasm," Ping replied. He poked the bird.

"Well, do something! This crowd didn't pay to see a tea dance! They will burn us alive if we don't give them their clash of titans!"

Ping made a despairing face and bowed to the rooster. "Oh fierce and mighty brain of the great Goliath, please forgive this worthless one for what he must now do."

He grabbed a couple of tail feathers and yanked as hard as he could. Ping almost lost an eye and half his face before managing to slam the kettle shut. He leapt to the ground.

"I believe I have managed to sufficiently motivate the bird brain," he reported to O'Flay.

"Excellent! Prepare the boiler."

The American grabbed a huge megaphone and sprinted to the center of the marked-off arena.

Ping jammed in the log. The gauges climbed. Across the room, Min labored at the final key turns for Iron Tiger. Her hair was elegantly styled, and she wore rich robes of bright colors. Ping sighed. This was a wonderful career he had stumbled into.

Ho Lai met O'Flay in the center, and each delivered a prepared speech, simultaneous with the other, in his native tongue through oversized megaphones.

"Gentlemen! Countrymen!"

The crowd quieted to a buzz.

"You are here today to witness a battle unlike any other in the history of the world." The crowd exploded in cheers. "You have the privilege tonight to see the dawning of a new age, an age where machines clash in a way that, before tonight, only men were thought capable of."

"These two mighty gladiators will vie for the privilege of destroying each other for your amusement and gratification. Let the battle begin!"

The entrepreneur and the inventor each ran for cover as their assistants hit the respective mechanisms that would unleash the energy embodied in their engines of destruction.

Goliath barreled forward like a runaway locomotive, while Iron Tiger swept ahead like a god of death, dancing to meet his victim. Each stopped short of contact, choosing instead to circle, watching for a weakness or a chance opening.

Iron Tiger struck first, going low to sweep an enormous leg into his opponent, seeking to unbalance him and even knock him over. Despite Goliath's enormous bulk, his own legs bent in a piston-fast motion and propelled him upward several feet when he straightened them. This allowed Iron Tiger's leg to pass harmlessly under the steam man's bulk.

The entire structure shook when Goliath landed. Onlookers fell off their seats, and people rushed to save the tinder-dry building from overturned torches. The audience went wild! This was the grand spectacle they had been promised.

Iron Tiger recovered and punched Goliath's side, spinning him twice around. When faced in the right direction once more, Goliath closed in and delivered a thunderstorm of piston-powered blows to Iron Tiger's midsection. Echoes from the blows drowned out even the crowd's hysterics.

An open-handed downward chop to Goliath's head left a huge dent in the kettle but served only to infuriate the chicken within. The fowl tried for a punishing uppercut but Iron Tiger rolled over backward in a smooth motion to escape the sledgehammer blows. Goliath chugged forward to continue his assault, but Iron Tiger had cart-wheeled around Goliath's flank, which allowed him access to the boiler in the back. Hard as he tried, Iron Tiger could not penetrate the rolled sheet metal body, so he kicked behind Goliath's knee.

Somehow the wily gamecock anticipated the move and bent Goliath's knee just in time to trap Iron Tiger's foot. Iron Tiger hopped on one foot as Goliath sought to crush the captured foot in his knee joint. This death dance lasted for another minute until Iron Tiger dislodged himself by falling down and using his free foot to extricate its mate.

Goliath turned in place but found his opponent had rolled away and regained his footing. Again they circled, offering feints and half-hearted kicks. Iron tiger bent back till he was balanced on his hands then shot his legs under Goliath's arms, lifting him off the ground. The steam powered leviathan flailed helplessly as he was pulled Iron Tiger and flung toward the cheering crowd. The metal giant wound up landing on his back but used his momentum to roll to his feet, a move few would have thought possible for one of his size. The metal shell which encased Goliath's Brain intensified his outraged squawks to something resembling a war-cry as the behemoth strode back into the fray.

Iron Tiger released his hands from their wrists where they dangled on strong cords. He quickly set them into deadly motion, swinging them at his sides like twin maces. The detached fists drummed on metal man like a chorus of gongs.

Goliath, in turn, let his left arm drop in a pendulum motion and continued the arc behind his back and up over his head, extending an extra foot as it did so. The blow came down squarely on Iron Tiger's head. A clang shook the rafters.

A hush fell over the crowd as the head of the Chinese champion cracked open on one side. Small gears went flying and left an exposed spring-wire vibrating from the blow. Tattered silk hung off shards of shattered bamboo.

Iron Tiger twitched in jerky spasms as his hands retracted back into his arms. Sensing victory, Goliath closed. With a sudden, unexpected burst of speed, Iron tiger met him with a spinning kick that sent the kettle head and fowl brain flying from great metal shoulders, tumbling unceremoniously to the ground. Goliath froze in mid-stride as his twitching counterpart danced an epileptic jig toward the scrambling gamecock. There was a defiant crowing and brandishing of heel spurs, cut short by the crunch of a brass boot grinding into sand. The fight looked to be ended in a puddle of blood and feathers.

The audience was beside itself with emotion. The clapping, whistling and cheering bounced off the distant walls. Some cried, some danced and others exchanged large sums of money.

Then, above it all, came a harsh yet musical voice. It was the sound of an insane calliope, and it issued from Iron Tiger's battered face. "I need my key, I must be free!"

A hush came over the arena as the mechanical man gyrated wildly toward Min and his aged inventor. Ho Lai ran to meet his creation with consoling words and promises that he would never use his poor Iron Tiger thusly again. Iron Tiger picked up the old man in both hands and ripped him in two, sending the halves flying into the audience in scarlet streamers. His gaze returned to the girl, and he resumed his crazed dance forward.

"I need my key! I must be free!"

Panic reigned as several thousand patrons tried to flee the carnage.

Ping and O'Flay ran at the insane artificial man, but too late. Iron Tiger took the outstretched key from Min's trembling hand and casually backhanded her. Her broken form went flying several yards to where she landed on the dirt floor.

Iron Tiger turned and plucked a loose gear from his head. With one swift, graceful motion, he flung the gear, sending it deep into O'Flay's neck. Blood gurgled from the American's mouth and jugular. He staggered another step before collapsing in a well-dressed heap.

Ping barely managed to dodge a killing blow by diving between the monster's legs. The boy threw himself atop Min's still form and waited for a final strike.

Iron Tiger, however, had already lost interest in them as he stalked toward the fleeing hordes. Once again, the mad calliope voice cut through the din. "Where are you going? You haven't heard my poem about rust yet!"

Min's eyes fluttered, and Ping bent close to hear.

"Please," she whispered. "Do not let this slaughter be how my master is remembered." She breathed out one last time, and Ping smelled rose petals and honey.

How could a death this ugly smell so sweet? A tear fell onto her rigid cheek, and Ping felt more helpless than he ever had.

He looked and saw Iron Tiger crushing hapless audience members as he recited his poem. He also saw the unmoving form of Goliath, still poised for battle, and an idea formed in the back of his mind. He could see that it was a stupid idea almost immediately, but, as no other presented itself, he decided it would have to do.

Iron Tiger held a patron aloft by his throat so that the man might better appreciate the nuances of his verse. That the man was dead seemed not to concern the automaton at all. "Red and gritty thou art, and the destroyer of all that gleams. The very air conspires with you to ..."

A voice from a large megaphone broke Iron Tiger's concentration. He turned to see who might dare interrupt his poetic masterpiece.

It was Goliath with a small, four-limbed pimple on his shoulders instead of a head.

"Come back and face me, mighty warrior." Ping hollered through the open-ended cone. "We still have matters between us and, besides, your poetry is quite terrible!" He threw aside the megaphone and pressed buttons until Goliath lumbered forward.

Iron Tiger ripped the head off the man he held before him. In one swift, fluid motion he was back in the arena, crouched in a fighting stance. Ping hit the punching buttons as fast as he could and barreled straight ahead.

Ping had never considered himself much of a fighter, and with good reason, but this attack seemed his best bet. He had to buy time while the steam in Goliath's body built to critical.

Iron Tiger bounded across the floor, arms flailing in savage lunges that would rip his foe to pieces. They met in a great clash and clanging of metal that almost sent Ping flying from his perch. Punches rained down on each other's bodies, neither able to topple the other.

Ping's legs were wrapped around what was left of the kettle latch, his hands free to hit buttons. Finally, above the screams of terror, above the sound of metal hammering metal, he heard the slight squeal of escaping steam and knew it was time.

He shifted Goliath's stance to straight up and let loose a haymaker to Iron Tiger's head. Enraged, Iron Tiger took a wild swing at Ping himself but missed when Goliath ducked into a low crouching position.

Ping rolled off Goliath's shoulders and hit a lever. All the pent-up steam power was released at once into the leg pistons to power one enormous jump. Goliath shot up through the roof in a cloud of expended water vapor.

Seconds later, the steam dissipated, leaving the 14-year-old boy sprawled on his backside, facing the unstoppable, clockwork monster. He scuttled back, forcing Iron Tiger to step closer. The metal man raised his foot above Ping and held up the key to show his triumph.

"I have my key and now I am fr—"

He was cut off by a high-pitched whistling sound. Ping rolled madly away as Goliath's metal body plunged back through the hole in the roof it had made seconds before.

In that instant, before the wonder of the East was crushed by the hurtling Goliath, Ping thought that he saw a puzzled look come over the rigid metal face of the mighty Iron Tiger — but perhaps it was only a trick of the light. The collision sent off a shockwave that knocked over anyone unlucky enough to still be in the building. Then, literally, it brought down the house.

The next day, the authorities searched through the rubble, rescuing survivors. Chunks of twisted brass and steel were found a

128

mile away. Those responsible were thought to be dead, victims of their own greed and hubris.

But Ping had managed to evade the falling debris and angry officials who sought someone to blame this all on. Fearful that he might be recognized, he stowed away on the first conveyance leaving the city that presented itself: a hog wagon bound for parts unknown. That suited Ping just fine.

His heart was heavy as he turned to a porcine companion who seemed to be an especially good listener. "I am an utter failure as a pugilistic promoter – no, it's true — and I failed Min as well." He rubbed away snot and tears with his sleeve. "Surely there is something, someone in this world, even for one such as me, but I can't see it at the moment."

The swine grunted and rutted in the muddy wagon.

"Yes, perhaps you're right. Maybe tomorrow will be less interesting." Ping snuggled in next to the hog for warmth and watched the sun as it slowly set.

CHIN SONG PING AND THE HUNGRY GHOSTS

Ping hated mules more than he hated horses. "Esmerelda, I offer fair warning, if you do not move this instant, I shall be forced to live up to my job title as mule-skinner ... literally. I shall have no qualms about turning your hide into several pairs of unfashionable boots."

Esmerelda swung her head from side to side emitting a loud, long bray that sounded like laughter to Ping's untrained ear. There were four mules in the team that pulled the dynamite wagon Ping was driving through the Sierra Mountains, but Esmerelda was the lead. When she decided it was time for a break, the rest of the mule union went along with her.

This was Ping's first actual encounter with mules, despite the lies he had told to get this job. In the five years Ping had roamed the United States, after leaving his native China, he had never met a horse that liked him. He had been kicked, bitten, thrown and just plain ignored ... but at least horses were noble creatures. He understood their disdain of a scoundrel such as himself. Mules, however, were scruffy and foul smelling ... Ping considered them in no way his social betters. And, he hated the way they laughed at him.

"God damn it, Ping." Harry, the other driver, and Ping's boss on this expedition, raised up from his nap among the crates of explosives. "You are the worst Mule-skinner I've ever seen."

Ping jiggled the reins furiously. "It is not my fault that you have recruited the most obstinate team of mules in Nevada. I am accustomed to working with a more professional class of jackass." In truth, Ping knew he would never have been hired if *anyone* else had volunteered.

Harry shifted, careful to protect his right arm encased in a colorful bandana sling. "Crap! Maybe it's just as well. Sun's getting low and it don't hardly make no sense to go falling off this mountain, with all this dynamite, in the dark." He chuckled softly. "Hell, I'd hate to have to explain something like that to ol' Saint Peter... damned embarrassing."

Ping knew this referred to one of the Christian deities. As much as the people in this land professed to believe in only one god, they certainly invoked any number of them when worked up. Jesus, Mary, plain old God, and occasionally this Peter, were all fervently advocated by practitioners of this religion. It made little sense to Ping, but then few religions did.

###

Camp was a simple affair, bedrolls and a cooking fire over which Ping made pan biscuits. It bothered him that after two months as a cook in an Oregon timber camp, biscuits were still the only thing he could reliably make that was edible. He had lost a tiny chunk of ear to the thrown axe that had served as a termination notice to that career. He offered Harry a plate of excellent biscuits and barely palatable beans.

"Harry, I apologize for my earlier impudence. I know that I am a disappointment to you with regards to my driving skills ... My dear mother felt the same about me in general."

Harry spit a bit of gravel out of his mouthful of beans. "Well, mules will have that effect on a man. Fact is I'm just glad I finally found someone to share the chore with. Ain't no way I could have got 'er done alone with this busted wing." He moved his sling so he could hold the plate more easily. "This time of year, over this here pass ... Hell, I wouldn't do it if they hadn't waggled that huge bonus in front of me."

Ping had his own reasons for taking the job but... "Why, exactly is that, O honorable boss?"

"Why, the Donner party, you ignorant heathen."

Ping had learned to ignore casual cultural insults. He would have little time for anything else had he not. "Thank you for this worthy information, now what sort of party is a Donner party?"

Harry set down his plate and rubbed his hands together, a wicked gleam in his eyes. "Now, that is a tale not for the faint of heart."

Ping leaned back and gnawed on his biscuit.

"Way I heard it, back in '46 a feller named George Donner set out to lead a whole passel of folks from Missouri to the Promised Land in California. George got hold of some bad advice and had them folks wandering around Utah like the children of Israel ... that's in the bible. It added a couple of months to their travels. By this time they'd

131

lost a bunch of cattle and horses and were just desperate to get across the Sierra-Nevada Mountains any way they could before winter set in. True to form, old Donner had them head up into the mountains and straight into the worst winter in history. Well, sir, they got stuck … right about where we are sitting at this very moment … and there they stayed."

Ping's eyes narrowed. He didn't care for the direction this story was headed.

"There were a bunch of rescue attempts but the snow up here was as high as Abe Lincoln in that top-hat of his. Months went by, and the food those folks had brought was long gone. They ate up the livestock and chewed on boot-leather and belts. In the end, only about have those folks made it out alive. Why don't you ask me how those poor souls managed to survive that awful winter?"

"I feel certain you will illuminate me whether I ask it of you or not." Ping set down his plate and shoved it gingerly to one side.

"They survived by eating the ones who didn't make it! Ain't that something?"

Ping pinched the bridge of his nose. "Why take this route then? Are there not others we might have taken? Is this not late October with the whiff of snow already in the air? Are you quite insane?"

Harry laughed and swallowed a mouthful of biscuit. "Well now, let's see. There was cheap dynamite in Nevada and hardly no dynamite in California, where the Central Pacific is blasting away, trying to poke a hole for the railroad to go through these here mountains. And, this was the quickest way to get 'twixt the two. At least three others lit out, loaded with explosives, just like us, but they took the southern route. We can beat them by a week and make out like bandits selling this stuff."

Without a word, Ping rounded up his few possessions, which he tied in a bundle and slung it over his back. Running in the dark was risky but his eyesight was keen and he was very nimble. Most of the way was downhill and if he maintained a steady trot he felt sure he could reach safety within three days. Despite everything Ping had seen in his short life, he was not a superstitious man. Ghost tales meant nothing to him. And, while tales of cannibalism were repulsive, they didn't stir any real terror in his breast. What he could not abide was missing his business in San Francisco. Also, he did not relish the thought of spending the winter in such a god-forsaken place subsisting on fillet of Harry Dodge and Esmerelda stew.

"Hey, wait! Where in the Sam Hill do you think you're going? We got us a contract." Harry was on his feet and all humor had fled his eyes. "Look, winter is still a couple of weeks off. I can feel it in my bones and my bones ain't hardly never wrong. We'll be sitting pretty in California long before then."

Ping bowed low. "I fear I do not know your bones well enough to trust them. I know Esmerelda just well enough to not trust my life on her speed. What I do trust is my own cowardice. It has seldom failed me." He turned to walk off.

"I'll double… triple your wages."

Ping halted. "My cowardice could be bought off with nothing short of a percentage of the coming reward." It would certainly be better to arrive in San Francisco as a man of means rather than as a ragged pilgrim, weary from his trek and empty of pocket.

It was a great moral dilemma for both Ping and Harry Dodge, survival versus the cleansing power of greed.

"I'll go twenty five, seventy five and not a penny more, you thieving owl-hoot." Dodge stuck out his hand to the young Chinese man.

Ping eyed the hand like it stank of leprosy. "A thirty, seventy split would do much more to bolster my waning courage." Ping could almost hear the beads of the abacus in the man's head as he calculated the plusses and minuses of the situation.

Finally Harry's eyes came to a sharp focus and a grudging grin split his face. "Done! Put her there, partner."

Ping was sure that his luck was finally turning. In one week's time San Francisco was to host the largest F'an T'an tournament ever to be held in America and Ping just had to be there. Now he might even do so in style.

In recent years he had come to prefer poker to the venerable Chinese game but still… There were rumors that the Imperial

Nephew himself might attend, incognito of course, and his pockets were deep indeed. All of Ping's once-fabulous fortune had been long since pissed away. He saw this as a chance to reclaim his standing as a man of substance, and surely if he were once again wealthy he could win back his lovely Louise.

For two years Ping and Louise had lived high on the riches he had won in a poker game with the trickster-god, Coyote. When the last of it was gone they had been happy living by their wits, turning a mostly-legal dollar here and there. Louise, granddaughter of a Voodoo Queen, seemed as well suited to this life of adventure as he was himself.

Then, two weeks ago, Ping had bet everything he had on a horse race. Unfortunately his luck with the equine species had run true to form and he lost everything. Even more unfortunately, that "everything" included Louise. She was not pleased to be used as barter in this age where slavery was supposedly long dead. When the winner showed up to collect his due, she bought herself back with the money she had squirreled away hidden from Ping's impulses. Then she purchased the man's pistol from him and went to find Ping.

Even here, lying under the stars, with Harry snoring loudly nearby, Ping was sure that, in her heart, Louise still loved him ... why else would she have missed him six times?

It was still the dead of night when Ping's slumber was rudely interrupted by Esmerelda. Even Ping could tell she was not laughing this time.

By the dying embers of the fire, Ping could see his new partner sitting upright in his bedroll, His one good hand in the air and eyes wide with terror. Arrayed around the camp were unshaven men in large hats, with large guns. Ping knew the hats were called sombreros which probably meant that the men were Mexican bandits. He was pretty sure about the bandit part because one of the men had a pistol pointed at Harry's head and another had a shotgun pointed at Ping.

There were several bandits, most of them rummaging through the wagon.

"Paco, there ain't no gold here. The gringos got a wagon full of dynamite." A bandit jumped down from the wagon, slapping his hands together in disgust. "I say we shoot them and get back to that cabin. It's damned cold out here!"

The one with the shotgun pushed back his sombrero and scratched furiously at his scalp. "Madre! What sort of fool carts explosives through the mountains this time of year?"

Harry looked unable to answer so Ping stood slowly and bowed low to the one with the shotgun. He seemed to be in charge. "If we have trespassed unknowingly on your lands, we humbly beg forgiveness. The most fearful load of dynamite, which you have correctly divined is not gold, is bound for California and the railroad."

The men all had a good laugh at Ping's explanation. Paco moved the weapon away from Ping. "Our land? Do we look like fur trappers? I am Paco Gonzales and these are my men, surely you have heard us?"

Ping looked thoughtful for a moment then shrugged his shoulders. "I fear I have not."

The bandit leader looked enquiringly at Harry, who shook his head reluctantly.

"Look, that one is ignorant and has a broken arm. What good is he? Kill him."

Before Ping could protest, a shot rang out and Harry Dodge slumped sideways. Blood poured from the large hole in his head, his eyes still wide open, now and for eternity.

Gonzales turned back to Ping. "Have you heard of me now, shit-for-brains?"

The young Chinese man forced back the bile that was rising in his throat. "You are Paco Gonzales, emperor of bandits, and I assume I will soon be dead."

The bandit came over and patted Ping's cheek. "I like you. You're a funny fellow." Gonzales then began yelling orders at his men. "Hide the mules and bring the food but leave the wagon here. Tomorrow we will unload it and try to finally get the hell out of here." A wind moaned slowly through the pine trees and all the bandits froze in fear. "¡Vamonos! I don't want to be standing out here scratching my cajones when the ghosts get here. We have to get back to the cabin pronto."

135

Ping followed along submissively, but not before pulling Harry's blanket over the dead man's face. Oddly, Esmerelda would only let herself be led by Ping.

The cabin was run down but solid. More than that, it was relatively warm. Ping was at least glad not to be sleeping outside again. The bandits dug into the stolen food supplies like they hadn't eaten in days.

Ping decided that his lot could hardly worsen by trying to satisfy his curiosity about what was going on. He bowed to the bandit chief. "Forgive my ignorance, but why is the emperor of bandits hold up in this shabby excuse for a palace, so far from his border kingdom? And, though I see saddles strewn around, why are there no horses tied outside."

Paco wiped bean juice from his mustache. "You ask a lot of questions, but I still like you so I will answer them." He kicked at a small man shoveling rice into his face. "We are here because of Ramon ... who I should kill, but he is my sister's worthless husband ... had a brilliant idea to escape the Federales chasing us. Hide in the mountains, he said. We can lose them, he said. We did lose them eventually, but it took three days and got us hopelessly lost. The horses were eaten by ghosts."

Ghosts? Yes, the man had mentioned ghosts before. Ping had thought it merely part of the man's colorful use of language. "I see. In China we had feasts for hungry ghosts. My mother would leave out plates of food to appease them, but I've never heard of any ghosts that actually ate the offerings. It was more about helping those who were unsatisfied and unfulfilled in life who took these feelings with them into the next life."

Gonzales stared at Ping, open mouthed. "I don't think these ghosts are going to be bought off by a couple of plates of rice and beans. When we found this cabin a week ago, I thought we'd stay the night and leave the next morning. That night we tied up the horses and were awakened by their screams in the middle of the night. They were being torn apart by things we could barely make out in the dark. Two of my men ran out to save the horses." His voice got quiet and the symphony of slurps and gulps died down as he continued the story. "They were torn apart for their trouble, a snack for the hungry ghosts. We locked ourselves in and said our rosaries. Then they came through the walls like they weren't even there, and whispered to us. I don't know what they were saying, but at least they didn't eat us. They won't eat us in here." The men looked at the walls and trembled. "Next morning we found only the bones of the men and horses. We ran down the mountain. It was daylight. What sort of self respecting ghost comes out in the daytime? But, there they were. They caught Felipe and ate him while the rest of us ran back for this cabin. Here we sat for a week until we saw your campfire an hour ago."

Ping had seen many strange things and these did not seem like fanciful men prone to making up stories. "Perhaps the ghosts have left. You were able to go to and from our camp without being molested."

The bandit closed his eyes and cringed. "I don't think they've left, senor."

Ping felt his heart go cold then a phantom hand came out of the front of his chest. The rest of the arm followed suit as a translucent form crawled through him. Ping screamed. The cabin was filled with wraith-like forms, coming through the walls and ceiling. The dimly lit room was alive with loud, insistent and incoherent whispering, audible even over the screams of the tortured bandits. Ping folded himself up like a babe in its womb but nothing could shut out the dry rasps of tongues long dead. He felt the cold go through him several times and when he dared open an eye there was a gaunt face staring back. It had once been a woman's face. Her cheeks were sunken and her eyes were hidden by the caves of her eye sockets. Ping saw the room beyond her clearly as through smoked glass. Her lips trembled with a passionate need to be heard.

"I fear I cannot understand you O fearsome spirit," Ping stuttered, "please speak more clearly and I will do whatever you ask."

The ghost screeched in dry frustration but Ping had an idea. "I believe there is one who might help us understand each other. Look on the trail above here for the spirit of Harry Dodge. He has died only recently and may yet speak the language of the living."

Suddenly the room contained only the living once again. All around, Ping heard terrified moans and his nose caught the acrid stench of urine. He now understood too well both reactions. Ramon sat rocking back and forth, knees drawn into his chest. Only Paco Gonzales seemed to still possess all his faculties.

"That was a short one." The bandit stuck out his chin defiantly.

After several minutes, the clean-up began. What supplies they had had been knocked over in the men's thrashings to escape the whispers from Hell. It seemed futile but at least Gonzales was a good enough leader to realize that the routine of work could help counteract the horrors of the last quarter hour.

Ping straightened up the saddles piled in one corner and quietly went through saddlebags to see if they might contain anything useful... though what that would be he had no idea. Then, without warning, Harry Dodge appeared, sitting comfortably on the topmost saddle. He looked well, both arms in good working order.

"Just because I made you my partner don't give you the privilege to whistle me up any time you want. I was half way to the Pearly Gates when that skinny lady found me."

Ping fell over backwards and several bandits rushed over to see what had happened.

Paco looked around nervously. "What's the matter, Gringo, afraid of a few little ghosts?" This got the expected laughter from his men.

Ping stuttered, "Can't you see him? Harry! You shot him a while ago."

Harry shifted on the saddle. "Look, Ping, I don't give a rat's ass about these Mexican hooligans, but I figure I owe you for getting you into this mess. Tell them to shut up so we can talk."

Ping turned to Gonzales. "The spirit of Harry has asked that you shut up... please. He has spoken to the other ghosts and may be able to help."

The bandit chief didn't look happy about it but he quieted his men. "Tell your friend that I'm sorry I had him shot." Ping just shushed him.

"That's better. As I said, I was halfway to Heaven when I got stopped by a woman leading the mangiest bunch of ghosts I ever laid eyes on. You remember I told you about the Donner party?"

Ping nodded. "Are these then the poor unfortunates who were eaten by their friends?"

"Hell no. These are the folks that did the eating. This is the cabin where they stayed that winter and when the survivors died of natural causes, years later, their souls were drawn back here. Seems they're bound to this shack where they are damned to eternal hunger. If you're just passing through they have to let you be, but if you use their cabin you are fair game."

"I was dragged here against my will, surely they would not eat me?" Ping felt indignant. This wasn't fair on any level.

"Partner, they didn't make the rules, they just follow them. This here damned cabin saved their lives and now it damns them for eternity." Harry scratched his ghostly head. "If I see God I'll ask him about this, but till then it looks like your best bet is to blow your brains out while you're safe inside here. At least that way you won't become no hungry ghost yourself. Well, I got me some harp lessons to get to." And the ghost of Harry Dodge disappeared as quickly as it had come.

Ping stood quietly for a moment, his head hanging low he turned to Gonzales and his band. "Harry says we should all kill ourselves so at least our souls might remain free." There was a low growl of grumbling at this. Ping raised his head and gave a wolf-like smile to the bandits. "I do not care for this plan at all, and have thought of another. If the emperor of bandits will trust a humble scoundrel such as myself, we might just get out of this with our skins."

Ping patted his makeshift bundle carefully. He adjusted it again to make sure he would have easy access to it without crushing the contents. "Have the spirits come back yet?"

Ramon stood at the dirty, smudged window keeping lookout. "Si. They are gathering now, it won't be long."

Ping turned to the young bandit, Louis, who had been chosen as the best runner and helped the man adjust his bundle. "Remember, head downhill wherever possible." Louis bobbed his head vigorously

139

in affirmation, though his eyes were wide in terror. "Do not use your ammunition to excess, it must last you." Ping had his doubts about the man.

"We all know our parts. Don't be such a mother hen." Paco was getting anxious for things to get started "I still don't see why we can't use the mules? Francisco can hitch up a team faster than anyone you've ever seen."

Ping exhaled nervously … his plan seemed less brilliant with each passing second. "I do not doubt the worthy Francisco's skill or speed, only the work ethics the stubborn Esmerelda."

Ramon tugged the ragged curtains back over the window. "Madre! Here they come." He instinctively reached for the worn rosary beads he knew very well were no longer there.

Gonzales slapped Ping on the shoulder and grabbed for the door handle. "I'll see you in Hell, amigo."

AS the door was flung open Ping plunged through. "I hope not." He said as he grabbed at the overhang on the porch. He let his momentum swing him in an easy arc up onto the roof. Though the shingles clattered under his feet, the roof held under his weight. He took this as a very good omen. He climbed swiftly up to the peak where he could steady himself. He was pleased to see that his skills as an acrobat had not eroded too badly. He often thought he would be a great acrobat playing in the pleasure halls of Beijing if he had not been caught in bed with the head acrobat's wife. *Sigh.*

As hoped, more than half the ghosts veered off to attack Ping. He was no longer protected from their appetites by the wooden walls. They had almost reached him when he plucked something warm and round out of his bundle. He threw it hard as he could and the ghosts followed it. What hungry being, dead or alive would not prefer a warm biscuit to a stringy acrobat.

There had been some debate as to whether biscuits or tortillas would be the best distraction, but it was Ramon who reminded everyone that Missouri ghosts might not know what a tortilla was. Though the dough preparation and baking conditions were below Ping's usual standards, the bread had come out quite light and fluffy.

Ping glanced down the slope of the roof in time to see Louis sprint from the cabin, throwing biscuits as he went. He wanted to shout *save your ammunition*, but he had more pressing matters of his own to attend to. The ghosts were heading back his way.

He rolled down the backside of the roof and sprang into the gnarled pines that surrounded the area. The ghosts were almost on him when he launched another flour and lard missile. Like a squirrel, he jumped nimbly to another tree and then another, where he was surprised by a lone ghost and dropped a biscuit. Fortunately the ghost followed the falling food. Ping knew that this was a combined game of fetch and tag, and that he'd have to be more careful if he wanted to win it. Before his next leap, he saw Gonzales and the rest of the bandits jogging up the slope on their assigned mission. Good.

Ping kept to the trees, flinging biscuits only as needed. That the apparitions gave off a faint glow was just enough to keep track of them, and stay one step ahead. It had been a long while since he had had this much exercise and it was beginning to show. He had barely made his last jump. He could tell the land was sloping downward and saw ahead that the trees came to an abrupt end ahead. Buddha be praised.

From somewhere left of him he heard a scream and the sounds of struggle. Ping threw another biscuit and headed for the scream.

From his perch he saw Louis lying still on the ground, one leg torn off his body and half his face missing. Three of the ghosts gnawed at the bandit's flesh but the rest were fighting over the biscuits that had fallen out of his bag. Ping dropped lightly to the ground.

It was a horrifying tableau but Ping felt only pity for the ghosts. They were not evil demons, but ordinary people who had lost their way, and were now eternally cursed for that mistake. He had felt like a hungry ghost himself since his mother had thrown him out at fourteen, telling him that he would never amount to anything. His aspirations to be a great gambler, or acrobat, or cook, or any of the dozens of other failed careers he had aspired to over the years, were just his way of showing the world that he was not worthless. How could anyone, how could Louise, love a man who was worthless?

As the spirits finished their feast, he saw the rest of the ghosts were returning from above. Tears welled up in Ping's eyes as he held up a biscuit and yelled. "I am hungry too! Catch me or I shall eat these wonderful biscuits all by myself and fart at you for your efforts." He bit into the biscuit and took off running in the direction he had seen the forest end.Not his most rousing speech but it served the purpose, the ghosts were all hot on his heels.

Ping didn't throw any more tasty grenades but relied instead on speed. Before long he felt icy scratches on his back and tucked himself into a roll sideways. He bounded spryly to his feet and pulled out a length of cord comprised of wooden beads and worn crucifixes. The cord clattered as he twirled it above his head. The ghosts gave the beaded string a wide berth, unsure of what Ping was up to now.

He had their attention, now for the pitch. "You do well to fear these holy relics, Rosaries personally blessed by the head Pope man in Rome. They would burn the flesh off such wretches as you have become... if you had flesh. Saint Frances the sissy asked for a holy communion dance with your Jesus himself while wearing these. Peter Paul and Mary sang at their wedding" He was quickly exhausting his meager knowledge of Christianity, but the shades seemed to maintain their respectful distance as he twirled his "holy relic" in a ragged figure eight. Suddenly, one of the ghosts surged forward into the path of the twirling beads. Whether the move was brave or suicidal on the ghost's part, Ping could not say, but the effect was not unexpected. Nothing happened.

Of all the curse words Ping knew, an American one seemed most appropriate at that particular minute. "Shit!" Ping hurled the cord at the ghosts and ran. It couldn't be far, and then, there it was right ahead of him. He skidded to a stop, amid flying gravel, just short of the precipice of the cliff looming before him. He plucked off the bundle and spun in place to build momentum before he threw the thing far out into the valley below. Once again the ghosts, slaves to their baser instincts, ignored him and went chasing after the bag of biscuits.

Ping put his hands on his knees and gulped lungs-full of the cold night air. It would be a while before the ghosts found the bag, but they would find it. They might spend some time squabbling over its contents, but they would be back eventually. Ping stripped off his wool coat and threw it into the valley after the specters. With one last deep breath he turned. He would be more than warm enough running back up the mountain.

###

Paco Gonzales cracked his whip to no avail. The mules had decided to stop a couple of hundred feet from the cabin and could be coaxed no further. "You motherless offspring of a jackrabbit and a dead horse, move! I am the driver, I have the whip. I say you move or I swear I will shoot you dead and maybe then you'll move."

This was the scene Ping witnessed as he rounded the cabin. He stopped, breathing deeply through his nose. Had his instructions not been clear? Apparently not to an egotistical, maniacal bandit leader, eager to show everyone that he would not be bossed around. Ping stalked straight to Gonzales and raised a furious finger into his face. The bandit at least had the good grace to turn an embarrassed crimson. Ping counted backwards from ten to one in Chinese before he turned and stalked over to Esmerelda. He started to point his finger at the mule but realized the futility, so he stretched up onto his toes to whisper in the mule's ear.

The wagon lurched forward as Esmerelda and her team-mates strained at their harnesses. Ping jumped on her back as the wagon gained speed. They had almost reached the structure when Ping urged the mules sharply to the right. As a result, the wagon slid sideways into the building at full speed, destroying half the wall as it did so, but, miraculously, not exploding.

All the bandits let out a loud whoop and started grabbing crates of dynamite to plant strategically around the cabin, inside and out. This had to be done right if there was to be any chance of success.

Gonzales was measuring out lengths of fuse but seemed torn about their lengths. "I don't have much experience with this sort of thing, amigo. Should I make them long or short?"

Ping had unhitched the mules and slapped their flanks to send them on their way. In the distance there was an angry wail which got louder by the second. "I think short fuses would be most excellent."

Once the dynamite had been placed, all the bandits gathered around Ping as their chief lit the fuse. Ping could see they had come

143

to look to him for guidance. What would a great leader say at such a time? *Run?* Yes that seemed sound advice. "RUN!"

It became a madhouse. The vengeful ghosts came screaming in as the bandits dispersed in all directions, often running into each other. Ping made for a large boulder set some distance to the left of the house. He heard screams behind him but did not turn to discover the screamers' identities. He focused all his energy into his aching leg muscles. Something cold ripped through his shin and he stumbled. He rolled over to see the spirit that had slashed him wheel around to claim his prize. Ping pulled a half eaten biscuit out of his pants pocket and threw it back toward the cabin. Once again, hunger trumped revenge and Ping crawled to the boulder. With much effort he made it to the stony top and let himself drop to the other side.

He lay there huffing, looking up at the sky when he saw a glowing shape glide over the boulder and descent toward him. He had no more running in him. The thing drifted closer and Ping wanted to scream. Finally the apparition was almost nose to nose when he realized it was the ghost woman he had tried to communicate with earlier in the cabin. Her mouth opened and a strained whisper, dryer than a grave, came forth. "Thank you." She kissed his forehead.

And then the world exploded.

A wagon load of dynamite was an awful lot of dynamite. The huge boulder Ping had hoped would protect him rocked back and forth threatening to crush him at any moment. Then he could see nothing for the smoke and falling debris. After several minutes he started the task of digging himself out of the gravel heap that had come to rest on him. He stood tenuously, slowly putting weight on his injured leg. No major damage, thank Buddha. He staggered his way around the boulder to see what was left of the cursed cabin.

There was only a large hole, a crater, to give any credence to its once having existed. Then, in the smoke he saw Gonzales and two of his men. Their clothes were in tatters and covered in dirt but they all limped toward Ping.

"Pretty good thinking for a shit-for-brains gringo," the chief laughed through his coughing, "If you can't kill a ghost, kill the place that keeps them hanging around." He bent over to pick up a shredded sombrero lying at his feet and put it on Ping's head. "What do you think? You would make one great bandit. What a team you and I would make."

Ping removed the hat and bowed as he handed it back to Paco. "It is a most kind offer, coming from the emperor of bandits as it does, but I have business back in Nevada. It is timed I stopped being a hungry ghost."

Paco dusted himself off with the sombrero. "Well, if you change your mind, my throne room is just the other side of the Rio Grande." He motioned to his men. "Play-time is all over, muchachos, we got us some mules to catch."

Ping sat down on the rim of the crater and watched the bandits disappear into the smoke. After a time he felt a nuzzling on his neck and turned to see Esmerelda and a faint figure standing beside her.

The figure spoke in a dry whisper. "What in tar-nation did you say to this critter to get her moving?"

"Harry!" Ping sprang to his feet. "Why are you not in your Christian Heaven?"

One corner of the ghost's mouth quirked up. "I might have stretched the truth a mite about being at the Pearly Gates and all. I just been sort of fading away here and I don't know what's next no more than the man in the moon. So, what did you say?"

Ping stroked the mule's coarse grey fur. "I told her that there was a very large sugar cube inside the house and that an Arabian stallion was about to eat all of it if she did not hurry."

Harry's laugh sounded like rolling sagebrush. "I recon that'd get 'er done." Then he was gone.

The ride back to Nevada was a cold one without a winter coat, but Ping kept himself close to Esmerelda's neck to share her warmth. They had come to an understanding, of sorts, back at the crater and there had been no work stoppages since.

Ping stood in the early morning hours, staring up at the window of the Carson City hotel where he and Louise had lived, before his hasty exodus.

Surely she had already moved on, or perhaps she lay up there

145

sleeping in the arms of another ... a man who would certainly shoot him on sight.

Perhaps he should steal some clothing and a good breakfast before knocking on door number 218?

No.

He knew that despite the wisdom gleaned from the hungry ghosts, he would always be a gambler. He licked his palms and slicked back his hair. This was a hand he must play. He was done with bluffing.

SECTION THREE

SURF'S UP

Jell'Ah'Dahree blinked her front eyes more rapidly than polite society normally demanded. She often did this when she was really upset and Molli'Ma'Molian had just unloaded a bigger stink-bladder than she had ever smelled.

"Are you insane? That's the stupidest stunt I've ever heard of. You'd be signing your own death warrant on live visi."

Moli's eyes seemed to glow with an inner madness and his mouth formed a huge grinning "O".

"That's the beauty of it, no one's ever even thought of it!"

"No one's ever thought of it because it's INSANE!"

Fifteen cycles ago Jell' had signed on to be manager of Molli'Ma'Molian, The most knuckles-down surfer on the Western Rim. Surfing had been the hot new craze with that young generation of Taurins luxuriating in the newly acquired wealth of their parents. The average Taurin could, thanks to the new technological boom, now afford to send their young to good schools, give them the advantages and free time their generation had never enjoyed. Of course, the kids pretty much squandered their privilege on fast scooters, intox sludge and surfing.

A Taurin surf board consisted of a long lightweight plank with two flexible wings on either side. A surf bunger Taurin stands on the board with his back feet while grasping each wing with his middle limbs. The front arms are used for balance and waving obscene gestures at other surfers. It was wisest to surf backwards because that's where the wave was coming at you and stereo vision was most needed. A few glorious bastards surfed face forward and laughed at the fates. Moli'Ma'Molian the most glorious bung bastard anyone had ever seen and everyone wanted his endorsement. Enter Jell'Ah'Dahree who had made Moli one of the richest Taurins to ever walk the planet.

Of course, that had been fifteen cycles ago and Moli' was easily bored.

"Let me get this straight," she closed all her eyes to keep from blinking, "You finance most of this government space mission to whichever gas-giant they want to go to, and in return you get to go along."

"Right as formic rain, Jell', my little temple bell." Moli danced his famous beach bomba as he spun in place—proceeds from that dance alone had brought him his first million credits.

"Right," Her middle digits twitched, much less embarrassing than blinking. "And when you get there, you go surfing in the upper atmosphere on an ion propelled board that research developed just for you? And if—I repeat, if—you aren't crushed by the pressure, corroded by some chemical in the atmosphere we've never heard of, or eaten--you use the footage of your jaunt to promote...?"

Moli's right fore-limb waved in front of Jell's fore-eyes, digits waggling madly.

"Our new line of flying surfboards, silly."

Jell' opened one eye to see past the dancing digits, into her boss's eyes. "Those don't work. Your top scientists say they never will. Twenty Taurins have wound up in serious medical condition testing those stupid things, and you want to go space surfing to promote them?"

Moli' settled onto his favorite lounge cushion and started plucking eight his string wah-stick. "If there's one thing I've learned in all my years surfing the choppy seas of West Rim--as well as the choppy seas of business--it's that you have to take a wave when it comes or it will wind up taking you."

"What the hell does that even mean?"

Moli' strummed a bold power chord and smiled.

It means that Moli's gonna go space surfing, baby!"

The rumble throughout the ship let Moli' know that the ram-scoop was being retracted. The captain had scooped up enough fuel material from the dense layer of gasses that surrounded them, to make the long trip home. That meant he would get the drop signal any moment now so he toggled on the camera and sound pickup array situated all about his "board". Showtime.

"Hey, hey, all you zipperheaded sixes and sevens out there. Your big bunger buddy, Mondo Mojo Moli', is live here on the good ship Gleea'Al'Nonna somewhere in the way upper atmo of the biggest beach of all—Claa'Asha. Any moment now I'm going on the craziest ride of anyone's life, so let me give a little tour of my one-of-a-kind space board. Once the bottom drops out," he pointed his finger cams at the wings. "These ion spitting outboards will let me maneuver around some until I find a nice wave-front. Once I've caught a gale-force gas pipe to hang out in, the engines go off and I am surfing. I've got sensors on every square inch so I can scientifically plot my optimum course. Is that total flinch or what?"

What was taking so long? Is it that hard to retract a scoop? Moli' knew he had to stretch so he figured some more tech talk was in order.

"The whole bottom of my super board is composed of high density heat shield, so if I can maintain the right angle I should just about manage to not burn up like a floogle candle. Don't worry, zipps, Moli' has been riding monsters since before his hair grew in—and my atmo suit has enough heat resist built in to survive a few spills and frills. Anyway, while I risk life and limbs for your entertainment, Gleea'Al'Nonna is going to be to be circling the planet doing all kinds of cool science stuff. Once they make it back to this neighborhood, yours truly will lay down on the board and fire off this insanely large rocket pack, strapped to my torso, and take off to rendezvous with my ride home. Piece of shnogoff, huh?"

And then he saw it, the light flashing at his hind feet. Just enough time for one last plug.

"This is where I should say 'don't try this at home, but akk that. You can try it at home on your brand new Bungo Inc. sky board coming sometime next year."

The light stopped flashing and became a steadty glare.

"The sound's about to cut out because who could hear anything over all that screaming—and I don't know which scream will be louder, me or the alien winds".

Suddenly the ship was gone and Moli' was tumbling through the pandemonium of an alien food blender. Every sensor went dead as last week's news.

He would have been thrown off the board in those first few seconds if not for the grapple pads that held all four of his lower limbs firmly attached to the board's control surface. He might have gone insane staring into that swirling hell, but his eyesight was even worse than the average Taurin.He had endured a lot of brine soakings as a surfer, and he couldn't make out a lot of details around him.Besides, you surf with your body, not your eyes, and sensors were for ashgogs. His lifelong reflexes snapped to life and saved his scales once again.

The ion boosters kicked and roared, in a death-match with the buffeting gasses as he slowed enough to feel patterns of movement all around him.

"It's just another ocean." He said, though no one could hear his words. "Don't fight it, stroke it like a hatching egg. Let the ride hatch itself and watch out for the edge of the shells."

That was it. The wing jets cut out. No more ion training wheels. Either he found the wave front or he was toasted walla. And then he felt the cut of the board into something substantial. Well, gaseous but substantial. He lost it for a second but there it was again, and the ride was on.

He pulled at the board's left wing with all his might and the fireball that had threatened to engulf him disappeared. Okay, the trick seemed to be to keep the nose up more than he was used to. And rolling his weight back and forth to compensate for side currents. Breathing did not come so easily though. The suit mostly evened out the atmo pressure but there were micro pressure fronts passing over his body continuously. On a hunch he pulled in a gulp of air to expand and detach his upper ribs, as though he were ready to mate. That helped—and in a way he was making love to a whole world.

Then it all went calm. There was a tremendous sense of speed but the world had stopped trying to crush him. Even with his poor eyesight he could see the way in front and behind him was clear as a Launtan daybreak. If there was a surfer's heaven, this was it.

He noticed he wasn't alone. Ten arms to his left there was a small armada of translucent kites with long, spiraling tails. They paced him for a time but seemed to grow bored and sped up. He could tell that they would soon pass him by, leaving him to eat their wake.

Akk that.

He was The Mighty Moli' and it didn't matter what world he was on, he took second place to no one. He pulled both wings high then slammed them down with all his weight. He leaned hard to the right, in the hope that he could tack the edge of the pipe. It worked. He was once again snout to snout with the kites. To make sure things stayed that way he slung his torso low onto the board and wriggled like a coonoo dancer. It was a move that had won him many a trophy.

The board scooted into the lead as Moli' waved his finger cams at the receding Kites. In the distance he could just make out another flotilla of larger things that looked more like thrown discs than kites. They slowed down and buzzed all around him like summer snutches. When they buzzed out tiny chunks of his suit and board and Moli' started to get annoyed. So, he pulled a maneuver he had only done once—successfully—in all his life. He grabbed the board's nose and pulled hard while flexing the right wing forward and the left one backwards. The corkscrew that followed sent the discs flying in all directions. He righted himself again like the champion he was while the discs reformed into a V formation. They wobbled for a moment, like they were mocking him, before they spun faster and whirled out of sight.

Had they been mocking the greatest surfer who'd ever lived? Moli' felt sure they had. He could think of only one thing to do.

Nimble fingers detached the rocket packet on his chest. This was no longer about a great ride, and screw science, this was a point of honor. He secured the pack to the board near his hind feet, the thrusters pointed back the way he had come. He settled in low so his center of gravity was in front of the rocket. His middle right digit hovered for a moment over the button that would ignite the rocket.

"Damn sky boards probably never would have worked anyway. It's better this way. Who wants to die of boredom at a shareholder's meeting?" His raw gurgle of laughter almost drowned out his last words. "Sorry, Jell."

The skin was pulled tight across the bones of his face as he slammed through the group of saucers on his way to eternity.

###

Jell'Ah'Dal.ree tapped a digit on the grating over the voice enhancer. She was not fond of speaking in front of large groups and this memorial service was the largest Taurin had ever known.

"We are here today to honor a brave Taurin. (Stupid Taurin, more like. She thought.) He was a shining beacon of the Taurin ideal of pushing boundaries and finding the greatness that is in us all."

She held up a strip of sealed writing film.

"Before he left on his final adventure, Molli'Ma'Molian, left a last message to be read in case he should meet with misfortune."

A hush fell over the enormous crowd. She popped the strip open and read what it said. Her mouth quivered into the "O" of a smile as she tucked the film into her pocket.

"Molli'Ma'Molian leaves us with these words to comfort us. 'Always look to the next wave and let yourselves ride into the glorious future that Taurin will find in the stars."

The audience exploded into a thunder of open palms beating on inflated chests as Jell' made her way down the ramp. She tapped lightly at the folded strip hidden in her pocket and thought about the words that were really written there.

AT LEAST YOU'RE RID OF ME NOW, JELL'. RUN THE SHOW THE WAY YOU SEE FIT. AKK IT!

Two days earlier the research department had finally cracked the skyboard stability problem so the company was soon going to triple in size. She wondered silently, for perhaps the thousandth time. "How can someone so brilliant be such an idiot?"

153

UNIVERSES LIKE CHAMPAGNE

"Copy that, Comsit. I have active 'brane flux on grid alpha, coordinates 89 by 43." Linda wiped hair from her damp forehead for the third time in the last minute or so. She swore to herself that she'd get a buzz-cut if she made it back. "I am commencing shuffle sequence and will go in two minutes if conditions persist within stable parameters."

"Everything on this end looks good, two minutes and counting." There was something in Calvin Tweed's voice that, even at a moment like this, made Linda feel like she should pop a beer and stop worrying. Maybe it was his slight Jamaican lilt. "Say, girl, do you know what the cosmic zombie said to the theoretical physicist?"

"No, Cal, what did the cosmic zombie say to the theoretical physicist?"

"Branes, Braaaanes!"

"Copy, Comsit. Ha hyphen ha hyphen ha. That one never gets old."

Linda Cline leaned back into her harness and closed her eyes. She was suspended in a spider's web of straps, designed to hold her in place within the transparent bubble, constructed of woven nano-tubes. This would soon be her universe away from home. The web could swivel to any orientation necessary, so she could have total maneuverability and still keep as much distance as possible between her and whatever would soon be on the other side of the bubble. Previous unmanned probes had given her team only a limited idea of what to expect in the universe next door.

A lot of the accepted laws of physics still seemed to work over there, but there were differences that no one had fully figured out the ramifications of. Gravity seemed to act oddly, it had a slight spin to it, and the speed of light wasn't quite as constant as it should be. The Omniverse Project complex had been built out here, near Pluto, so the solar system's gravity wells would exert minimal effect. The idea was to gently nudge our membrane universe into the one right next to it, like a peck on the cheek, allowing the Cue Ball One sphere to slide from one to the other. There was initial speculation that such a

154

touching of two realities might be fatal to both, perhaps even initiating a new Big Bang. The project had only been nervously green-lighted when Linda had proven mathematically that our universe, at least, was made of tougher stuff than that.

She pinched the bridge of her nose and quickly scanned all the virtual readouts that seemed to surround her. It was too early for this. They had scheduled another year of unmanned probes, but their budget had been cut off and re-prioritized for the war effort. If she didn't go now, the chance was lost forever. She blinked her left eye a few times to adjust her contech lens and bring the virtual displays back into sharp focus. "Do we have any further word from Duffy?" she asked, "I can't believe that those bastards commandeered our listening post at a time like this."

General Ben-Iman's voice broke in, harsh and impatient. "Doctor, I'm sure this little experiment of yours is very important to you and your people, but back in the real world there's a war going on to preserve freedom. You may have read about it, it's in all the 'casts."

"General, please..." Cal tried to reassert communications control.

"Cline, we've allowed you to tie up a vast amount of equipment and personnel out here in God's bunghole, but I'll be damned..." Ben-Iman's voice trailed off into static.

"Sorry about that, Cue Ball One, I've managed to put a cork in God's bunghole, which should keep him off your back till transit. Thirty seconds and counting, at my mark—mark."

"This is Cue Ball One, I copy you. Cal, don't let him pull the plug on me before the deadline, we can't back down now." Linda's hands trembled slightly as she triggered the final protocols.

"We'll handle things here, boss. You've got enough on your plate." Cal made sure that his voice carried all the confidence his heart was lacking at that second. "Transition shuffle in 3 – 2 – 1..."

"Goddamned scientists!" General Ben-Iman's mission had been simple; come out to this huge waste of government resources and dismantle it. Sitting across from his battle cruiser was the repurposed mining platform that constituted the major holding of Omniverse. A partial list of the assets they were wasting on their little science project included two of the biggest plasma generators in the system, a moebius accelerator powerful enough to drive a leviathan, and a sensor array equipped with the latest probability wave collapsing tech. That wasn't even counting all the brain power that could be put to better use, defeating the Sanger Evolutionaries. At least they had dismantled the so-called listening stations.

"Did you feel that?" He turned on his XO. "By god, the universe just flickered and we can't do a damn thing about it. They said 'no side effects'! Bullshit! Get on the horn and get me authorization to act before those maniacs destroy us all!"

The XO hadn't felt anything. "Sir, if we send a signal sunward, we paint a bull's-eye on ourselves and Omniverse," he said quietly. "All communications have to be bounced and buffered, you know that."

The general snarled and straightened his collar. "Very well, we wait. I'll be in the wardroom, you have the con." He glanced at the crew. "Run a drill or something, might as well be ready if the universe is going to end."

And, suddenly, Linda was alone except for the stars that seemed to twinkle all around her.

"There are stars here; the colors seem to pulse from red to blue with a period of whiteness in between. Like Christmas tree lights twinkling on a...." She stopped and frantically checked her panels. "Holy crap! The stars *are* twinkling—I'm in an atmosphere! If these readings are right, I could step outside this bubble and I'd be okay, except for a little giddiness from the extra oxygen." She rotated herself three hundred sixty degrees to make sure. "I could go for a walk except there's no planet in sight." Linda laughed out loud in sheer glee. "Feels like there's a slight tug in one direction, and the instruments confirm gravity, but I have no clue what's causing it."

Cue Ball One wanted to drift in the direction of the pull and she could see no good reason to prevent it. A little spatial variance shouldn't matter when it came time to snap back into her own universe. Slowly, reefs of clouds, almost like spun cotton candy, came into view. "Well, this is new! It looks like condensed vapor but..."

The sphere nudged into a bank and its course altered slightly. "There's substance to it, the sensors say carbon compounds. Curiouser and curiouser."

Color wove itself into the clouds, which were quickly taking on qualities of a landscape, comprised of ever larger gatherings of clouds, oriented towards the gentle gravity pull. The sense of openness remained though, thanks to large canyons separating things. Stars became harder to see as an Aurora Borealis-like effect lit the sky in the distance. She checked her chronometer to see how much time the mission had left, but it said only a few minutes had passed since her arrival. She wondered if time meant exactly the same thing here.

Then there were bubbles everywhere. Pulsing and glittering, hundreds of them. A few were almost as large as Cue Ball, but they went as small as an exercise ball. They seemed to pay no attention as they drifted past, with Linda deftly navigating the sphere's path to stay out of their way. Instruments said they were solid throughout, and yet almost completely empty. "I'm not even going to comment on these readings, which make no sense at all, except that I wouldn't be surprised to wind up at the Mad Hatter's tea party any time now."

She glanced at the mission timer. Her one hour mission was now seven minutes into overtime. Either something had gone seriously wrong or time flowed differently here. She crossed her fingers and hoped it was the latter. Curiouser and curiousier...

Out of the corner of her eye she caught movement across the now expected axis of orientation. It looked like there were several new shapes moving quickly, and then they were out of sight. Calling up the sensor view from that direction, she spooled back and enlarged the picture. The complex shapes had large wing-like structures toward their fronts that might be providing locomotion! She could also make out tendrils of some sort trailing behind them, touching others in the group as they moved.

"Life!?" Linda could barely breathe. This was something they hadn't even seriously considered from the probe data. There was always the stuff about finding mirror versions of yourself in another universe, but that had always seemed better science fiction than science to her mind. Yes, the math supported the possibility, but the odds were infinity to one. But, life of some sort? Why not? There were specialists back home trained in this whole first contact business, should any neighbors ever drop by. Not that there had ever been any first contact outside of microbes, but the possibility was always tantalizingly there. Heck, she told herself, even if there was life, that didn't necessarily mean sentience. She might wind up trying to make first contact with a herd of cows. Unconsciously, she started working kinks out of her hair.

###

Cal glanced nervously at the chrono that had been synched to Cue Ball one. "General, the clock says fifteen more minutes! If we try to induce snap-back now, there's no telling what shape she'll come back in." Suddenly, a panel over a young tech's head bulged inward and snapped off its braces, sending the young man flying from his board. "Django, are you all right, man?" Cal jumped up to tend to his fellow worker.

Through the buzz and hiss of interference, he heard Ben-Iman's angry retort. "I can't properly engage these bastards and protect your ass! You will shut down your class project, engage the machine shields, and evacuate now!" The hiss spiked for a moment. "... Losing the assets is not an option." The noise overcame the general's voice until it was lost in static.

Cal helped the young tech to his feet, checking his head. "Kid, you're going to have a goose egg, but you'll be okay. I need you to round up whoever you can find and get to a pod. I'm going to hit the alarm—that ought to get everyone going—and I'll make sure all that precious equipment is shielded. You understand?" The tech nodded a little blearily and headed out the hatch.

Cal looked at the shambles all around him, blown panels everywhere and most of the peripherals deader than his first marriage. The Evolutionaries' stealth ships had popped in from nowhere about ten minutes into the mission. Sanger Evolutionaries believed that when they died in a righteous act of wanton destruction, they would evolve into a god. Given that, they had no fear of using stealth shields that would kill you inside of a year. It was just another path to enlightenment. So far they had only used concussives in hopes of taking prizes, but if the battle went too long, there was no telling what they were capable of. "Shut down the listening posts, what a good idea," he mumbled to himself, and continued to splice systems until he got readouts on the main monitor system. He looked at the chrono again: ten minutes left. An hour had seemed like such a short window for the mission when they had agreed to it.

The beings—if that's what they were—became more numerous but kept their distance. The bubbles also became more numerous, and the aliens seemed to avoid those as well. As Linda drifted by, she could see two groups in the distance, one with red tendrils and the other with purple, as they ran into each other. There was much jerky motion, then they started whacking at each other until the incident became a full-blown melee. Tendrils were torn off, and something vaporous leaked from the many wounds inflicted. A herd of bubbles went whizzing past Cue Ball, barreling toward the rumble. Just as they were about to smash into them, the bubbles gave out a roar and swallowed up each individual fighter until there were none left.

Linda was horrified.

She couldn't be sure of the meaning of all she'd just seen, but the violence shocked her. Yes, nature tended toward violence back in her world—eat or be eaten—but this place had seemed so tranquil. Her sphere drifted on, and she watched as the bubbles wobbled in place for several minutes. Then, just as the scene was almost lost behind a cloud, she saw the bubbles flow away, leaving the former combatants to re-gather into their groups and sheepishly drift away from each other.

Linda cleared her throat before commenting, "I can't even guess about that incident... Weird, that's my considered scientific analysis, weird. I'm going to try to initiate interaction, if I can get close enough to one of the native life forms. They may view Cue Ball One as just another bubble, so I will do what I can to draw some attention and let them know that they have a guest. I hope this is a good idea."

As it turned out, it didn't take much at all to attract their attention. With the next group headed in her direction, she activated the exterior speakers and began playing sequenced tonal pulses. The group slowed, so she increased the volume.

That seemed to get their attention.

They flowed around the sphere frantically, as if looking for something. One of the beings stopped right in front of her, looking her over with a keen interest. This was her first opportunity to actually observe one of them close-up and at rest. She gulped but started recording her observations.

"My first impression of this being is of an achingly beautiful eight-foot-tall butterfly with iridescent soap-bubble wings flowing gracefully about him. The wings are incredible, catching the light in ever-changing patterns, seeming fragile, almost insubstantial, but giving the body locomotion. On each side of their flattened, hourglass bodies, dozens of elegantly expressive tendrils move purposefully, individually or in unison, acting as arms, legs, feet, and hands. All of them are carrying objects of varying types. The tendrils are able to manipulate moving parts on these artifacts with incredible dexterity. They have graceful swan-like necks that blossom into beautifully shaped oblong heads with small mouths and tall, sensitive ears, or maybe antennae. They move with a grace I've never seen outside of a dream."

The being cocked its head and seemed to smile at her. "But, it's their eyes that are the most remarkable. They have two of them, just like humans, but much larger, covering the upper part of the head and wrapping around to each side. Their irises have an outer rim that starts as a Maxfield Parrish blue and moves inward with gradients of color that seem to reach into infinity. Their skin has a luster like a pearl and is translucent in intriguing places, giving the impression that they are as beautiful inside as out."

Suddenly this being, who seemed content to stay still while she gave him a thorough inspection, was pulled away by his fellows. Linda rotated herself to see what all the fuss was about and saw that they had congregated at one of the almost microscopic microphone pick-ups. The one she had been studying, who seemed to be the leader, tapped gently at the mic to assure himself he had the right location. Linda was prepared for almost anything except the sounds that that came from his lips.

"Hello, Linda. You're looking very well. Say, would you mind turning that racket off? It's awfully distracting."

Three minutes left. Cal had donned his EVA gear and had another suit all prepped for Linda when she returned. The hull of the facility had been breached, and atmosphere was leaking like crazy. Only the emergency lighting was operating, and that flickered. Ten years' worth of his life lay in shambles all around him. There was still some chance that he and Linda could survive this and start over, incorporating everything she might have learned on her journey.

They could use Cue Ball One as a lifepod. Something made out of nano-tubes was almost indestructible, and it had some maneuvering capabilities to escape whoever emerged victorious. Even if Ben-Iman managed to win the battle raging outside, their work would be co-opted by the military, weaponizing travel to other universes. He shuddered to imagine what the Evolutionaries would use this technology for.

He looked at his watch. "If that other universe looks any good at all, maybe you'd be better off putting in for a permanent Visa," he whispered.

Linda opened the hatch carefully, trying not to bump into any of the Li'Cha—that was what the aliens called themselves. She wore a portable breather so the high oxygen wouldn't start her giggling. She could barely restrain herself as it was. She had tethered herself to the sphere's interior so she could be instantly reeled in through the automatic hatch in case a quick getaway was required. She was awed and delighted, not stupid. When she was clear of the sphere, Ja'al, the one who had spoken to her first, looped a tendril around her waist to steady her.

"Okay, let me get this straight, you've met me at this spot one hundred and fifty three times before. Then, after the subjective two hours that I will remain in this universe, you go back in time to meet me again, and each time you learn more from me. Isn't that dangerous, what with paradoxes and all?"

161

Ja'al's wings fluttered "Paradoxes! You always ask that! It's so cute. No, what is cause and effect might be more of a problem in your universe, but here it barely translates. It took a lot of iterations before I was able to grasp your language, but since then I've learned more. This is the last time loop needed though, so I thought I'd give you the opportunity to ask me questions."

Without Ja'all using his wings to impede their progress, the sphere and the entire group had drifted further toward the elusive center of gravity. Off in the distance, Linda saw a structure that must have been huge if the other dot-like shapes she saw were more Li'Cha. "So everyone here just travels back through time whenever they get the urge to shuffle the deck and improve their hand?"

Ja'al looked puzzled for a moment. "Ah, 'Shuffle the Deck'... Your language is so flexible, and yet everything else about you seems so incredibly solid. To answer your question, no. Time traveling for more than a few seconds requires some very expensive machinery." He extended the irregular glowing shape he carried. "And a lot of training to use it. I was only called in just before your first appearance ended. I went back immediately to get this process started."

As they got closer to the structure, Linda saw that it seemed to be a semi-rigid frame supporting dizzying patterns of strings winding their way through and around the more solid struts. It was huge. She tore her attention away to focus again on what Ja'al was saying.

"We finally figured out that your universe is expanding while ours rotates, even on the quantum level. I can't even imagine the bizarre effects that an expanding universe would have, but a rotating one has always allowed for some form of simple time travel."

She glanced at the approaching structure again and saw that hundreds of Li'Cha were ducking in and out of it randomly. She pointed over his wing. "Is that one of your buildings? It's incredible!"

He looked behind him. "Yes and no. It's a place where we can gather and tether those things we wish to be able to easily find again. It's spatially anchored so that it doesn't drift. It doesn't provide shelter for us though, nor would we want it to. There are dangerous things in our world, and long ago we had rigid, enclosed structures, much like your Cue Ball One, but then we created what you call the soap bubbles."

Linda was suddenly aware that there were a number of the bubbles lagging a good ways off, but obviously following them. "Yeah, I saw a bunch of them swallow some Li'Cha who looked like they were fighting." She bumped her fists together to demonstrate. "Then, after a few minutes, they spit the Li'Cha out and drifted off. What are they?"

Ja'al stretched his mouth into a large grin. "They are small, semi-sentient universes." Linda's eyes got very big. "They were created, almost by accident, about a thousand life-spans ago. Up until that time, we could only create mini-universes that lasted for perhaps an hour or so before they would destroy themselves. Those were interesting but not very useful. Then, Alla'mor, the wizard of K'la, as he is called, changed one so that it was aware of itself."

Linda looked back nervously at all the bubbles that had gathered behind their party. "Intelligent universes?"

Ja'al cocked his head. "I wouldn't go so far as to call them *intelligent,* but they are certainly sensitive to all the aspects of our universe. As I was saying, it was aware of itself, so when it came time to self-destruct, it decided to split in two instead. Much to the alarm of some, the baby universes kept multiplying. One day, there was a completely unexpected attack by a herd of wild M'ir, and many Li'cha were caught out in the open. Sensing that there was danger, the bubbles engulfed the M'ir and transported them to a place where they would do no harm to us. I rather think that you saw something very much like that. Sensing the violent behavior of the youths—if they acted like that, they were probably still quite young—they simply pulled them apart and gave them a chance to think about their actions before releasing them."

Linda opened her mouth but couldn't think of what to say to this.

"I see that this troubles you. Perhaps these things impose some morally judgmental tyranny upon the Li'Cha?"

"Well, yeah," she said quietly.

"They very rarely bother adults, though. They're very easy to shoo away for a mature mind. Everyone gets angry or upset at some time, but an adult has learned to control these destructive urges and

163

channels them into something more useful. This was the case long before the bubbles were created." He gave a reassuring smile. "I once found myself in a bubble when I was very young and stupid. I was in a place of nothingness, no light, no dark really either, but it wasn't frightening. On the contrary, it was boring, except for the occasional wave of concern from the universe around me. It's difficult to maintain a good mad-on under those circumstances."

She nodded, and the bubbles drifted a bit further back. "If you've been questioning me for such a long time, by your frame of reference, then you must know that I'm probably not the last of my kind who'll find their way here. You must also know they won't all behave like adults, and that they have some terrifying resources."

"You have explained some unusual concepts to me; greed, war, bigotry, religion, and they do sound daunting, but we have many advantages over any treachery—time travel to name one. Change doesn't frighten us so much as it does your people." Ja'al smiled.

"Don't underestimate us. You live in an environment that provides for your safety so you have no real gauge of what the combined stupidity of mankind is capable of. Individually, we can be wonderful, embrace high ideals, create great works of art and science. But get a bunch of us together and watch out." She gestured to indicate the world around her. "I don't want to be the one that opens the floodgates that will destroy all this!"

Ja'al released her from his tendril and, automatically, she was reeled back toward the sphere. "It's time," he said. "I know you have no choice in what will happen in your universe and have reason to fear the worst, but we are an optimistic people by nature, and I believe that only good will come from this meeting of minds."

A tear formed in the corner of her eye as the hatch sealed behind her. "What universe are you living in, pal?" She climbed back into her rig, checking virtual readouts, and prepping Cue Ball One to leave this reality. The Li'Cha moved away and waved their tendrils at her, wishing her a safe journey. "Damn!" she yelled, and brought her fist down on a panel as the audible count down began. *Ten—Nine— Eight—Seven—Six*—and suddenly the exterior of the sphere was covered by bubble-shaped universes, slowly penetrating the nano-tube hull. She barely had time to react. "Shit—" and then the universe went *sproing!*

###

"Sweat dripped down Cal's forehead, though the suit's cooling system was functioning normally. *Five—Four—Three—Two—One!*

In the vehicle bay, the sphere was just there, but he couldn't see Linda or much of anything else. Instead, it appeared to be full of bubbles, and they were multiplying at an alarming rate. Some seemed to ooze through the hull, but too slowly to accommodate the new ones. Then something happened that should have been impossible— the nano-tube skin of the craft ripped itself to shreds. The bubbles shot through the walls of the station as if they weren't even there, causing no further damage to the cracked and tattered station. All that was left was the small, fragile figure of Linda Cline, struggling to free herself from the free-floating straps of her harness, gasping for what precious little air still remained.

Cal was stunned, but only for a second. He flung himself toward Linda and forced a mini-breather mask into place so she would at least have some air. His gloved fingers deftly released the harness latches until he was able to toss the whole rig away from his friend. She had gone limp—hopefully just passed out—which made it easier to get her into the suit and seal everything together. The sphere-as-lifepod idea was no longer an option, so he zipped her into an evac body baggie, tucking her limp form under one arm and made for a hallway. His hunch was right; it didn't take long before he found a hole big enough for both of them to squeeze through.

Outside the sky was full of bubbles, passing like ghosts into the ships of both sides. It was eerie, in the silence, how the ships had just somehow stopped in place. The debris from the damage to both sides continued along its trajectory, ignored by the spell that had been cast upon the ships by the bubbles. Within moments, only a few bubbles remained visible. They seemed to congregate for a moment before heading off toward the sun and the inner planets at a speed that would have made Einstein uncomfortable.

###

Linda woke to a sky strewn with shimmering, undulating globes

165

and drifting war crafts. It was as though some giant child had gotten tired of playing with her toys, deciding instead to blow soap bubbles "Oh—my—god!" she whispered.

"Are you all right, girl?" Cal saw her nod through her faceplate. "What the hell are those things? What have we done?"

In a rasping voice she replied, "I think it means that it's about time we grew up."

Another voice cut in "...vin is that you? Did you see what happened out there!?"

"Django!" Cal practically screamed the name.

Linda broke in, "Are the rest of you okay?" Django's reply was more a whoop than an affirmative, but she got the idea. Wearily, she nodded as Cal gave her a thumbs-up, turning on his homing beacon. "Look, whatever you do, stay mellow, like that damned song Calvin always plays. Don't worry; be happy. Trust me, and please, just come get us, guys. We'll talk when you get here."

Linda reached out a hand to Cal, who clutched it hard through his glove and the body baggie, a tear forming in one eye. "You always did like to make an entrance. Just tell me we can all survive this one," he said, blinking furiously.

Linda was silent for a moment before she whispered a reply. "I don't know, but I'm betting a lot of rules have just been rewritten. What worked over there might not go over so well here, but we had to hit puberty sooner or later." Her voice trailed off in wonder at the faint lights glinting off the ghostly bubble-like universes that swirled around her.

After a moment more of silence she continued in a louder voice. "Whatever comes of it though, it looks like being an asshole is about to go seriously out of fashion."

LIFE AFTER WARTIME
By Laura Givens and Nicole Spencer

The left side of the hover transport heaved up under Cassie as though a giant child was trying to flip it over. Cassie Clement was damned if she was going to lose her cargo while she was in a supposed green zone. She hung onto both joysticks like they were the horns of a charging bull, trying desperately to regain control as the vehicle spasmed again and again, the left side slewing higher each time. "Somebody secure the stabilizers before we go turtle."

Zhloh, the mechanic, lunged into the repair shaft with a multi-wrench and a pry-bar, nearly slamming into Lucy, the medic, in his haste. Whatever they had hit was still trying to flip them over, so she took a deep breath and decided to try something they hadn't taught her in transport drivers' training.

"Hang on!' She nosed the hover-transport upwards at a degree that the specs did not recommend and slammed the main thrust hard while cutting the blades full to the right. If she'd tried that at ground level, she would have rolled over, but with a little air under her. She managed a very lovely corkscrew maneuver, just like an old Earth-movie stunt. Pulling an air-born corkscrew on a hover-bike, or even a sled, was stupid if fun. With a seventy-five ton hover hauler -- the word *suicidal* came into her mind.

"Stabilizers!" she screamed as the metal monster came into upright position again. She hit the down-blow and said a Hail Mary through gritted teeth. They hit the road with a heart stopping WHUMP and bounced once before spinning to a stop a hundred yards off the road in a thicket of thunderweed.

For a few seconds, Cassie just breathed and tried to slow her heart rate. "Is everyone okay?" she finally managed.

"I'm all right," Fren said tightly from the shotgun seat, her fingers dug into the armrests. "But I think we lost Lucy."

From overhead a huge centipede skittered silently down into the cab. "Lucy survives despite the physics experiment you call driving." The voice came from a grid installed beneath the centipede's eyes. "Lucy also would like to discern health of his fellow travelers." Cassie

167

gave a sigh in relief and raised her hand. The centipede caressed the outstretched fingers and began to crawl over her, looking for signs of injury or shock. Lucencian Lurok didn't have a license to practice medicine on this planet, but one of the reasons Cassie had hired him was his tremendous medical expertise.

"No permanent damage," he proclaimed. "I feared brain damage, as indicated by that bone-head landing maneuver, but found no apparent symptoms." He crawled off Cassie to examine Fren before heading down the repair shaft to see about Zhloh.

Cassie and Fren shared a knowing smile; they knew exactly what was coming next. A few moments later, yelling and banging came from the shaft as Lucy scurried back into the cab, followed by a thrown multi-wrench and a string of curses. "Zhloh also remains in good health. At least his throwing arm and dislike of being examined by me are unchanged." Zhloh had a thing about being touched, especially by long, hairy aliens.

The centipede looked around to find that he was speaking to no one. Cassie and Fren were already over the side, trying to determine what the hell had happened. "Ah well!" he sighed. Someone had to keep watch, so he snuggled down and raised a feeler as sentinel.

A heavy-haul hover transport looked a lot like a flying saucer. Cargo space was arrayed all around the lower perimeter so that loads could be evenly distributed for stability. Sitting in the middle of the cargo ring were the main engines, three of them, providing thrust and lift through the miles and miles of swamp where roads appeared and disappeared like fleeting mirages. On top of the engine sat the cab, a compact living and control complex with retractable cowls in case of bad weather.

Tightening a loose bolt, Cassie thought she heard a snoring sound coming through an overhead vent. It didn't take much of a detective to realize that Lucy was probably curled up asleep on the driver's seat. When it came to basic mechanical repairs, Cassie knew that the centipede was pretty useless, but he was a great medic and a good driver.

"Boss, number three got jolted loose a bit, but I'm pretty sure she'll make it to Shippa if we don't push it too hard." Zhloh limped to

168

where Cassie was running her seat-of-the-pants diagnostics on the lift exhausts. "Same with the stabilizers, they just don't know what to do with abrupt angle deviations. These three-eighties are just funky that way."

Cassie grinned. The translator chips they all used were a marvel, but where did they dig up words like *funky*? "Well, the fans look workable, and the cargo is intact." She pulled her head out of the cowling to look at Zhloh, noticing the slight limp. "Any idea what happened back there on the road? Dispatch said this route had been swept clean days ago. How do you miss a mine right in the middle of the road?"

"I couldn't find a blast hole," Zhloh replied. "Whatever it was left no traces. The government coverts used something like this on us at Bremmon. Disruptives. That was the official name, but we called them chiggers. They spring up and attach themselves, then send out pulses designed to wreck whatever they're attached to but leave it mostly intact. I saw a heavy artillery piece flip right over once, for no apparent reason. Crushed three good friends." Zhloh had been a rebel guerilla before signing on as Cassie's chief mechanic.

"Chiggers? Damn! My little stunt must have dislodged it somehow." Cassie blew a piece of thunderweed off her cheek. "We'll report that to Dispatch quick as we hit free skies."

Fren came around the curve to join the discussion. "Don't count on it, Cass. Just before the com went dead a few miles back, the weather report said that a whole front of aerosol flak was settling in over this region. Probably won't let up for a couple of days."

All during the hostilities, the rebels had released vast amounts of aerosol signal jammers into the atmosphere, making satellite imaging, radar, and even wireless communications virtually impossible. It helped to finally turn the tide for guerilla freedom fighters but was a pain in the neck for everyone else.

Fren came close and whispered in Cassie's ear, "Hey cheer up! On the bright side, we're all okay and I look very sexy by flak light." Cassie blushed, starting to reply when Zhloh raised a hand for silence. They all heard the rustle of undergrowth and the slight sucking sound of boots in mud.

169

"Fren, honey, why don't you go topside and prep the engines?" Cassie had caught a glint of mottled sunshine off something metal, maybe a gun barrel. "Whatever these guys are selling, I don't think we can afford it."

Zhloh and Cassie climbed atop the cargo ring as the three strangers approached. She felt helpless with only a wrench as a weapon, but the light arms stashed under the command seat wouldn't help much against the black and red armor that marked the strangers as rebel elite. The rebel elite were supposed to be on their side, but it seemed an awful coincidence that they had appeared from nowhere so quickly after the "accident." Rumors of rogue units were everywhere these days.

"Having trouble, comrades? We'd be happy to take a look." The largest of them smiled and bowed. "Captain Grell of the People's Fourth Elite, at your service." His silvery blue skin was scarred with marks denoting the number of men he'd killed.

"No problems." Cassie worked hard at keeping her smile in place. "One of my team noticed this lovely patch of thunderweed over here. He has this great recipe for thunder pie, so we thought we'd stop and pick a few bushels. We appreciate the offer but we're just fine, thanks loads."

"Ah, then maybe you'd care to exchange recipes with Agla here," Grell gestured towards his companion. "His thunder bread makes even blue beans quite palatable." He raised his weapon and stepped a few paces closer. "I would bet you have many things worth sharing."

Zhloh stepped in front of Cassie. "Comrades, we have nothing you'd be interested in. All we're carrying this run are used medical instruments, some canned food—which we'd be happy to donate part of to the cause—drainage pumps, and insulating fabric. We revere you as heroes of the revolution. Please don't soil your glorious legacy for a prize such as us."

"As it so happens, I could use a good drainage pump to keep Agla's bedroll dry at night," the rebel captain said, waving his weapon at a hatch. "Why don't we take a look and see if you have anything that goes with his armor."

"Crap!" Zhloh looked back at Cassie, who shook her head.

"We need to stall them for another couple of minutes," she whispered, "till Fren gets things back on line. There's no way they can catch us once—"

A war cry broke the tension. Overhead, three more of the elite rebels came arcing out of the sky toward them, jump packs blazing, feet first, weapons brandished. There was barely time to flinch before the first man buckled into an invisible wall a foot over Cassie's head. The other two also met the invisible barrier, all three sliding to the ground in crumpled heaps. Suddenly there were bullets flying everywhere. The aerial threesome had been joined by others charging the vehicle from all sides. None of them got to within a foot of the transport, and two of soldiers were thrown down to the ground from the force of their own ricochets. Their leader yelled for them to cease fire.

"A force field?" He pounded his hand into the solid nothing. "Where the hell did you get a working force field?"

Cassie uncurled her arms from over her head and looked around with one eye. "Oh y-yeah," Cassie stammered, "Force field, couple of plasma cannons -- we are one badass transport, don't mess with us... Isn't that right, Zhloh?"

Zhloh spit in the rebels' direction, but that too hit the invisible barrier, "You aren't worthy to wear those colors! Since when do comrades prey on comrades?"

"Comrades? Bullshit!" the captain screamed. "For ten years I've fought in the name of freedom for all Mazzah against the government thugs and their off-world masters! So what does our glorious newly elected president do? He declares that we will now open trade negotiations with the alien allies of the deposed regime! He wants us all to become good little farmers and miners to carry on trade with that bunch of imperialist hooligans."

Zhloh knelt and spoke in a softer voice. "The war has been over for three months, Captain. We won. Maybe the new order won't be a worker's paradise but we won, damn it. Go home."

Agla, a sergeant by his markings, pushed forward. "Our homes are gone! The war doesn't end for us."

The rebel captain snarled, "We're organizing a counterrevolution to see the principles we fought for finally triumph. Join us, comrade. We can use this vehicle, and you won't have to take any more orders from this off-world bitch." He glared at Cassie, then back at Zhloh.

Zhloh stood and glared back at the rebel. "I trust this off-worlder. The fighting is over, and you're too stupid embrace the victory we have won."

"Look," said Cassie in as reasonable a voice as she could manage, "There's a town that needs these supplies if they're going to have a crop this year. This is your victory right here. These villagers can get what they need and just get on with their lives. They can raise crops, raise families, without fear of being dragged away in the night by faceless government killers. That's why you all fought this war, right? It's time this world got back to some semblance of normalcy."

A cloud came over the captain's face for a moment, and he growled "You'd like that—wouldn't you, bitch? You'd take by treaty what you couldn't get through force."

Cassie got very still. "Look, I've been on this planet for five years, working my ass off for your cause because I believe in it as much as you do, so don't try to hang that off-worlder imperialist crap on me."

"Oh yes!" the captain barked. "Let me kiss your pink toes in gratitude while you reduce proud warriors into lap dogs like that 'man' beside you."

Zhloh shook his head angrily and spit at the captain once more. This time the spittle hit the rebel square on the cheek.

"Oh shit!" Cassie whispered.

"Grab something, we are go!" Fren shouted from the cab above.

"Thank god!" Cassie cried as she and Zhloh grabbed at hatch handles as the lifters shuddered to life, the craft taking off like a bee-stung berl, followed by a hail of bullets.

After a couple of miles, the craft slowed down to a brisk crawl, and the two clambered back up into the cab. Fren sat at the controls, her silver-blue skin an ashen gray. Her tone was flat with terror, "Number three almost came loose," she said mechanically, "We should be okay if we keep it at a reasonable speed, but our sprinting days are over." Cassie leaned over and gave her a big hug.

"We have a force field?" Fren asked.

From the back of the cab came a clicking nervous sound. Slowly, all of them turned to Lucy, who was curled around a seat, trembling and tapping the metal frame as he did when someone yelled at him or he was in pain.

"It's a personal shield. Where I'm from, everyone who is anyone has one implanted once full growth length is reached."

Cassie gestured for Fren to get them underway again and sat down on a chair near Lucy. "You said personal shield -- what you did back there was a lot bigger than any personal shield I've ever heard of."

"My field is bio-impelled, anger and surprise activate it automatically, but I can also access it by an act of will. I just imagined the whole ship as an extension of Lucy and that it all needed to be protected."

Cassie shook her head quizzically. "Think of a human lifting something very, very heavy," Lucy continued. "Normally the weight might be too much, but you might do it with great effort, in adversity, but not for very long, and you might hurt yourself doing so."

Cassie stood up. "I see... Is there anything else we should know about? Super strength, invisibility -- anything like that?"

"Please understand, my people don't speak of such things, they are private -- much like the sexual exploits you have with Fren when you think we are all asleep."

Cassie blushed, and Fren cleared her throat.

Zhloh finally broke the awkward silence. "Well, this is good. Comrades getting to know each other better is healthy... It helps us all be better -- comrades." He coughed. "Is anyone else hungry? I'm starving!"

Suddenly, Lucy fell off his perch and lay twitching on the floor, secreting green bile from one eye.

Cassie scrambled to his side. "Somebody get his med-kit!" she yelled, but Zhloh already had it open.

After a mad search through the kit, they finally had to admit that they had no idea what they should do. Fren had stopped the transport and gone searching for a blanket; it was all she could think to do.

Eventually the twitching and secreting stopped.

Cassie finally broke the silence. "I can't tell if he's dead or alive, but I vote that he's still alive." She tucked the blanket more soundly around Lucy. "We need to get out from under the flack so we can radio for medical advice. I looked once -- he has medical files on how to treat us but nothing about treating him."

Fren wiped tears from her large violet eyes. "That sounds about right. Was he really a famous surgeon on his world, like he always boasted?"

Cassie shrugged her shoulders. "Who knows -- and let's not refer to him in the past tense just yet."

Zhloh eased into the driver's seat and started the engines. "We should stay off the road for a while longer just in case our belligerent friends decide to try catching us." He looked over his shoulder and growled softly, "He can't be dead. He owes me money."

###

Once night set in, their pace slowed to a crawl. Cassie was all too happy to relinquish the driving to Zhloh. They'd moved Lucy to the below deck sleeping quarters, where Cassie kept one hand gently on his blanket, imagining that she felt a slight tremor every now and then. Who could tell?

Cassie pinched the bridge of her nose, closing her eyes for a moment. Lulled by the quiet hum of the engines and the soft swish of vegetation beneath the transport, she could almost imagine that she was back in Iowa, curled up in the back of her dad's combine. She'd loved that farm, but after her folks had died and she'd been forced out by the bank, she found herself at loose ends and at odds with the world for a couple of years. It was about then that news started breaking on Terra about appalling social conditions on a backwater planet called Mazzah and the popular uprising aimed at removing its oppressive oligarchic regime. Something about the plight of Mazzah's peasants and townspeople really spoke to her, and it wasn't long before she found herself selling everything she owned to make her way to Mazzah and the revolution. What the hell, if it had been good enough for Hemingway...

Cassie glanced over at Fren dozing in the corner. The young

174

Mazzah's skin was a pale silver in the subdued compartment lighting, a small spot of spit shining from a corner of her lovely mouth. The earth woman couldn't help but raise the corners of her own lips in a smile. When they'd first met, Fren had been hiding in a dumpster, on the lam from rebel troops after they had stormed a government-sponsored cathouse near the capital. The fact that she'd been indentured into service, like so many young Mazzahi females, would not have prevented them from killing her as a collaborator. Cassie risked serious grief herself to smuggle the young fugitive out of the fire zone, hidden in a large duffel bag, to another city where she could make a new start. But it never crossed her mind to do otherwise or that she'd run into this girl again after hostilities had ceased.

Yet that is exactly what happened. Without resources to return home and facing sudden peacetime unemployment as an ambulance driver, Cassie began making moves to put together a freelance heavy-haul operation. Much to their mutual astonishment, she found Fren among the first in line to apply as a relief driver, newly authorized operator's certificate in hand. Taken aback in surprise and admiration, Cassie followed her gut once again and hired the young rookie on the spot.

Fren turned out to be a damned fine driver and a good friend, fiercely loyal to the earth woman who had saved her. Feelings of trust and affection sprang up between them almost immediately, quickly blossoming into something much deeper, if a little complicated.

Cassie was glad that their relationship was out in the open. Mazzah had no taboos about off-worlders or partners of the same sex, but the whole silly prohibition on bosses fraternizing with their crews still bothered her. She had such a small crew to begin with.

Sometime in the middle of the night, Cassie was awakened by the sound of explosions in the distance. Carefully untangling herself from Fren's tree frog embrace, she pulled on pants and a top and went topside.

The transport had stopped, and Zhloh leaned over the railing watching the distant light show. "It started about five minutes ago. I guess the counterrevolution has begun. That's got to be Shippa, our destination, getting pounded out there."

Cassie pulled her fingers through her hair. "With all the flak cover, that fire has to be local in origin. Want to bet that our pals from this afternoon are the ones playing with firecrackers?"

"I think your money would be safe in such a wager. Anyway, it made no sense to keep heading into their sights, so I stopped." Zhloh plopped back down into the driver's seat.

Cassie tapped her fingernails on the railing. "That insulation we've got below, is that fumar?"

Zhloh's eyes narrowed. "Yeah, great insulation as long as you don't put it under high compression. Should keep the school they're building in Shippa comfortable all year round—if it hasn't been blown up yet."

"You ever work a drainage pump?" She asked lightly.

Zhloh smiled humorlessly. "I'm not in that line of work anymore, and you were an ambulance driver for most of the war."

"I've got my hover bike stowed in compartment C if you feel up to a little flak light ride. I make it about an hour's trip with the two of us and a little baggage."

"What if Fren gets jealous?" he laughed.

Cassie's voice got very quiet. "Those folks out there don't deserve what's happening to them. The war's over. Those 'elite' rebels need to have that explained to them in detail, and we're the only ones with blackboards and chalk."

"Comrade, if I had any idea what you were talking about, I'm sure I would agree completely."

Without another word, they scrambled over the side to prepare for one last charge into the valley of death.

###

During her time driving ambulances, Cassie had earned the nickname "Dodge Ball." Many of her passengers threw up at some point during their journey, even ones who had never before been troubled by motion sickness, but she never lost an ambulance and almost never a patient. By comparison, this was nothing. She kept low, zipping through trees and rocks that Zhloh could barely see. Most hover bike riders preferred big growling engines that were

176

intimidating from a block away, but Cassie kept her bike tuned to purr like a kitten. It was a little unnerving, whipping through the treacherous countryside almost blind and in near silence. But Zhloh knew that if anyone could pull off this mad charge without getting them killed, it was her. She had blazed into heavy fire in the middle of the battle of Alibin to get him and three of his men out of harm's way and to a med station, only to rush back in to evacuate more his comrades still lying wounded in the field. He just wished his stomach believed in her as much as his heart.

Before setting out, they had awakened Fren, leaving her as a guard under heavy protest. Cassie finally convinced her that someone had to watch over Lucy and that they had to go on this mission if Lucy had any hope of reaching a doctor. When Zhloh instructed her to return to dispatch if they weren't back by morning, she told him flat out to go screw himself. Cassie was very proud of how far this girl, whom she loved so much, had come from cowering in a dumpster.

The rebel camp wasn't hard to find. There was no need to be inconspicuous -- they were the only military force left in the entire sector, and they knew that, with the flak cover, the townspeople couldn't call for outside help. After parking the hover bike some distance away, Cassie and her comrade covered the rest of the distance to the camp's perimeter on hands and knees.

"Mortars," Zhloh whispered as they came up on the edge of the clearing. "And it looks like they are using bam-bams. Makes sense -- lots of noise, lots of light, but limited concussion. They want to loot Shippa, not level it."

"So, what's the plan?" Cassie asked.

"Hey! You're the boss!" he whispered back.

"Okay, I just promoted you. Come on, I know you have a plan."

Zhloh mussed her hair and pulled up the bag carrying the doctored drainage pumps. "Okay, we've got three of these things, and there are five mortars -- so you need to plant the pumps between the mortars. It probably won't destroy them, but it should mess them up pretty good. If we get lucky, you'll set off all the loose ordnance, and that's all she wrote."

Cassie tried not to smirk at the translation. "So," she asked, "while I plant the pumps, press the five-second timers and run like hell, what will you be doing?" She examined the devices to make sure she knew exactly where to activate each timer.

Zhloh pulled out two small blasters. "Diversion."

Cassie's eyes went wide. "Please tell me there's more to your plan than those things! You couldn't put out your own eyes with those pea shooters."

"Trust me, boss. I am a war hero, after all." Zhloh's eyes narrowed. "Wait for my signal. I don't think you'll miss it." With that, he disappeared into the surrounding foliage.

Five minutes passed, and Cassie became acutely aware of how badly she needed to pee. This always seemed to happen. Then, across the clearing, she heard someone let out a blood curdling scream and saw her comrade blasting full speed toward the clearing on her bike. The Elite rebels scrambled for their weapons and armor.

Bowling through the men who were not engaged with tending the mortars, Zhloh reached the center of the clearing. Jamming the down thrusters to full, he shot the bike straight up into the air, jumping off at the zenith of its ascent and dropping a match into the open gas tank as he did so. The effect was quite spectacular.

"Shit! He blew up my bike!" Cassie thought as she jumped to her feet and dashed toward the pandemonium that was the rebel camp. Everywhere there were flaming bits of debris and wild gunfire, though for the moment none of it was directed at her. She ran past the first mortar and dropped the first device after hitting its timer. Then the second device -- so far so good. The first pump exploded as she sprinted for the area between the last two guns, almost throwing her off her feet. She lurched toward her final drop zone, but no longer unnoticed. Bits of charged plasma whizzed past as she triggered the third device's timer. The second explosion went off even more spectacularly than the first -- it must have gotten the ammunition -- throwing her to the ground. Scrambling to her feet, she felt a burning sting in her side but knew that she had to move if she wanted to survive the next three seconds. Then the entire world all around her lit up, and a giant hand sent her flying through the air. She hit the ground with a dull thud, sinking into darkness to the lullaby of

178

automatic weapons fire.

The sun was coming up as Lucy's eyes fluttered open. Fren smiled and stroked his carapace under the voice-box. It had been a terrifying night. Every breeze had been a skulking assassin, and the noise in the distance just seemed to get louder and louder. Then the noise stopped, completely. She'd carried Lucy topside just to have someone to hold onto.

"Hey! Look who decided to wake up!"

Lucy looked around, somewhat confused. "What happened? I feel absolutely awful."

Fren was about to give the centipede a big hug and a kiss when the bushes started to move. Suddenly Lucy was suddenly alert. "Stay close by, and I will try to extend my shield around both of us."

She was ready to protest but a small hover sled broke through the shrubs driven by a heavily bandaged Zhloh. Behind him was the prone figure of a human woman, badly burned on her right side.

When Cassie finally came to, it was in a small hospital ward. Asleep, slumped on the chair beside her, was Fren.

"She's been here since we brought you in." Cassie turned painfully to her left toward the voice. There sat Zhloh, with an arm in a sling and bandaged in several places.

"We're alive," she noted.

Her erstwhile comrade laughed and winced at the pain it caused. "After that third pump went off, most of the rebels were pretty banged up. I'd found decent cover behind a rock and kept shooting enough to keep them guessing. If they'd known I was one guy with a couple of pop guns, things might have gone differently." He handed her a glass of water and waited till she'd finished. "Anyway, the commander, captain Grell, and that guy, Agla -- remember Agla -- they got into a shouting match about lost causes. Well, to make a long story short, Agla shoots his commander in the head and wants to talk terms. In exchange for safe passage and a sled, I agreed to give them all two days head start to disappear, to make their way back home."

Cassie nodded her head. "I thought Agla was the guy who had no home to return to."

"I asked him about that, and he said he'd sell his armor -- he'd heard there were already collectors. Then he'd look for his nephews and make a new life for himself somehow. It was time."

The door opened, and Lucy crawled in dragging two medical charts. "Ah! The patient lives. Alas! I have lost another bet." He crawled up the foot of the bed and across Cassie's left leg. "That is how I lost my fortune on my home world, you know, betting against my patients surviving. I am just too great of a healer for my own good, it seems."

Cassie looked on in amazement as the centipede went to Zhloh's bed and proceeded to crawl all over his wounds, checking the dressings. Zhloh made no fuss, but merely shrugged, saying, "I made him promise to wash his feet before he crawled all over me."

To her right a sleepy voice joined in, "Pay up, bug."

Mazzah had survived a long, soul-searing war and now maybe they'd figure out how to survive the peace. Hell, if someone like Agla could leave the war behind, maybe the rest of the planet could make it as well. That was the trick, after all, realizing when you'd won -- learning how to live again.

TURTLE SOUP

Orrey's tentacles moved frantically, propelling her through the dark water in a tight orbit of the spacecraft.

"You're kiddin'. Zoey and fifty-four other colonists are really crammed into this fragile, little metal ball?" The thing wasn't hardly large enough to fit five Torts her size. Small as it was, it was more metal than she had ever seen in one place. Now that it had cooled enough from its plunge through the atmosphere, she wanted to see every inch of the landing pod. Two hundred and eighty-five shuttle pods had fallen all over this section of Kepler-36b but this was the pod that held her friend.

"That's what the ping address says, kiddo." Her father, Jabbo, was the chief of communications, in charge of the last cycle's worth of real-time dialogues with the colony-ship *Armstrong*. He had made his young daughter a deputy comm, after days of pleading, and assigned her to the craft's night shift. That was how she had gotten to know Zoey. For some reason, Zoey always seemed to pull graveyard comm shift. "Honey, don't get too close. If you bump that thing too hard you could breach its hull integrity. It's had a rough enough time just getting through the atmosphere. We don't need any colonists squashed like grape polyps by the water pressure, now do we?" He'd pulled a couple of strings to ensure they were both assigned to tow in the pod that Orrey's new best friend was on.

Orrey swam back to her dad's side. "Sorry, it's just so exciting. The first regular humans finally on K-36b, I can't wait to see them."

The rest of Jabbo's team moved in with nets to scoop up the pod so it could be transported to the gigantic ceramic structure known as Hab-1, docked safely out of the drop zone. For a hundred miles in every direction, crews, just like this, were ferrying other newcomer pods to their new home, the only livable place for Homo Sapiens on the whole planet.

"Let's just get them safely to the habitat first. There'll be plenty of time to socialize, once we make sure humans can survive in that thing. The numbers say it should work fine but the real world is the only test that counts."

Orrey rolled her eyes. She knew better than to get into an argument about the hab with her father. His design input had been voted down by the council twenty Earth years earlier and he had been grumping about it ever since. She was only sixteen Earth years old but her mother was fond of ribbing dad about the length of time he could maintain a pout when he didn't get his way. She knew Hab-1 was perfectly safe.

Orrey had seen plenty of sims of what Earth humans actually looked like and knew how delicate their physiology was. Heck that was why the Tortesie breed of human-variants existed on K-36b, to build an environmentally sound place for baselines like Zoey. Orrey's kind had been genetically engineered to withstand the crushing pressures of these oceans, but they weren't considered colonists— never had been—they'd been born here and raised by teaching machines more than thirty-five Earth years ago. No, with their turtle-like shells, enormous eyes and long, prehensile tendrils, Torts were classified as Heralds. Their job was to make way for those who were to come after.

Jabbo and his team were busy coordinating update information from the pod—-there were hundreds of items to cover before it could safely dock—-so Orrey, there strictly as an observer, was bored almost immediately. Since no one had actually forbidden her to do so, she tingled at the personal frequency she and Zoey had been using to communicate off-shift.

"Zoey, you in there?" she sent quietly.

"Uuuugh! Why is there an elephant on my chest?! Could someone please turn down the gravity?" A young, breathy female voice sounded tired as it tickled at her aural receiver. "Girl, that was the freakiest thing I ever want to do. I'd ask about turning around and going home, but then I'd have to back through that goop you call an atmosphere. I looked up the crazy orbital dance this rock does with its ice giant neighbor, close as it gets, I'd at least demand dinner next time."

Orrey giggled, not a very professional response. "Don't be such a tadpole. There are double the gravity baffles once you hit the hab and I made sure to put a mint on your pillow and turn down your bedclothes."

"Now that's service."

"Watch out though, those close encounters with Kepler-36c can get everyone's hormones going."

A laugh came over Orrey's comm, then there was a moment of labored wheezing before Zoey could reply. "Ewww, the guy a couple of bunks over threw up three and a half times on the way down—don't ask--and now he just tried to scratch his nose, I think he dislocated a shoulder. What a moron."

That was what Orrey liked about Zoey, she never took anything totally seriously. It was almost like she had a Tort sense of humor. Mom said Tort humor came from the dolphin genes spliced into their matrix.

"You should have seen your splashdown from out here. There was a seismic wave that I could have surfed for miles and…"

"Look, could we continue this witty banter later? My lunch wants to come out and play." With a retching sound, the connection was cut off abruptly.

Dad was right, baselines were pretty physically fragile.

It was a good hour's swim, with the pod in tow, to the place where Hab-1 had been anchored. It was a mile-long structure that could be moved as needed, completely designed to make survival not only possible for unaltered human colonists, but downright comfortable. It was almost a self-contained world and had taken a full twenty years for the Torts to build from scratch.

Boredom soon raised its ugly head again so Orrey swam back to talk with Bimbo, a Tort who was only a few years older than her. He had pulled rear guard duty. When she was younger, she'd had quite the crush on the strapping young Tort, with his spiky shell plates and long, sinuous tentacles. He was promised to another now—*sigh*—but at least he still took her more seriously than the others did.

"Wow, is this cool, or what?" she swam rings around the young heart-throb.

Bimbo didn't smile. "Hey, Orrey. Yeah, this is pretty historic, but I'm not so sure how cool this will be for us."

"What are you talking about? As of today, K-36b is a full-fledgged colony world. We're citizens, you big goof."

Bimbo looked around and set his comm-caster to mute. He motioned for her to do the same.

"Did it ever occur to you that now that real humans are here, we're just going to become second-class freaks? To them we aren't real people at all. Sure, we get a block vote when it comes to policy, but when you read the fine print, the baselines can veto anything we propose. I've heard rumors, that on other worlds, the Heralds die out as a species within a few generations of baseline colonization. Really, it's easy enough to do, just slip in an expiration date when you design the species."

Orrey was stunned. She'd heard, and ignored, such bilge over the last year but she'd never expected to hear crap like this coming from Bimbo.

"That's crazy. Colonists couldn't survive five minutes on K-36b without us. I just talked to my friend, Zoey, and they're helpless as tads in a trim-tank."

Bimbo snorted and pointed several tendrils at the pod they were following, "Friend, that's a good one. Are you going out reef-hopping with her this weekend? Sharing a polyp salad? Hell, no. Once they're safe in the habitat that we built for them, the only use they'll have for us is as janitors and repairmen. Maybe they'll let us run errands for them. You've read Earth history, we're just the happy little darkies on this plantation."

"What a hateful thing to say!" She slapped at Bimbo's eyes. How could she have once liked him? He turned and grabbed at her flailing tendrils.

"Grow up! In their eyes we're monsters, leviathans of the deep, bred and domesticated for their needs. Educator drones taught us to think like humans, and yeah, ninety-two percent of our DNA is human, but an Earth chimp has a higher percentage in common with homo sapiens than we do."

Orrey shook herself free and sped off from the tiny convoy. She didn't even want to share the same ocean with Mr. Bimbo Haley right at that moment. This was supposed to be the best day ever and now it was ruined.

She swam for several minutes till she was sure she was out of comm range. Who was going to miss her anyway? Off in the distance ahead she saw another pod being ferried to Habitat One, Probably the delta four team. She hid in a reef of pseudo-coral rather than explain why she was cut wandering around so far from her own assigned group, during the biggest event in K-36b history.

It couldn't be true, she told herself. *Humans weren't like that, certainly Zoey wasn't like that.* Maybe she should swim back and see if Zoey felt like talking. Bimbo was a creep for spreading such vicious lies.

She hung behind the spiked growth, miserably watching as the other convoy made its way past. It was sure to be a madhouse once all these pods started docking with the habitat. She shouldn't just stay hiding here like a cowfish while there was so much work to be done.

In the distance, moving toward the delta four convoy, was a shrikefish, a true leviathan. These bad boys were five times larger than a full-grown Tort and covered with sharp-toothed, articulated mouths that fed on everything in their path, sending all that food to the great central stomach it dragged in its wake. In the early days, these monsters had been the bane of Tort existence, but once a sub-sonic frequency was found that repelled them, they weren't much of a threat at all. This one was a biggie, and was getting closer than she'd ever seen. Usually they would zoom off once they got in range of the sub-sonics, but this one was just putting on more speed.

"Hey!" she literally screamed into comm-set, "Crank up your sub-sonics. That shrike isn't slowing down!" She knew she was casting on the right frequency but all she heard in reply were frantic orders and the sounds of panic. Before she could even register a response, the shrikefish gobbled up the hindmost Tort. The others quickly turned to face the menace, but their gigging spears and plasma shells were no match for all those mouths. The defenders were all gone in under a minute and the great fish began gnawing at the floundering shuttle pod.

Orrey stared in wide-eyed horror as the thing's teeth scraped along the metal hull. It was strong, but after its plunge through K-

36b's corrosive atmosphere, and the splashdown impact, the hull integrity had to be badly compromised. After a few moments of frustrated chewing, the shrikefish wheeled around and slammed its enormous gut into the metal sphere.

What happened next was horrible. The pod ruptured and started to explode, but the pressure of the waters around them reversed things almost immediately and the ball twisted in on itself. The implosion compacted everything that had been a part of it, or lived within it. All that was left was a small mangled hunk of meat and scrap metal, barely an appetizer for the ravaging giant.

*Oh god, oh god, oh god!*She turned and fled, desperate to get back to her father's team. It was at least a couple of minutes, at her top swim speed, before she was in comm range. The shrike was already on her tail, but at a distance. At least her sub-sonics seemed to be keeping it at bay.

All those colonists, dead! Thoughts kept ringing in her head. *Trillions of miles to be snack food for a monster.* She'd known a couple of the Torts in that group. *Why hadn't the sub-sonics worked?* On the contrary, they had almost acted like a dinner bell.

"Orrey Salinas to convoy delta six, come in. Emergency! I repeat, emergency!" She prayed she was close enough to be heard, the monster was still on her tail.

"Orrey, Honey, what's the matter? Where are you?" Her dad's voice sounded frantic.

"There's an insane shrikefish headed right for you. It destroyed delta four--Torts, colonists and everything. Dad it's after me, coming right your way." She was already exhausted, terrified and out of her mind with worry. "Daddy, what should I do?"

"Veer off, kiddo." Jabbo's voice sounded strained. "There's a megalith forest ten degrees south. If you can make that, you'll be safe till I can come get you."

"Okay." She replied weakly and flicked all her tendrils into the water at once, executing a perfect ten-degree turn. Orrey put everything she had into speed, not letting herself dwell on what would happen in she didn't make it. After a few seconds, she finally dared to glance behind her. The fish wasn't there. It had streaked on, ignoring her and making straight for dad, Bimbo, and Zoey.

"Dad, it didn't follow me. Get out of there!" Once again the dinner-bell image struck her, the shrike seemed so focused on getting to that colony pod. *Oh crap!* "Listen, I think the shuttle is putting out something that cancels the sub-sonics and actually attracts shrikefish."

There was a long pause. Orrey wondered if her dad thought she had cracked up.

"Honey, I want you to keep heading for that forest. You understand? I can't just leave these people." Another pause, "I love you, baby." And the comm went dead.

She didn't even stop to think, but lit off after the receding shrike. Screw the forest, her father and friends were in danger.

With a speed she didn't think was in her, she caught the creature, or at least its bulbous stomach. Her plan, such as it was, involved using her gigging spear to slice open a hole in the thing's gut and shove in all the plasma shells she had. At best this might give the damned fish a stomachache bad enough to stop his attack. At worst it would annoy Mr. Shrike and make him chase her instead, once she turned off her sub-sonics.

The third scenario hadn't even occurred to her. Orrey's spear broke with her first stroke, and the shrikefish didn't even notice.

She could just make out Zoey's pod in the distance ahead, floating free. Had her dad abandoned them?

Her private comm tingled. "Orrey? What the hell is going on out there? The crew is trying to shut down all the systems, but they keep injuring themselves getting to the controls. Morons! Did they not read the instruction about staying in their couches? No one will tell us anything!" Orrey had never heard such a panicky edge in Zoey's voice before.

"There's a humungous shrikefish out here that wants to eat the pod, or at least crush it. We think something that the pod is broadcasting is attracting it."

"W-w-what?!"

"I don't see dad or any of the others, but I'm coming. Hold on, I'll find some way to stop it." Orrey did not say this last part with much

187

confidence, but it just had to be true.

"No! No you will not." All panic and false levity was gone from Zoey's voice. "I just looked up shrikefish on my pad and you have zero chance against something like that. I think the other Torts had the right idea and I order you to get the hell out of here too."

Suddenly, out of a patch of stew-weed, four Tortesie streaked, each holding a corner of the net that had been used to haul the Earth pod. Within seconds ten more followed, whooping and taunting the shrike. More than half the shrikefish's lethal mouths were caught in the net's tough filaments as the first four sped through the deadly maws in a corkscrew pattern. The rest were harassing the thing, though their weapons had little real effect.

Orrey laughed out loud. This was Tortesie humor at its finest.

"Hey Zoey, You remember how you were trying to explain cowboy movies to me? I think the cavalry just arrived." With a flick of tentacles, she propelled herself into the fray.

The thing about shrikes that always baffled the Torts, way back when, was their lack of sensory apparatus. No eyes, ears, noses or manipulators to touch with. Just all those mouths. Turns out their eyes and ears were in their mouths. Dad had told her that when she was six, and it looked like he remembered now as well.

Spears, tipped with primed plasma shells, stabbed into mouths causing some actual damage to the thing. Orrey followed suit and attached a shell to what was left of her spear and made for the nearest mouth. The mouth had seemed to have a life of its own, bobbing and weaving. Several times, it was a close thing whether the mouth would bite her before she could feed it a plasma lozenge, but she eventually did and it made a satisfying sizzle as slime drooled out of the orifice.

In the middle of her victory dance, she felt sharp pain in three of her dorsal tentacles. Another mouth had grabbed her when she was distracted. It didn't bite through the appendages but held her tight so it could drag her toward its other waiting maws. A spear tip sliced into the mouth and it let go abruptly. She turned and wrapped her injured tendrils around her savior.

"Dad! I thought you'd died or run off."

Her father held Orrey tight for a few seconds before releasing her. "If we live through this, you are so grounded."

"We're going to beat this thing, right?" There was more pleading in her voice than she would have liked.

"If I had fifty Tort marines and a few bazookas… maybe." He swam with her away from the battle, toward the still floundering pod. "Look, all my comm gear got smashed by the shrike so I need you to contact your pal, Zoey, on that personal frequency you two cooked up, and see if they still have any form of propulsion that works. The further away they can get, the better their chances of survival." She could see Bimbo, part of his shell crushed in, waiting for them. "We're going to hold laughing boy off as long as we can, but I want you two to get this thing moving any way you can. Understood?"

They both said their *Yes, Sirs* but Jabbo had already turned back to the fight.

Bimbo winced, "I checked the whole pod out and I think there are a couple of places strong enough to hold up under some nudging. That's the best plan I have."

Orrey nodded curtly. "Okay, let me call Zoey, like dad said, see if they've got anything."

Suddenly her comm came to life and she realized Zoey had probably been listening all this time.

"Okay, I asked the captain already and he said these things weren't paddleboats—-his words, not mine-—about all there is might be the auxiliary retro pack, if it didn't get burned up. It wasn't used during descent but if we fire it down here, it'll probably just punch right through us. Sorry, Orrey."

Bimbo had switched personal comm frequencies and was listening in. what more was there to say, so they shared a miserable moment of silence. Then, all at the same time, three voices broke the stillness in unison. "I just had a really stupid idea."

"Yeah, Cap says you're hovering right over it. It's the red packet."

Bimbo's tendrils twitched in frustration. "In this light, everything is shades of grey. don't they teach you anything in Earth schools?"

"Bite me, turtle boy!"

"Can we focus here?" Bimbo and Zoey had known each other for

189

two minutes and already they were arguing like an old married couple. Orrey could see that the struggle with the shrike still continued and it was closer than before. There were five Torts floating, unmoving, in the water. The net was shredded in more places than she could count. What good was a stupid plan if no one was left to watch it fail?

"Okay, The captain says it should have a big triangle on it and say something like 'Danger, this thing will kill your ass.' I'm paraphrasing, of course." It sounded like Zoey was beginning to warm to her new role as liaison.

"Got it!" Carefully they undid the fasteners and slid the retro rocket out of its casing. "So, how do we detonate this thing?" Orrey found two metal tabs that had to be contacts.

Zoey breathed a labored sigh over the comm. "That part had the captain stumped, but I might have a thought on the subject. One of you takes your comm receiver and attaches it to the two leads you see. Then, when one of you shoves the rocket up that thing's ass, the other one yells something nasty, a tiny charge goes through the receiver, boom."

Orrey and Bimbo exchanged a look. "Well, other than a shrikefish not actually having an ass, per se, I like it." Bimbo started to remove his commset.

Orrey grabbed it from him. "With your shell all banged up, you don't have the speed, but you still have strength and can get the pod far enough away to maybe minimize damage to it. I'll do my own yelling too, if you don't mind. I know lots of nasty words."

He stared into her eyes.

"Shut up. You know I'm right."

Zoey's voice spoke up, "Damn it Orrey, I don't..."

"You shut up too! This round's on me and that's all there is to it." She took the comm and stuck it on the improvised bomb. "Bimbo, toss out a scatter signal and get pushing." She didn't look back to see if he'd done what she said but soon there was a shriek sounding through the water that every Tort knew the meaning of.

As she zipped toward the monster, the Torts broke off what they were doing, grabbed fallen comrades and lit out in every direction.

They may not know why the scatter signal had been triggered but their response was trained in from childhood. The shrike struggled to free itself from what was left of the net. At the last moment she changed trajectory so she would miss all the snapping mouths and come up on the thing from behind.

It was a shame she couldn't say some brave last words to Zoey, to pass on to her father, but she was afraid it might set off the retro before she was ready. She knew that, not only was there not a convenient anal opening, but the way the fish was thrashing, she was going to have to hold it in place herself to make sure it did its work.

Through tears, she searched for a likely spot on the swollen gut of the creature. Then she noticed something odd. There seemed to be something leaking out of the disgusting gut, not much, but noticeable. It was hard to see with all the movement, but there it was. Her little gigging spear had done more damage than she had thought. She slipped two small tendrils into the hole—*yuck*—and pulled as hard as she could. The fish jerked and the retro pack went flying. *NO!*

But a tentacle was there to catch it.

"Not only are you grounded, no allowance for three weeks." Her father grabbed one side of the tiny rip and Orrey grabbed the other. Soon the fissure was big enough and Jabbo slammed the rocket pack deep into the thing's stomach. "I don't know what the plan is here, kiddo, but I bet it's a doozy. We good to go now?"

Orrey nodded and they were off.

Fifty yards a hundred and suddenly a triumphant squeal erupted from dozens of mouths and she knew the shrikefish was free. She redoubled her efforts and screamed into her comm microphone. "DIE, Motherf… !"

The ocean behind her became a solid thump, which sent her reeling. Her last memory before the blackness closed in was of a great gout of meat bouncing off her shell.

It was weeks before Orrey got the complete story on what had happened. What was attracting the shrikefish turned out to be its signal beacon, set to a very low frequency to travel further in the oceans of K-36ɔ. It was an unused frequency, chosen completely at random. Eight other convoys had been attacked, three of those survived the engagement, though none as ingeniously as the Delta Six team had.

"I look like a freak." Orrey wiggled the mechanical tentacles that replaced the ones bitten, and infected by the shrikefish. Her father had shielded her from a lot of the blast that killed the shrike, he was still in intensive care, but doctors said he'd be okay.

"Gripe, gripe, gripe! You are such a wuss." The hologram of Dr. Zoey Graves examined the area where she had attached the prosthesis tendrils to her friend's ruined ones. "I don't hear Bimbo complaining about the shell-cast I put him into."

"That's just because he's all relieved to hear that he won't have to learn *Camptown Races* on the banjo." Orrey slid out of the med bay, kind of an oversized drive-through CAT scanner hooked to the outer hull of Hab-1. Zoey's holo-face looked puzzled. Orrey laughed "Oh, you know, order 7-C, the one that makes us full fledged citizens. He was sure you guys were coming down with whips and chains."

Zoey's image enlarged till it was about the same size as Orrey. "Yeah, well, that wasn't so far off with the first couple of Earth colonies and I was shocked 7-C hadn't already been implemented here. Bureaucratic morons. Fortunately, we humans learn from our mistakes eventually. Baseline human doesn't mean much these days." She blinked all four of her eyes and rubbed her bald head.

'We humans', Orrey liked the sound of that. She had already decided she would be the captain of the first Tortesie star ship. There were a lot of planets out there for 'we humans' to explore.

WISHES & DREAMS AND TWILIGHT'S LAST GLEAM

John Carew sat on his back porch and looked at the pitch black sky. Three stars were all he could see. Then he looked at the picture of those three stars on his TV set. It was a really good TV and showed three-hundred-sixty-degrees in every direction at once. Yup, three. There'd been ten last time he'd looked. He was relieved. Being god was getting old. He was such a lame-assed god and was anxious for it all to be over with… finally.

He needed to be sure, though, so he tried adjusting his spectacles and got up to turn the TV to several other channels. They were all running the same program. He felt around for the TV controller so he could fine-tune the reception. Where the hell was it?

"Teddy, did you eat the remote again? Hah! Kidding. Well, Teddy old pal, looks like the big show's almost over. Maybe it'll take me with it if I'm lucky.' He looked around but his bulldog, Teddy was nowhere in sight. "Oh, Christ! I forgot to Manifest Teddy again this millennium." He pinched the bridge of his nose. Bringing Teddy back for the end of the universe seemed like more trouble than it was probably worth.

Once before, maybe a couple million years ago he'd been sure all the stars had gone out. He'd created manifestations of Einstein and Newton for the occasion only to discover that he'd let the TV's focus drift. When he tinkered with the remote just a bit, though, sure enough, there were still hundreds of pinpoints of light, impossibly faint, from unimaginably far away, but definitely still there. It was embarrassing to say the least. He wasn't of a mind to be fooled again.

John sagged with weariness as he hobbled back into his bungalow. Where had he left that controller this time?

He knew the house was a construct, another manifestation of his own mind, so the filth and clutter all around him was a disturbing reflection of what he had become.

He lifted couch cushions littered with potato chip crumbs. There were bits of cookies and colorful candy wrappers for sweet carbohydrate abominations that hadn't actually existed in untold eons, but no controller.

For a long time he'd lived in a mansion large as a planet. He filled that place with every diversion imaginable, again, manifested by the power of his mind alone. The mind of god... yeah right. The diversions ceased to divert him after the first million years or so and the upkeep had been too much bother. So he'd let his mansion fade away and created this dump.

He pulled out drawer after drawer, shaking them empty onto the floor with no success. There were simulations of car keys and scissors and restaurant menus whose numbers might be called to deliver Chinese food... if those eateries had still existed. The TV remote, however, was nowhere to be seen. Simply creating another was too much like cheating.

He went through piles of dirty clothes and pushed books off their shelves, nothing. This was beginning to annoy him. None of it was real, including the missing controller, so why couldn't he remember where he'd put it? He checked in the fridge, even the vegetable crisper, still nothing.

He noticed he was out of beer, and then it hit him. A week ago -- or a millennium, whatever -- he'd gotten good and drunk to relieve the boredom. There were vague memories of dancing around naked and pissing on all his belongings to affirm that, though they were imaginary, they were his and his alone.

Alone.

Mostly, that feeling of aloneness had ceased to bother him, but he had always been a morose drunk and remained so, even with no actual physical body. Yeah, he had a body but it was just one more damned manifestation.

At some point during that foggy interlude he decided he didn't give a shit anymore and threw the controller into... Oops, now he remembered.

The pretense of eating still had some comfort for him, as did the inevitable consequences thereof —- accuracy was, after all, the key to making all this sham of normalcy sort-of believable.Sitting, reading the Sports Illustrated Swimsuit Issue from 2052, for the billionth time,

194

as his illusory bowels moved was soothing in its way.

Where better to toss the thing that could bring his lunatic vigil into crystal clarity?

He wiped the controller clean and flushed, almost instantly regretting it. The waters overflowed their porcelain reservoir.

"Christ," he muttered, "nothing works right in this place anymore." Still it beat floating around as a disembodied super-mind. He knew, he'd tried it for half a million years or so.

Back on the porch he adjusted the wire rims of his glasses and set the controller to infinity. "Oh yeah," he nodded, "still only three stars." He wondered if he would notice a difference once they too were gone. He knew, of course, that the actual stars were long kaput. That is the dynamic nuclear ovens themselves had long ago ceased to burn. He was just waiting for the final photons released on that fateful day to reach his simulated eyes.

He'd picked a fixed point at the edge of the universe... well, as close to an edge as was possible when dealing with infinity. Here he had created a place to wait for the last glimmers to reach him.

How long had it taken for him all the light of a once living universe to get to this place? He'd tried to do the math once, but ran out of patience long before he'd run out of numbers. He sometimes wished he had kept up with marking the days off on his calendar but after the first billion years or so, it seemed pointless.

Well, he still remembered the date when he'd snuffed out all the energy in the universe like so many candles on a birthday cake. He supposed that was something. April 1, 2053—April fool's day--the irony still made him wince.

Dr. John Carew had been the wunderkind of astrophysics during the mid-twenty first century. He turned the field on its ear by introducing sentience into the nuts and bolts of quantum physics, in a big way. He'd postulated that if an event didn't actually collapse into reality until it was observed, then sentience must actually be a universal constant like the speed of light. Otherwise nothing could have happened on any cosmic scale until consciousness made it so. However, since sentience didn't travel anywhere, it was omnipresent——like god, but without all that worshiping nonsense. It had gotten him onto lots of talk shows and earned him the disdain of a number of his colleagues.

To be honest, he wasn't even sure if he believed his own theory back in those days -- the math was shaky at best -- but Amos True certainly believed him.

True was a fundamentalist Christian who converted to being a Radical Muslim and then a Nazi Buddhist. None of these were fanatical enough for him so he founded the Church of the One Mind. Determined to show the world his faith, he took over the Roswell Nuclear facility and threatened to blow it sky-high.

He coordinated his effort to coincide with the April Super Bowl, (There were four a year by 2053.) buying ad time just before the half-time show. He announced his intention to cause a nuclear meltdown at the Roswell plant right after the second half kick-off. He claimed he would contain it by the power of his mind alone —- that and some powerful hallucinogens.

John Carew, much to his annoyance, had been adopted by True as the prophet and first saint of the Church One Mind. Carew had tried to get a restraining order of some kind against this new religion, to stop them from using his name and image, but it turned out that forced sainthood was not against the law. In a last ditch effort the scientist was rushed in by the authorities to talk his unwanted acolyte and assorted True believers.

Instead Carew was captured by the fanatic and force-fed an LSD/wipeout cocktail. (LSD being a sacrament in True's church and wipeout being the latest in designer drugs.) Once the astrophysicist's mind was properly expanded they began their sacred ceremonial experiment. Amos True ordered his followers to activate their explosive vests.

Not a very scientific experiment.

Carew lay there; tripping, mangled and dying, the only survivor on that long-ago afternoon. The nuclear core was going into total meltdown so he decided he might as well do one last thought experiment. Einstein had been very big on thought experiments. What could it hurt?

196

Proposed: If his mind —- as part of the universal consciousness -- could theoretically absorb all this terrible energy now consuming his body, how would he go about doing so?

He imagined that he would need to do away with, or absorb, all nuclear reactions everywhere and then he could collapse probability into something more manageable. Yes, if there were no nuclear reactions possible he would be out of danger. He could feel his mind expand, becoming one with the universal mind and by extension, the whole universe. It was the sort of idea that seemed feasible when one was that thoroughly stoned and dying.

And somehow it happened--just like that. His mind encompassed the entirety of the universe, time and distance being irrelevant to god-like, omnipresent sentience. He then just mentally erased all traces of nuclear reactions everywhere. For good measure, he made sure they wouldn't ever start up again. About eight minutes later he felt the last rays of the Sun's light strike the Earth and knew that it had become an inert, dead thing.

Carew had not remembered to be careful, though, about what he asked the quantum Genie for. Energy could not just be destroyed, it had to go somewhere.

He screamed as the power surged into him, infinite power, but with no meaningful way to access it. He felt, more than knew, what had happened.

He had murdered the very universe itself to save his own life. In the blink of an eye, every star, every nebula, every black hole, everywhere, had ceded its ability to produce electromagnetic energy potential. Though his body died that day, the essence of John Carew became the new de facto god.

Gravity, being a different type of force, still held the utterly inert matter together. So, while the corpses of stars and planets still existed to populate this new universal graveyard, they could never again produce new light.

Somehow, the photons already in transit remained immune to the new god's edict. They continued on their way at the cosmic snail's pace of 299,792,458 miles per second, acting as a cosmic funeral pyre. Corporeal life on earth had ceased soon after the sun went bye-bye.

Dr. John Quincy Carew had his thought experiment results.

So many times, during that first trillion years or so, he had tried to generate a new Genesis. For all his power he couldn't figure out the trick to getting things going again. He visited every corner of his cosmic cemetery. He rubbed the husks of black holes together like a boy scout trying to light a campfire but failed to ever get his cosmic merit badge. Everywhere he went he was the only spark... and he couldn't share it, or even give it away.

All he could do with that power was create an illusion to live in and watch the long-deceased stars wink out one by one as the last photons of each celestial body finally reached him. Those orphaned particles were the last evidence there had ever been a living universe. John Carew, failed god, had become the center of all creation out on the edge of creation. Whoopee.

One star left. He decided to check the fridge again and this time there was beer. Maybe things were looking up. He lounged back in his hammock, strung from the porch roof, popped the can and let the foam cover his knuckles. "Here's to you," he said as he raised the brew in a toast to the last glimmer of light, "You were a good universe while you lasted." He took a long, cold swallow and let it swish back and forth in his mouth.

Without any pomp or ceremony the last light from the last star was gone.

John Carew cried till he had no more simulated tears. Maybe there were other universes out there somewhere -- he liked to hope so. True, these potential neighbors had never stopped by for a visit in all this time. Maybe they were shy or simply too appalled at the condition he had let the place get into. He lay for a long time, trying to remember the universe as it had been, then closed his eyes and, for the first time since April 1, 2053, he slept... perchance to dream of a new sky.

SECTION FOUR

PROFESSOR CHAMPION
AND THE STRING THEOREM

The telegram from the Professor should, under other circumstances, have come as no great surprise to me. He had come to consider me as sort of an unofficial chronicler of his work since that *hidden world* affair. No, I had come to expect the odd mysterious summons from him.

My consternation and surprise, at this particular invitation, was due to the well-publicized declaration of Champion's death. He had been lost at sea some three months earlier in a mid-Atlantic shipping accident.

The demise of Geoffrey Edward Champion had been mourned throughout the empire as the loss of a great mind and an intrepid soul. I had wept unashamedly at his wake after having consumed an obscene amount of ale.

Yet there I was, in a fishing boat, ten miles off the shore of Scotland, awaiting the arrival of a presumably dead legend.

"Ye'r sure this is where you wish to be?" The captain of the tiny, dilapidated vessel asked--for the fifth time in the last hour.

I pulled my Macintosh more tightly around me. "Sir, I merely follow the directions given to me, the coordinates from which I have relayed to you. So, perhaps it is I who should ask you if this is, indeed, where I wish to be?"

Captain McHaddon huffed out a cloud of smoke from the vile pipe clutched between his teeth. "Laddie, I've fished these waters since I was a wee pup. I can find a cork from a bottle of brew drunk by Lord Admiral Nelson hisself, tossed into the ocean a hundred years before you was sucking at your mother's teat. And, I can do so in a gale that would strip the hide from a lubber like you."

I sighed, "I meant no disrespect, sir. I suppose I'm a little embarrassed to have been gulled into playing along with such an obvious and cruel hoax. We'll give this another ten minutes. Then, I promise you, we shall head back to shore."

McHaddon grumbled and chewed his pipe stem.

"Don't worry," I assured him, "you will receive the full sum we contracted for. You have done your job well, I'm sure. It was I who was a gullible foo…"

At that moment the ship lurched violently to the port side and I was flung unceremoniously to the un-scrubbed deck. From this vantage I could see the waters on the starboard side bubble like a volcano ready to blow.

It was a clear night with a moon full and gibbous. I saw every detail as the great metal sphere broke the surface. It measured at least ten feet across, made of brushed steel and, where one might have expected rivets, holding the various plates together, the thing was encrusted with pearls. On the very top of the ball was a shallow dome of some translucent material from which were appended tentacles of the same substance. They enwrapped the sphere ornamentally, almost sensuously, giving the impression that they might squeeze it till it crumpled like an eggshell in the fist of an overexcited child.

I scrambled back to the bulwark where the captain stood swinging a gaff hook at the thing, screaming oaths of defiance and terror. I, for my part, leaned on the railing goggle-eyed, laughing like the village idiot. This was so like the man.

The top dome popped open on a swinging hinge and the shape of a singular man rose into view like Aphrodite from the sea. He looked to have lost some weight, but the defiant spade beard, the barrel chest and a head proportionate to his ego were exactly as I remembered them.

"Maloney! My dear fellow, I'm so pleased you could join us. I do so hope you remembered the brandy and cigars. I am so damned tired of smoking seaweed, you have no idea."

After a few minutes of maneuvering Professor Champion's unlikely conveyance alongside my rented craft, there was a period of hand-clasping, back-slapping, and short introductions. I presented the still bewildered McHaddon, who reluctantly shook hands with Champion and his two companions. Both men, whose names I was told, but would not care to assay pronouncing--much less spelling. They were dark of skin, with fierce beards and eyes that had a certain fanatic's gleam. The two said not a word, but began to transfer unfathomable electrical and mechanical devices from the sphere to the deck of the fishing boat.

Champion made himself at home on a pile of ropes and nets. He lit, with no small delight, one of the Havana cigars I had brought and gestured for me to join him. His men silently assembled what the Professor called his *pulse actualizer.*

"Where do I start?" he leaned back to savor the Napoleon brandy the Captain had so kindly poured for us.

"Well," I cleared my throat, "There is the small matter of your ship sinking and you being reported dead."

"Ah, yes. Is that what the papers reported?" He jumped to his feet and grabbed a shiny apparatus as it fell from the hands of one of the men. He yelled loudly, in a tongue I was unfamiliar with, and gingerly secured the whatsis to some thingamabob before returning to his seat. "Now, where was I?"

"Your death?" I prompted

"Just so. As it turns out, all those wild stories about a sea monster sinking ships are absolutely true. Except, of course, there is no monster, as such, but rather a quite remarkable chap, goes by the name of Captain Noman. It's he and his crew who have been sending men to their watery graves these many months. I suppose that does make him a monster of sorts, what?"

He puffed his cigar thoughtfully and I said nothing. Better to let him have his way with a tale than to risk his derision. "Noman has built himself an undersea boat of tremendous power, calls it the Odysseus, which he has equipped to ram ships. Bloody diabolical, but it certainly does gets the job done. The man seems to have his sights set on revenge against the whole western world in general."

"Good God." I murmured, "So he sunk the Excalibur, but how did you survive and how have you escaped him?"

"Strictly speaking, I am still his prisoner. These are two of his sailors." Champion indicated the two men constructing whatever it was they were constructing. "I imagine if I were to jump over the side and swim for it, they'd shoot me in a heartbeat."

"Dear Lord!" I looked at the two in a new light and saw the

strange side arms slung low on their hips.

"When the Excalibur sank, I alone managed to swim strongly enough to escape the undertow. Well, after an hour, I had fought off two sharks and was still treading water so Noman surfaced to see what I was about. The blighter might have tossed me back right then and there, but I recognized another man of science in him, insane perhaps, but inspired. I surmised that if I could tickle his imagination enough he might keep me around and even stop sinking ships for a while. So, I posed him a scientific puzzle that he and his leviathan of a vessel might help me solve. "

McHaddon, who had been seated nearby, was speechless, and indeed I worried for his continued sanity. I, however, had been adventuring with the Professor before, so my mind was a bit inoculated to such things.

"My lord, what could you propose that would stop a madman from the pursuit of his insane endeavors?" I asked.

He got up to stretch and take in several deep breaths of good clean sea air. He then stepped over to inspect the work of his cronies. He continued his story as he did so.

"A couple of years ago I met this fellow at my club, brother of one of our members--seems he was a policeman, or detective of some sort. I thought he had far too keen an intellect for such mundane matters. The blighter actually beat me, Geoffrey Edward Champion, at several games of chess. We got to talking about the mental restlessness we both seemed to share and he claimed that playing the violin often helped him compose his thoughts. Well, the violin was out of the question for a man with hands like mine." He held up one hand, wriggling fingers the size of sausages. "At any rate, he suggested the bass viol."

I had no idea where this might be going, so I pulled up my collar against the cold breeze and took a long gulp of brandy. The Professor seemed satisfied with the progress that had been made and rejoined me.

"I have scant talent for music, but I did come to enjoy the sensations caused, within me, by the deep vibrations when I played the thing. One night, lost in a piece by Beethoven, it occurred to me that the vibrations produced by each string affected the vibration of every other string. It also affected my mind, transporting it, as it were. I reasoned that the brain might have strings of its own, incredibly tiny strings, to be sure, but strings that could resonate and affect my perception of reality. It wasn't much of a leap at all to then postulate that reality itself could be composed of infinitesimal strings whose vibrations formed the very fabric of what we perceive as the world around us." He chuckled and motioned to the dazed Captain that he was ready for another brandy.

"Professor, forgive me, but what the hell are you talking about?" I exclaimed.

"I thought it a lovely theory--explained a lot don't you see--but how could I test something on such a mind-staggeringly tiny scale? After a few more snifters of port and some hurried equations, it came to me that it might only be tested on a truly mind numbingly large scale, the very large and the very small being much the same in many ways. So, that's what I proposed to Noman and that is what we are here to witness this night."

I glanced nervously at the machinery that seemed to be nearing its completion. Coming from any other man, I might consider all the stuff about bass violins and such as the meanderings of a feeble mind. But this wasn't *any other man*. "Professor Champion, what exactly is it that you have done, and why am I here?" I managed to croak out.

The Man clapped his massive hands in almost childlike delight. "I convinced Noman that he could use his undersea craft to secure one end of a failed attempt at a trans-Atlantic cable to the ocean's floor. Thus secured, he might pull the other end taught with the measureless power of his ship. With that accomplished, it would be a simple matter to send an electrified plasma pulse through the cable, in effect plucking it like the world's largest bass violin." He indicated the machine. "That is what my pulse actualizer is for." Then he reached over and patted my knee. "I argued, successfully, that while he is in his submersible boat, right under our feet, stretching the damned cable, I needed real cigars, something decent to drink and a ship to stand on to observe the historical moment properly. Hence, he allowed me to contact you."

204

"P-P-Plucking it like…" I stammered

"That's right, my boy, produce a note so significant that it would alter the very fabric of reality. Why, I convinced old Noman that we might create a new reality where justice and equality would prevail among the nations of the Earth.Of course, there's the off chance it might just cause earthquakes, tidal waves and typhoons worldwide, but why dwell on the negative?"

Perhaps the constitution of my imagination was not as robust or jaded as I have previously let on. I leapt up, dashing my brandy to the deck. "I can't stand by and allow this. Science should be brave, not foolhardy. I demand you cease this wild and dangerous experiment right…" But before I could finish my speech, I felt a blow to the back of my head. I dropped to the deck like so many netted cod fish had done before me.

When I recovered, Champion was busy at the controls of the strange apparatus and my hands were tied behind my back. I lunged at him but was stopped by one of the two intense men flanking his sides.

"Professor, Geoffrey… Please stop this. You have no clear idea what effect something like this might have! At the very least this is bad science… mad science." I pleaded.

His hands moved over several buttons and switches until his right hand came to rest on a large lever and there he hesitated. "It all seemed like such a good idea when Noman and I discussed it, but I do see your point about this seeming a little rash. Perhaps we should wait a bit, do the math, work out the finer details." And then I noticed the glint of moonlight off a knife the other man brought up to the professor's throat. Still the professor stood frozen. "Mr. Maloney, sometimes my scientific zeal gets the better of me, which is why I so value your level-headed input. Unfortunately, I seem to no longer have any real say in the matter." He said calmly.

The knife wielding sailor barked out a string of harsh words, the only one of which I recognized was Noman.I saw the knife move ever so slightly and a crop of blood appeared on its tip.

Champion bit his lip. "Did I mention the part about Noman being quite mad?"

I struggled against the man who held me tightly, to no avail.

The Professor, however, was a man of deeds as well as words. He twisted to one side and brought his enormous fist into his captor's chin.

The smaller man with the knife pivoted, to lessen the impact of the blow. He grabbed the Champion's lapels. Using the professor's own momentum against him, he sent scientist sailing across the deck.

Without hesitation the sailor threw the knife at the Professor and grabbed the lever. Pull as he might he could not budge the thing. The device had been made so that only someone with the strength of a Professor Champion could activate it.

My assailant threw me across the deck and grabbed at the lever to add his strength. The two heaved at the switch till veins popped out along their bare forearms and foreheads. Finally, it began its ponderous descent.

They say that time slows to a crawl at such moments but no such thing occurred just then. It wasn't until later I found out what happened. Geoffrey managed to dig the knife out of the deck, where it had narrowly missed him. He threw the blade with an expertise I had not realized he possessed. It embedded itself right at the place where the lever met its contact, and at the very second that the circuit closed.

The night erupted in a shower of electrical sparks as the two grim men jerked uncontrollably in a dance of death, neither able to let go of the deadly lever."

"Thank god!" I gasped, but the Professor merely held his breath.

We did not so much hear what came next as feel it. There was no visible clue as to the vibration I felt, nothing shook or wobbled, yet every cell in my body seemed to resonate. Champion rose, the very embodiment of expectation. His cells vibrated too, I supposed, as did those of the fishing boat, the ocean, England herself, and indeed the entire world. However, only Champion could guess what those reverberations might herald.

And then there were three moons in a sky the color of mustard over our heads. As I regained my own footing, I saw that the machine had ceased to emit fireworks and its operators lay dead.

The deck beneath our feet lurched at a frightening angle as a metal mountain emerged from the depths. I could only assume this was the dreaded *Odysseus*. A man, in silk robes and a fez, with the same dark skin and wild eyes of the two deceased sailors, emerged from the top of the vessel. A shower of sparks erupted from the hatch right behind him but he didn't seem to notice in the least. He shook both fists in triumph at the strange sky.

"We have done it!" He twirled like a dervish on the deck of his craft. "Come, Professor, there is a whole new world to explore and re-make in Noman's image."

Champion waved at dancing madman. "That does sound like a jolly good time but I have to clean up this mess. A new world's omelet does require a few broken eggs." He pointed at the dead men and the machine. "What say I join you back on that charming island of yours next week? I am sure in this reality you will be revered as the savior of humanity."

"Ah yes, I shall be the benevolent Emperor Noman and I shall rename England Championshire--you shall rule it scientifically." With a loud whoop, Noman jumped back into the hatch from which he had emerged. In a moment, the vessel had slipped silently back into the stygian depths.

The Professor stood, hands on hips, like some hero in a penny dreadful. He laughed with a volume that could only be produced by someone with his great barrel chest.

I feared he had joined Noman in madness.

"Sir, what. .?" That was all I could manage to articulate at that moment. Too many questions filled my mind.

"Everything's fine," he came over and undid the ropes on my hands. "I should have foreseen this. Reality hasn't changed at all, we've merely shifted planet Earth into another universe. No doubt the effect will wear off when that incredible, earth-moving note we sounded has died away." He pulled out his pocket watch and studied it a moment. "Fifteen minutes, twenty at the most, and we should be back in our own universe, none the worse for the wear, I dare say." He laughed again. "By Gadfrey, what I wouldn't give to have a telescope right now!"

207

###

Sure enough, seventeen minutes later our old familiar moon and stars once again resumed their reign of the heavens.

We found McHaddon trussed up like a Christmas goose below decks. He helped us throw the infernal contraption overboard, along with the dead sailors. The brushed metal sphere had vanished back into the depths from which it had emerged. I feared the wrath of the man Noman might be upon us at any second, once he found out that things hadn't worked out as he'd hoped. Professor Champion assured me, though, that the electrical feedback from his actualizer would give the man and his submersible plenty to occupy themselves till we were safely back on land. He assured me that he would go on no more ocean voyages in the near future.

And so it was.

With no proof to speak of, we decided that our wild tale was best left untold, at least for the time being.

The rescue and return of the famous Professor Geoffrey Edward Champion should have made headlines throughout the realm, but the papers were full of little except the strange and alien sky witnessed by the entire world the night before. No rational scientific explanation being forthcoming on the matter, all was soon dismissed as mass hallucination, mesmerism of some sort. Within the week, the news once again focused on what was important--the latest sex scandals and brutal murders.

Still, the events of that incredible night are burned into my memory, so while the details are fresh I have decided to set them down.As I commit all this to paper I am on a train, once again in the great man's company. One would think I should know better by now. We are on our way to meet with a chap named Camphor — Cavor – something like that. The silly bloke wants to talk about going to the moon. Where does Champion find such crackpots?

THE STRAW MAN

I felt the slug as it hit me full in the chest and wondered how many shades of purple and yellow I would be tomorrow. I had to be more careful. A bullet proof vest can get a man to thinking he's invulnerable and once you get that idea in your head, you might as well start shopping for coffins.

A dead crime-fighter isn't much use to anyone.

I channeled all that pain into a banshee shriek and hurtled off the fire escape into the crowd of pissed-off policemen waiting below decked out in riot gear; shields, armor, helmets and truncheons. I landed full onto their upraised shields and brought them all down like cheap bowling pins.

They'd been chasing me long enough, through blind alleys, abandoned playgrounds and all-night liquor stores. I figured it was time to catch *them*... so to speak.

"Hey, why don't you guys pick on someone your own size?" I danced from shield to shield like I was doing a jig in an earthquake. "Go arrest some real crooks like the Petrolli gang or, how about the creeps on Wall Street those protesters are talking about! Oh, I forgot. They already got their paddies slapped!"

One officer, George Blake, big as a freight train, heaved up just as I landed, tossing me away like a rag-doll. "Dammit, Straw, This isn't your fight." Blake shouted at me. You are not helping anyone with all this crap."

During my almost four years of trying to bring a little justice to Pima City's streets, I'd learned to take a fall, so I rolled and was up on my feet in a flash, nose to nose with Dexter Hale from the mayor's office. Hale was the guy overseeing tonight's raid on the outlaw encampment that had been set up in the Park. He grabbed at my ragged poncho like it had lapels.

"You've put your foot in it this time, you bum. I have written instructions from the mayor himself to break up that little hippie-fest across from town hall and you are interfering." Hale bit his lower lip, eyes gleaming, and yelled at the recovering policemen. "Get this guy in cuffs, or do I have to do everything around here?"

I reached my arms up between his and forced them apart with a snap. He was left holding chunks of my signature black drape. The poor guy looked so out of place standing there in his three-piece suit, with a dumb look on his face. So, I took pity on him and judo flipped him into a pile of garbage the city had neglected to pick up. I figured he'd feel right at home among all the other filth.

"I decide what's my fight, and what's not," I hollered back at Blake, "like always." I didn't stick around for a reply, but headed into the darkness of the back alley before any of the cops could react. Dark alleys are what I do best.

I slipped through a near invisible opening in a sliding grating, and was gone. I dashed through the pitch black storeroom of the now defunct Jacobs Printing Plant. It had shut down four years ago, when magazines for kids went the way of the dodo. By the time the cops found the opening, I'd be through five more bolt holes, each one tougher to detect than the last. I'm a hard man to catch.

My name's Carl Meeker, though my close, intimate friends call me Straw. The newspapers tagged me with the name *the Straw Man* and it's the one that stuck in the public's mind.

I don't know if the reporter who dubbed me that really knew the meaning of the term or was just referring to me looking like a scarecrow. Understandable really, what with the ragged black blanket that I wear like a poncho, draped over the stick slung across my shoulders. My beat-up old slouch hat, which keeps my home-made mask in place, sort of completes the ensemble.

In the right lighting the effect can be pretty damned intimidating. You need a good gimmick if you want to survive in this line of work.

I've been back from Iraq for a little over five years now, doing super-dooper thing for the better part of last four of those.

Marla, my neighbor and confidant, says I should change my nom-de-guerre to PTSD Man. She usually says that when she has to patch me up, which happens way more often than I'd like to admit. Marla is a retired nurse, and a real pistol.

I slipped into the unlit entrance of my basement apartment. Things had gotten ugly tonight when the cops started tearing down

210

the protester's tents. Those tents had stood peacefully in John Glenn Park for the better part of the last month but that had changed at about three A.M. this morning by order of our illustrious mayor.

Mayor King was a total stooge of the Lyans Financial Group, which owned more than half of Pima City. Hale only moonlighted working for the mayor, his day job was chief enforcer for Lyans. Once the housing bubble burst, a lot of folks found themselves out on the streets and the streets are under my protection. Tonight wasn't the first time I had butted heads with Mr. Dexter Hale.

Anyway, when the tear gas, pepper spray and truncheons started flying, I charged into the middle of the action and harassed the boys in blue--they wear black really, but you know what I mean--until they started chasing after me. I thought it would take some of the heat off the protesters. Even as a short term solution my strategy had proven less than brilliant, but I couldn't just stand there and watch things get all Kent State.

I was glad to be home, rough night all around.

"Yo, Spartacus, front and center!" I knew well enough that it was the sound of the electric can-opener, and not my words, that brought the big Tabby running. "I forgot to pick up cat food, so it looks like straight tuna for you tonight, Fuzz-ball." The cat tolerated a few quick strokes of his fur before dismissing me, so he could attend more important matters. I noticed that Marla, bless her heart, had left a tin-foil covered plate for me along with a fresh bottle of pain killers.

I went to my tiny bedroom and carefully peeled away the layers of my masked crusader persona. The hat and bullet-hole riddled poncho were the first to go, then the loose weave gunny sack that covered my face with a painted-on maniacal grin and crazy eyes. I love these sacks. They're free when I buy potatoes or onions. The cool thing is you can see out clear as anything when you wear them, but they're pretty much opaque to anyone looking at me from the outside—no eye holes needed. Next was the home-made harness that held my trusty quarter staffs across my shoulders. I could screw them together on a moment's notice and, *voila'*, nice long pole. With the poncho draped across those oak rods, I looked bigger than life, which was the point. I stripped off my dark gray coveralls, wincing with pain, and finally unbuckled my kevlar undies to survey the damage.

"Spartacus, good news! Looks like George and his pals were using rubber bullets." It still hurt like hell but would heal in no time flat. "At least those kids won't get killed by some trigger-happy servant of the people." I mumbled. I could still smell pepper spray on the poncho.

The cat bounded into the room and managed to find the exact spot that hurt most to hurl himself at. After a few seconds of cursing I pulled him close in and hugged him for all he was worth. In many ways, Spartacus was responsible for my dual identity.

I'd first met him when I was living on the streets after my discharge. He was a beat-to-hell alley cat that always seemed to show up when I'd managed to score a burger. He sensed what a soft touch I was. I liked him right away. He was as down and out as I was but somehow managed to retain his dignity.

I hadn't taken long to fall into a victim's mindset. Folks like me, down on their luck, we're treated as though we were invisible, ready-made targets for the scorn and abuse of fearful, hateful minds. When you're in that position you learn real quick to take what life dishes out, suck it up, and say thank you. Dignity doesn't figure into the equation.

And that was who I had let myself become until that fateful August night.

I'd found a dark corner, in an alley that didn't stink any worse than I did, and was settling in for the night. There was Spartacus, nosing through cans for a late night snack. I was about to coax him over with the remains of a Big Mac, when all of a sudden a cop comes out of nowhere and drop-kicks the cat into a wall. I'd seen this guy before, always hassling street folks who were just trying to survive another day. Now, here he was, trying to kill a friend of mine and laughing about it.

Without thinking, I was on my feet and up in that cop's face. At that instant, I wasn't a homeless guy, I wasn't a crazy ex-ranger, I was just a guy who'd seen enough and was willing to put myself in harm's way. Someone had to stand up as champion for this furry victim of injustice.

The copper got in a couple of licks with his baton before I disarmed him. I put him on the ground spitting and squirming like a wild man. Okay, he was down, now what? I couldn't exactly call the police.

It would have been nice if I'd had more time for the planning phase of this operation.

Then something unexpected happened, the cop had a heart attack. I stripped his shirt and vest off, applied CPR, then used his radio to call for help. Still, I wasn't about to let the guy off the hook. No one should have license to be that much of an asshole without some consequences.

I took his gun-belt and threw it over a power line along with his tied-together shoes. He had a marker in his pocket so I left him a love note written on his chest.

"THERE ARE MORE THAN ENOUGH REAL VILLAINS OUT THERE TO VENT YOUR SPLEEN ON! STOP TAKING IT OUT ON THE STRAW-MEN OF THIS WORLD!"

I know, I've read way too many comics, so sue me. I wrapped Spartacus up in the vest, and got out of there before the flashing red and blue lights showed. Hiding behind a dumpster that night, I decided that I was, somehow, going to find a stable life for the cat and myself. No one should have to live like this.

Maybe I was still tripping on the adrenaline, but I also took a solemn oath that night.I vowed that I would always be there to protect those that had no voice and no one to speak for them. Funny thing happened that night. I had a dream that this beautiful Siamese cat came to me, said she was queen of all the cats –crazy, huh – and that she was granting me cat-like powers to fulfill my oath. I asked her if that power would allow me to lick my own balls? Well, in the dream she lunged at me and ripped her claws across my hand. I woke up with a start to find my hand bleeding from scratch marks. I know, bullshit. Yeah, but from that night on I've been able to jump and move in way that would make a thirteen year-old gymnast weep with envy.

Such as it is, that's my origin story and surprisingly enough no one has offered me millions to make a movie about me. Go figure.

###

Last year people started "occupying" Wall Street in New York. It hardly made a blip on the evening news. Then the Authorities decided to stomp down on them hard. All of a sudden the movement catches on and spreads and I thought, good for them. Three and a half weeks ago the tents started blooming here in Pima and, overnight, the rules of engagement had changed. These kids were on the streets so they were under my protection... but they weren't victims.

At first I'd stayed in the background, keeping the predators away, the way I always had. Something about "innocence" and "idealism" is like a dinner bell to a certain kind of scum. I'd had plenty of experience in dealing with that sort of thing. Give me something to punch and I'm a happy camper.

Tonight, however, hadn't been about fighting bad guys. It wasn't about taking on a few dirty cops either. George and his pals were doing their jobs... at least as the mayor defined it. Technically, the protesters were breaking a couple of city ordinances, but damn it, a little free speech ought to trump that. Right?

As I finished my shower, and swallowed a couple of ibuprofens, I knew the sun was coming up and hoped I could catch a few hours of sleep before the lunch rush hit. It didn't matter how I felt, there would still be dishes needing washing and even a superhero needs to pay the rent.

The papers that day said the tents and protesters had been *peacefully* removed from John Glenn Park the night before. My buddy, Hale, assured everyone that their city was now safe from the outside agitators trying to disrupt our way of life. I don't know why I expected anything different. My shift ended at nine and then the real work began again.

###

As I watched from the shadows that night, the tents, sewn and patched, were being resurrected by kids with bruised but determined faces. There were no policemen in sight but I could still smell the eaude' de pepper spray from the night before.

I spent the evening productively, stopping two young toughs

214

from stealing Annie McCoy's shopping cart, making sure a family of three made it safely to a shelter for the night, and talking a guy out of offing himself — the usual. Then, about three A.M., I heard noises from the park and knew instantly that another lop-sided confrontation was gearing up.

I didn't charge in this time, but watched to make sure no one would be injured too badly. That turned my stomach. Just how badly was someone supposed to be injured before it was too much? Damn it! I hate this moral ambiguity crap.

I recognized George Blake, even in his riot gear. I noticed he was hanging back. This had to be hard for a man like him.

Two years ago Officer George Blake had helped me break up a motorcycle gang whose favorite pastime was cutting up tranny prostitutes. That little adventure never made it to the eleven o'clock news and certainly never got George any kind of commendation. We'd crossed paths several times since and seemed to have come to an understanding. I'd always thought he was a stand-up guy.

Then I saw another familiar face, my neighbor Marla, the eighty two year old retired nurse who kept me running, standing arm in arm with men and women a quarter her age. I almost leapt to her aid when one of the cops pushed her, but I stopped myself. So, it was okay to go in and bust a few heads for the sake of a friend, but strangers would just have to take care of themselves?

Shit!

I knew, and respected, that this movement was supposed to be all about non-violent protest and civil disobedience. The last thing they needed, or wanted, was a guy dressed up for Halloween, coming in and leading with his fists. That had sure saved the day last night. Right.

Suddenly I felt stupid in my scary costume, ready to wield a big stick for justice. Here I was hiding behind a mask while those protesters stood there, never invoking an eye for an eye mentality, with everything on the line for the whole world to see. Now, that took guts.

I was about ready to slink away when I noticed a man sneaking around among the tents. He seemed even more out of place than last night in his three piece suit and hundred dollar haircut. Hale was more behind the scenes type usually, so I couldn't help but wonder what he was up to.

With my trusty little binoculars, I could see he was busy pouring colored sand from a large jar to form a circle with a five pointed star inside it. This couldn't be good. I couldn't hear him, of course, through all the chanting and yelling, but it wasn't hard to tell that some kind of a ceremony was coming down, a spell was being cast.

There'd been rumors that Lyans Corp. had used some sort of black magic, as well as shady financial practices, to consolidate their power here in Pima but... Well, this was just outright blatant. Hale must be pretty desperate.

Christ! I really disliked dealing with all that hoodoo stuff.

Suddenly the pentacle exploded in light and a two story tall nightmare appeared. Mr. corporate leg-breaker kicked at the sand to release the horror within, but it seemed he hadn't read the manual completely. The demon's first act was to grab Hale and bite his head clean off.

That got everyone's attention.

Suddenly tents were flying everywhere. It was obvious that anyone in close proximity, cop and protester alike, was next on the agenda. This looked way out of my league, but it was definitely not something non-violence and a people's megaphone were going to be able to deal with.

Showtime!

I pulled out both sections of my staff, screwing them together on the run, and used them to pole vault over and through the mass of people trying to get away, but only managing to block each other.

Okay, supernatural crap, I've dealt with supernatural crap before. This was a bit more than Papa Loa turning day workers into Zombies but... What works against a demon from hell? I tried to remember the stuff from my old Dungeons & Dragons books. I know, but it was probably as useful as what I might find on Wikipedia, and I'd left my smart-phone in my other life.

The monster had picked up a young woman in jeans and a tie-dye jacket, ready to sample the next course. I threw my staff straight into his one baleful, red eye. He dropped the girl and screamed in rage. I don't think I hurt the big guy, so much as startled him. Instantly, he pivoted and was on me before I could think how stupid a move I had just made.

Fortunately, my body reacts even when my mind is scared out of its skull. I tucked myself in and neatly rolled between the demon's tree-like legs. He was fast and grabbed at me but only caught a piece of my black blanket-poncho. It was so tattered that it just ripped away. I silently gave thanks that I hadn't bought a new one at the Bed, Bath and Beyond sale last month.

Think, dammit!!! No way could I out-muscle this thing. Though the Police had started firing at it, I was pretty sure Pepper spray and rubber bullets were not going to do the job either. Hell, if they'd been steel hollow points blessed by Dirty Harry himself, it wouldn't have made much difference.

I tackled the thing's ankle and shin but all I got for the effort was a sore shoulder.

Wait a minute, something about steel, no, no… Not steel -- iron! Cold forged iron, that was the ticket, at least if Gary Gygax and his D&D minions were to be trusted. Yeah, now all I needed was a nice iron sword or maybe a spear. How hard could that be to find in a camp devoted to your basic non-violent creed?

Two cops already lay dead on the blood-slick grass and I was beginning to feel stupid and useless again. Then it hit me and I dived for the nearest cooking area. I grabbed around blindly. No, Teflon is no good. Aluminum? Hell no! God, what sort of neo-hippies were these protesters anyway?

Then I felt the heft of a good, old-fashioned iron skillet in my hand, big enough to make a decent stack of flapjacks at one crack. Wielding it like a club, I turned, screaming a blood-curdling challenge at the two-story terror.

I was in the thing's hand, headed toward its mouth, before my challenging roar had faded. That was one fast demon!

The thing's breath stank of rotten meat and I almost vomited into my mask. The timing had to be just perfect or I was a Snackable. Sharp teeth loomed toward me but I stretched up and pan-bashed the thing's pig-like nose with every bit of muscle I could muster.

It was like I'd hit a piñata filled with slimy green blood.

That had gotten his attention.

His fingers opened and I tucked into a roll as I hit the ground. Blake helped me to my feet, green blood spattering on the plexi-glass shield raised over his head.

I looked at that shield and had a crazy idea. "You ever see that Russell Crowe movie, Gladiator?" I yelled to be heard above the din, pointing at his shield.

George looked at me for a moment like he wanted to administer a breath-o-lizer right there and then.

I did a little finger miming to illustrate my hare-brained plan. It took a couple of seconds, but comprehension lit up his eyes and a wolf grin split his face. "Make it good." He said as he knelt down, his shield at a gentle angle. "We're both going to look pretty silly at our funerals if this doesn't work."

I backed off ten paces and ran straight at George, jumping up on his shield at the last second. George heaved upward to add his strength to my momentum, sending me hurling at the thing from hell's exposed groin.

I smashed the demon's family jewels with my mighty iron skillet and watched as he folded like a cheap accordion.

I hurt everywhere that I could hurt as I landed in some bushes. Somehow, I still managed to scramble up once more, crawling onto the monster's face. I sat there, on the bloody ruin of a nose and aimed the skillet's handle directly down into the blood red eye.

"I swear, if you move a muscle I will ram this cold iron into your eye and you can spend eternity selling pencils on a corner in Hell!" Demon Boy's chest rumbled but he didn't move a muscle. "Why were you brought here? What makes Lyans so scared they'd risk something this stupid?" I snarled my best tough-guy snarl.

The demon spoke in a bass note that shook the trees. "Greed brought me here... A side-show of fear am I."

I spit some blood into my mask. "Thanks, that's a big help. I should let Blake take you downtown and do a proper questioning, but I don't think they have cuffs in your size... and I don't even want to think about how they'd do the body cavity search"

That actually made the monster laugh... not a pretty sound.

By this time, the skillet was getting heavy and I didn't know how long adrenaline was going to keep me upright. "Look, I'm willing to call this a draw if you are. Can you find your own way home, or do I need to show you the way?"

The giant head nodded slightly so I slid slowly back to the ground on a trail of green gunk. Ponderously, painfully, the Hell-spawn stood and made a mystic looking gesture which set the air in front of him on fire. As he stepped through he intoned, "Yours is the victory today, but demons are unleashed each day by those who hunger for more, more and more -— those demons are not so easily defeated."

The next moment, the demon and his fiery exit were gone, as though he'd never been there. The headless bodies scattered about were a pretty compelling argument that he had been though.

If he'd said no, I had no plan B.

I guess I passed out about then.

Next thing I remember was being frog-walked by George Blake through a pandemonium of uniforms and tie dye. I could tell I wasn't wearing a mask – Oh well, there goes the old secret identity. No one took any notice of me though, there were plenty of injured to go around. Without the outfit I was just another guy caught in a disaster zone. I passed out again.

Marla stayed by my bedside for three days, feeding me lots of soup, changing bandages and jabbing me with needles. She wasn't going anywhere, she said, until she was satisfied that I wouldn't embarrass her medical reputation by dying.

Thank god for Marla. Dishwashing crime-fighters have lousy medical plans.

On the fourth day Marla took me down to John Glenn Park. We stood in the rain with thousands of other folks, all quietly saying enough was enough.

I saw George Blake, who gave me a wink when our eyes met. He didn't have his baton or shield, he was standing arm in arm, as part of the crowd. Stand-up guy, like I said.

219

###

It was another month before news that all the Lyans board of directors had been slaughtered by Yakuza thugs. Seems the board had been working on a deal to acquire Pima for their Japanese pals, who wanted to build the world's largest casino, after bull-dozing the city, of course. Unfortunately, there was some local law going into effect real soon that would have made the whole plan useless. Those laws were the direct result of the tenacity of the protesters. Who'd have thunk, foiled by some pesky kids and their dopey dog … me.

So, I guess there is still a place for someone like the Straw Man. Some monsters have to be fought the way he fights.

Then again, there are even bigger monsters, and those can't be brought down through violence and force of arms. At least not without turning people into the sort of monsters they wanted to slay. Horrors like that can only be beaten by the likes of Marla Hoover and George Blake and even Carl Meeker, quietly demanding justice and refusing to take no for an answer.

Okay, sermon's over. I've got places to be and people to hit.

THE FORTRESS OF SOLICITUDE

"Okay, I'll tell the story but you gotta remember this was back before all these super-duper types wore fancy costumes and shot lightning bolts out of their asses." Duke Sandscott was a regular fixture around the Fortress of Solicitude Bar & Grill. At ninety two he could still hold his own in a bar fight and always had some outrageous adventure to relate. "I'd been a masked vigilante for about six months, Kong, the Avenger..."

Niles Carter, resplendent in his threadbare, broad-brimmed slouch hat, broke in, "You were a sight in that gorilla suit and skull helmet, twin sawed-off shotguns blazing away and cartridge belts slung like you were some Mexican bandit. Bad guys pissed their pants when they caught a sight of you but I could never figure out if they were scared or just pissed themselves laughing."

Duke took a sip of beer and cleared his throat. "So sayeth the Velvet Ghost! Look Carter, do you want me to tell this or not?"

Niles doffed his hat. Resting his chin in his hands he gave an innocent smile and fluttered his eyelashes. "I'm all ears."

"It was spring, nineteen thirty eight and Newark was in the grip of terror from the marauders the papers dubbed the Jersey She-devils..."

Winter still clung to the rooftops with icy fingernails of wind on the blackboard of a man's face. It had been a bitter season that seemed to carve cruelty into the souls of otherwise reasonable citizens. When murder and brutal assaults hit too close to home, it brought me to my decision to become a protector of the weak and innocent. The Hollyhock pawn shop was just a little Mom & Pop joint but it had been run by my Mom and my Pop. My old man had been shot down like a dog for the twenty bucks in the till of his cash register and I'd returned home from Hollywood to take care of Mom. I'd been a stuntman and I could really do all those things that movie heroes pretended to, so I made it my business to bring a little of the justice that the cops couldn't—or wouldn't—to Newark.

I'd gotten the gorilla suit as payment for some gags I'd done on a jungle picture that had gone belly up, and it had served me pretty damned well that winter. I had no idea what I'd do when summer came around and crooks could smell me sweating from half a block away. The skull helmet I'd found under an inch of dust in the Holly-hock back room, God only knew where it had come from. The sawed-off pump actions were from under the store's counter and the shells held everything from rock salt to hot peppers--I had no intention on adding to the body count unless I had to.

Harry came over with another round of drinks and much to everyone's surprise, Dirk Stone paid for the round. Dirk had been a spandex type back in the seventies but he was okay, and he loved to hear the old stories—this was one he'd never heard. "Yeah, yeah, Duke we've all heard your origin before, but you said this was about how the Fortress came to be." He wiped the foam off his lip, "We all come here week after week but no one seems to know exactly how a bar in another dimension came to be, much less why it only allows heroes to enter."

Duke rolled his eyes, "Not to mention that the door to this place seems to exist in every major city but they all open onto this joint. Well, if you would just listen, I was about to tell you."

"From the rooftop across the street, I was staking out the Rialto Theater, an art deco monstrosity that had been built at the height of prohibition. The Rialto had played host to everything from symphonies and ballets to bottoms up burlesque shows. Tonight the joint was swinging to the big band sounds of the Dorey Brothers Orchestra. The Doreys had been playing gigs all over the northeast but Newark was their home. Now I'm as hep to swinging sounds as the next guy, and it wasn't because I was too cheap to buy a ticket that I was parked on that roof.

For weeks the papers had been filled with stories of roaming gangs of monstrous women who would attack some hapless fellow and drag him into an alley. Once in the alley they would strip him, force him into unnatural acts of sex, and when he was at the heights of ecstasy, these women would rip him to shreds and dance on his

222

entrails. This, according to the eye witness account of a wino hidden in one of those alleys, had sobered him up real quick. Five times this had happened leaving five ordinary Joes eviscerated in a bloody mess of limbs and organs. Afterward in each instance the women would go dancing madly down the street, terrifying passersby until they would go into another alley and vanish. That was weird even for Newark.

The police were stumped, but not my Mom. Mom was Sherlock Holmes in an apron. She could do the Times crossword in twenty minutes flat—in ink. She never read more than the first couple of chapters of a mystery before she figured out whodunit, even with Agatha Christie books. Mom could put clues together in ways that made my head spin. She was my crime-fighting ace in the hole, so I posed this new killing spree to her as a puzzle to solve. She had me go to Mrs. O'houley, who saved newspapers, and bring back every paper for the last six weeks. For three days there were papers spread on every flat surface in the house and I was forced to eat at Millie's Diner morning, noon and night. On the fourth day the papers were gone and Mom sat down with me over ham and eggs.

"More coffee, Duke?" She smiled like a cat with a canary secret.

"Okay, what did you find out?" I poured us both a warmer and sat down to bask in her brilliance.

"Well," She began through mouthfuls of eggs, "I started with the victims, of course. No connections at all. They ranged from twenty five to fifty three and came from different parts of the city and various jobs from plumber to banker. No clubs, schools, sports, gambling… nothing in common. Zip, zip, zip!" She reached into her apron pocket and pulled out a small book. "Then I got to thinking about the killers, the women, and it reminded me of something I'd read about back in school."

She handed me the book, 'Myths Made Easy' and I opened to the page she'd dog eared. "Bacchus?" I asked.

"Dionysus to the Greeks. He was the god of wine and ecstatic revels. His women followers would go into fits of euphoria and rip men to pieces. Sound familiar?"

I read the rest of the page and it was interesting but I couldn't see what this all had to do with a killing streak in Newark, New Jersey and I told her so.

"Well, it got me thinking in odd directions and I started looking at the entertainment sections. Did you know that Kip and Steve Dorey and their band played in Newark on every night there was an attack?"

I shrugged.

"It might also be of some interest that all the attacks occurred within two blocks of where they were playing."

My eyebrows shot up. "Okay, but the Doreys have been playing Newark for years…"

She cut into my protest "Six weeks ago they hired a new boy singer and the first attack took place during his debut performance. His name is Dion Bach."

I smiled, "Yeah, I've heard of him, he's that guy that all the pimple face girls are going so crazy abou…" And it just hung there in the air for a few moments.

Mom nodded like the whole thing actually made sense. "Tonight the Dorey Brothers band plays the Rialto."

Sure enough, about fifteen minutes after the show started, a bunch of laughing, twirling young women burst through the main entrance and spilled into the street. I counted twelve girls in bright dresses who went off dancing wildly down the sidewalk like they had not a care or inhibition in the world. I was up and running to keep pace with them across the tightly packed rooftops. Rooftops are not well lit so it's a lot harder not to stumble in the dark and break your neck than it looks like in the funny papers. The revelers cut across traffic and headed down a side street. I figured where they were bound for and took a shortcut to get ahead of them. As I made my way to street level via a series of flagpoles and fire escapes, I could hear female laughter and panicked protests in a lower register. I made a last jump into a pile of crates, which broke my fall, and rolled to a crouching position. It was dark but I could make out a man being forced into the alleyway I'd just landed in.

The young ladies had performed a rather jarring quick-change during my descent and no longer looked like a bunch of hot honeys out for a night on the town. Their party dresses had been transformed into tattered white togas that barely hid their charms, while their carefully styled and coifed hairdos had become wild, unfettered locks that fell almost to the waist. The biggest change was the eyes which were wide and glowed in the darkness with a violet glint of madness. Without hesitation, I fired both my sawed off shotguns into that mob. One was filled with a blend of rock salt and sand that usually got a bad guy's attention. The other was my own home blend of ground up chili peppers I'd bought in Tijuana and black pepper from Mom's pantry. It was a pretty potent one-two punch that I followed up with a Tarzan yell and a direct charge wielding the shotguns like clubs.

"Run!" I yelled at the poor guy they'd shanghaied. His clothes were in tatters but he needed no further instruction and took off like a jackrabbit down the alley back to the street. A couple of the ladies tried to hold him but just got pieces of undershirt. As one they turned their attention to me. Wheeling like a flock of birds, they tore down that dark city canyon, their glowing eyes watering, bleeding from multiple scratches, screaming like banshees and baring fingernails that had grown to claws.

They hit me like a tidal wave! I swung the still smoking shotguns at heads and limbs, hoping to cut down the odds but with little effect. They bore me to the ground and began ripping through my leather and fur suit, peeling me like a grape. As claws dug into my flesh, twelve anxious bodies writhed over my naked form. My skull helmet was wrenched off my head and thrown down the alley as biting kisses engulfed my face and ears. I know guys who daydream about such things but, though my body was acknowledging the attentions, my mind was screaming in terror. I thought I was a goner, when suddenly a large truck came barreling down the alley, blaring its horn and ramming right into that mini-orgy of death, scattering my assailants and driving right over top of me with only inches to spare. In the distance were wailing sirens and the battered Bacchae—that's what Mom had called them--danced down the alley and disappeared into the darkness.

After a moment I heard the truck door open and a hand reached to pull me from under the truck. It was the man I'd saved. "Say, pal, are you all right?" I nodded. "Damn if that wasn't about the weirdest

225

thing I've ever seen!" He looked at my wounds and state of dress and said. "You want I should take you to a hospital or something?"

I blinked a drop of blood out of my eye and replied. "No hospital, but if you've got a blanket or an extra pair of pants, I'd be obliged." As he rummaged behind the seat I added. "If it wouldn't be too much trouble I got a couple of guns and a mask lying around here somewhere." He found them and then drove me home. I never asked his name and he never asked mine, we just shook hands as he dropped me off.

I snuck in the back way and Mom bandaged me up with a minimum of talk. She tucked me in that night like a little kid and I let her, but it was a long time before sleep came. Two thoughts kept running through my head—I was way out of my league here, and it was time I had a talk with one Mr. Dion Bach!

Bach and the Doreys played clubs in Manhattan whole that week, so I took the time to heal and make with some strategy before any sort of confrontation. So far there hadn't been any incidents outside of Newark and that pattern held so I used the time as best I could. Without the Gorilla costume, Kong the Avenger was pretty much kaput, but I still had the helmet and shotguns, so I got a black trench coat and became Skull the Avenger, which worked better anyway.

The Club Meow was where the band would be that Friday, and this time I didn't wait till the night's performance or cool my heels on a rooftop. Dion had just started his first solo of the rehearsal when I stepped out of the curtain shadows at stage right. He was skinny but wiry. With his hair in a lavish pompadour, a shiny suit, a bow tie and bedroom eyes, he was quite a sight. I had to give it to him though, the kid could sing. His voice had a smooth, dreamlike quality that wasn't loud but still somehow soared over the orchestra. As he caught sight of my skull-face he stopped in mid note and snapped his fingers with a sound like a thunderclap. The entire band froze in place. I wasn't sure what I'd expected but it sure wasn't what came next. Dion stomped his foot petulantly and kicked his microphone over, "Did Zeus send you?" he whimpered, "Doesn't that cat have better things to

226

do than send his titan goons to drag my ass back to Olympus?"

Sometimes the best reply is silence.

"C'mon," he continued, "I'm not hurting anything down here and Olympus has become square city. I know, I know, I'm a god and entertaining mortals is beneath me. Blah, blah, blah! Well, I won't apologize, I love jazz and especially when it swings like this! I mean, can you dig it? These solid sounds are like musical wine, they get your feet movin' to the beat and make your mind feel real fine." He stalked over toward me wagging his finger. "This is my scene if I ever had a scene and I had to do it down here because Zeus closed down my club up there. Right in the middle of my theme song he put a billion watt hurt on the joint and brought the house down. Mr. Vintage Voltage said jazz hurt his ears!"

That crooner got right into my face and glared into my soul. "Hold the pad, dad." His eyes got wide and he backed away. "You're a mortal."

I'd heard about enough of this guy's crazy talk. "Yeah, and you're under arrest, buddy. You've been hypnotizing a bunch of possibly underage girls to go out and commit homicide, ripping men from limb to limb. I don't know why and I don't know how but it stops right here!"

From all over the club, figures emerged from the shadows and dimly lit corners. They were a bizarre assortment of caped and masked men mixed with muscular fellows in jodhpur pants and safari jackets, but they all had a determined and ready stance in common. They were the pulp heroes—so called because their exploits usually only appeared in the cheap rags of the day willing to report the strange occurrences more respectable papers would never touch. I'd met Miles, the Velvet Ghost, on a case a month before and he had hooked me into the pulp grapevine. I couldn't call in the cops but I had my resources.

Dion didn't look so impressed, but he did look puzzled. "Hey, I did that whole Bacchae thing like twenty five hundred years ago! There's got to be some sort of statute of limitations for that stuff, besides I was a coo-coo young god at the time."

Out of the back of the room came a spooky laugh from a guy still

227

half hidden in shadow—I was flattered, he had actually showed up—then his voice boomed through the hall. "We aren't here about deeds done long ago! We accuse you of the foul murder of five men and the seduction of innocents into your web of passion and mayhem that has played out over these past weeks!"

Again Dion scratched his head, "All I've done since I've been on Earth this time around was sing and make people happy, so shoot me. The only chicks that could possibly be affected badly would have to be direct descendants of those original Italian babes I had go whacko way back when. C'mon, we're half a world away! What are the odds of a bunch of Italians, from a small little area thousands of miles away, winding up living here in New Jersey?"

And that's when the doors burst open and a swarm of screaming girls poured in! The instant they saw Dion they started transforming into the violet eyed psychos that had almost done me in. It happened way faster than it had before and they seemed even wilder and bigger—more powerful somehow.I got the feeling that this had slipped up a notch and we were playing on a whole new field.

The pulp guys jumped into their paths but were tossed aside like last year's rag doll. These nut jobs had one goal and that was Dion, and he just stood there looking stupid. I grabbed him by the arm as the first Bacchae grabbed his foot and he let out a scream as her claws dug in. Professor Peril tackled her low and managed to knock her aside while I dragged the singer into the wings. I looked frantically around until I spotted an open dressing room. Hustling Dion in, I latched the door and crammed a chair against it, then I grabbed him by the collar and slammed him up against a wall.

"Look, pal, maybe you are a god, I don't even care, but you better do something and quick!"

Dion looked stricken. "She scratched me! I'm a god, I don't get scratched!"

I slammed him again and then slapped him just to get his attention.

"Hey, watch the lapels." He yelled at me. Then the crashing of bodies against the door kind of got our attention and we both stared at it. I let him slip to the ground.

"I don't know," he sputtered, "It's like these crazy broads are sucking my power right out of me. They've got some kind of connection through that old spell, and I've noticed that women here in the U.S. of A. are a lot stronger willed, as a general rule, than your average Roman babe."

I added my own weight to bolster the quickly failing door. "All right, you cast the spell, so un-cast it!"

"Oh, man! That was a long time ago. How am I supposed to remember something like tha…"

The door flew off its hinges and sent me flying across the room seeing sparkly lights. When I came to, a minute later, the room was empty so I followed the sound of fighting out into the theater. When I got to the stage I saw that my masked associates had managed to grab Dion from the clutches of his fans. They had formed a battered and tattered human barrier around him and were facing off against a ring of glowing eyed fanatics ready to rip them to shreds.

I stared a moment, wide eyed, and tried to think like Mom. This situation wasn't about to be solved by strength of arms. I needed an idea, and then it hit me. "Dion, they're your fans, right? Well, sing to them!" I yelled.

I could hear him gulp from a hundred feet away, then he went into some syrupy song about lovin' only one girl. The reaction was instantaneous; the women all sighed "Diiiiioooon…" and plopped down onto the floor. By the time he got to the second bar, he snapped his fingers and the frozen Dorey Brothers band came back to life and began accompanying him.

They put on a two hour show, right on the spot, which gave Mysto the Mysterious and Doctor Hoodoo time to put their magical heads together and break the spell. Who knew that they could do real honest to gosh magic?

Eventually, the bewildered but happy girls were all given cab fare and sent on their way. Dion pledged his everlasting debt to us all and wanted to reward us for saving his godly hide. Of course we didn't do it for a reward, but he snapped his fingers and poof, we were all transported to a bar where our outfits were made whole again and the bartender was pouring anything that our hearts desired. He told us that The Doreys would go on without their boy singer from now on and he would return to his rightful place among the gods. He was determined to make Olympus swing, no matter what big daddy Zeus said. He said our courage had inspired him.

We were wary at first but soon settled in and knocked a few back. Most of us were loners by nature, but soon found out how great it was to be able to talk to others who understood what this whole hero thing was about.

Anyway, we spent the night jawing and toasting our individual crusades. Come morning, Bach told us that when we left by the front door we would each find ourselves on our respective home turf. Then he gets up on a chair banging a spoon on a shot glass and proclaims, "I shall leave this establishment as a safe haven for all those who would champion the right, though the very gods themselves might be arrayed against them. This world needs such men! It needs true heroes and you crazy cats truly are the closest I've seen since Jason and his wacky Argonauts. Can you dig it, man?!" Then, old Dion disappeared in a puff of purple smoke and the bartender, Harry, made sure we all had the right capes and told us to come back anytime.

About a year later some joker started calling the place The Fortress of Solicitude and the name stuck.

Dirk Stone emptied his glass and wiped his lip. "So, the Fortress is kind of a present from the god of getting drunk?"

The Velvet Ghost put his hat back on and raised his right hand as he made a cross over his heart with his left. "Swear to God... gods— whatever! It happened just like the man said, though I was much more dashing and heroic than he let on."

Dirk Chewed his lip a second. "What about Harry, the Bartender? He hasn't aged a day in the thirty five years I've been coming here. Is he a god?"

Duke shook his head and chuckled, "I asked him that once, about sixty years ago, he told me it was time to pay my tab and I haven't asked since."

Harry came over with another round as the door opened to admit several young men and women--battered, bruised and bleeding—

wearing skin tight outfits laden with high tech accessories. Harry had a round of drinks waiting for them as they eased into chairs at a nearby table.

Miles turned to face the newcomers. "Where's Julie? I saw on the news where you guys had a dust-up with Lord Lethal."

A well built black man lifted his face plate and took a long sip of beer. "Doctors aren't sure if she's going to make it, Miles." The others stripped off masks and helmets. "We came here to wait, where else were we going to go?"

Miles turned back to his companions, "I remember the Scarlet Scimitar wanted to call this establishment New Valhalla. A place for mighty heroes to brag about their bold deeds, he said." The old men smiled ruefully at each other, then slid their chairs over to the newcomers table.

"I don't know Julie that well," Duke sighed, "Tell me about her."

A half hour later, Harry brought yet another round. It would be another long night at the Fortress of Solicitude.

AFTERWORD

So, those are my stories and I'm sticking with 'em.

There will, no doubt, be more but I couldn't say when with any certainty. I'm thinking about doing a graphic novel as my next big thing—writing and doing the art for the whole darned thing. I know, lots of folks are doing graphic novels and some of them are pretty good too. Mine may be a little bit different though. If all goes according to plan it will be inscribed on a giant metal moebius strip and will have no actual beginning or end. Wait, you say, that's a cool idea but what if someone else steals it first? I can't imagine another human being silly enough to try something so blatantly foolish as a giant, metal moebius comic strip.

I've done silk screening. I've made a movie. I did improv comedy. I've done advertising. Cartooning, painting, digital art, book covers—been there, done that. I've done a billboard, my, gosh. I always want to tackle new creative challenges and this one scares the hell out of me. Cool!

It could be a disaster but I have a long history of averting impending doom at the last second. Hence this book's title. But, I've never averted those disasters on my own, and there are a lot of folks to thank for helping me in all these endeavors.

A list of my enablers: Nicole, first and always, Carol, Richard and Maya, Rose and Dave, Mike and Marilyn, Tim and Kaia, Lori, Mary, Lorna, Linda and Paul, Bob, Devon, Liz and Anna, Tom, Ron and Nina, Elaine, Melissa, Emily, Tyree, J, All the Daves, John, Michael, Eileen, Matthew, The nieces and nephews, Aggie, Lunell, Dana, Sean and Atarah, Jill, Dave and Eden, Jeff, Amanda and Owen, Angie, Jennifer, Jean Marie, Mary Rose and Marko, Hueso, Bill, Sarah, Ron, Connie and Courtney, Connie, Katie, Ed, Kent, Jenny and Jamie, The other Nicole and all the others who gave my sorry ass a shove in the right direction when I needed it.

If you want to check out some more of my art, go to my trusty on-line portfolio at lauragivens-artist.com.

One word of advice, laugh out loud as often as possible. It feels great and keeps the world on its toes.

Peace, out,

Laura Givens

Check out all of the Nomadic Delirium Press titles at:
http://nomadicdeliriumpress.com/blog/shop

You can find Nomadic Delirium Press e-books at:
https://www.smashwords.com/profile/view/nomadicde
lirium

Feel free to comment on any of the stories in this
collection by visiting our blog:
http://nomadicdelirium.wordpress.com/